BOND LAY FROZEN...

The creature reached his knee. It was starting up his thigh. Whatever happened he mustn't move, mustn't even tremble. Bond's whole consciousness had drained down to the two rows of softly creeping feet. Now they had reached his flank.

God, it was turning down toward his groin...

IAN FLEMING'S
DOCTOR NO

BERKLEY BOOKS, NEW YORK

This Berkley book contains the complete
text of the original hardcover edition.
It has been completely reset in a typeface
designed for easy reading, and was printed
from new film.

DOCTOR NO

A Berkley Book / published by arrangement with
Macmillan Publishing Company, Inc.

PRINTING HISTORY
Macmillan edition published 1958
Jove edition / May 1980
Berkley edition / May 1982
Fourth printing / December 1983
Fifth printing / May 1984

ISBN: 0-425-06394-1

A BERKLEY BOOK ® TM 757,375
Berkley Books are published by The Berkley Publishing Group,
200 Madison Avenue, New York, New York 10016.
The name "BERKLEY" and the stylized "B" with design
are trademarks belonging to Berkley Publishing Corporation.
PRINTED IN THE UNITED STATES OF AMERICA

CONTENTS

CHAPTER 1

Hear You Loud and Clear

Punctually at six o'clock the sun set with a last yellow flash behind the Blue Mountains, a wave of violet shadow poured down Richmond Road, and the crickets and tree frogs in the fine gardens began to zing and tinkle.

Apart from the background noise of the insects, the wide empty street was quiet. The wealthy owners of the big, withdrawn houses—the bank managers, company directors and top civil servants—had been home since five o'clock and they would be discussing the day with their wives or taking a shower and changing their clothes. In half an hour the street would come to life again with the cocktail traffic, but now this very superior half-mile of 'Rich Road', as it was known to the tradesmen of Kingston, held nothing but the suspense of an empty stage and the heavy perfume of night-scented jasmine.

Richmond Road is the 'best' road in all Jamaica. It is Jamaica's Park Avenue, its Kensington Palace Gardens, its Avenue D'Iéna. The 'best' people live in its big old-fashioned houses, each in an acre or two of beautiful lawn set, too trimly, with the finest trees and flowers from the Botanical Gardens at Hope. The long, straight road is cool and quiet and withdrawn from the hot, vulgar sprawl of Kingston where its residents earn their money, and, on the other side of the T-intersection at its top, lie the grounds of King's House, where the Governor and Commander-in-Chief of Jamaica lives with his family. In Jamaica, no road could have a finer ending.

On the eastern corner of the top intersection stands No. 1 Richmond Road, a substantial two-storey house with broad white-painted verandas running round both floors. From the road a gravel path leads up to the pillared entrance through wide lawns marked out with tennis courts on which this evening, as on all evenings, the sprinklers are at work. This mansion is the social Mecca of Kingston. It is Queen's Club, which, for fifty years, has boasted the power and frequency of its black-balls.

Such stubborn retreats will not long survive in modern Jamaica. One day Queen's Club will have its windows smashed and perhaps be burned to the ground, but for the time being it is a useful place to find in a sub-tropical island—well run, well staffed and with the finest cuisine and cellar in the Caribbean.

At that time of day, on most evenings of the year, you would find the same four motor cars standing in the road outside the club. They were the cars belonging to the high bridge game that assembled punctually at five and played until around midnight. You could almost set your watch by these cars. They belonged, reading from the order in which they now stood against the kerb, to the Brigadier in command of the Caribbean Defence Force, to Kingston's leading criminal lawyer, and to the Mathematics Professor from Kingston University. At the tail of the line stood the black Sunbeam Alpine of Commander John Strangways, R.N. (Ret.), Regional Control Officer for the Caribbean—or, less discreetly, the local representative of the British Secret Service.

• • •

Just before six-fifteen, the silence of Richmond Road was softly broken. Three blind beggars came round the corner of the intersection and moved slowly down the pavement towards the four cars. They were Chigroes— Chinese negroes—bulky men, but bowed as they shuffled along, tapping at the kerb with their white sticks. They walked in file. The first man, who wore blue glasses and could presumably see better than the others, walked in front holding a tin cup against the crook of the stick in his left hand. The right hand of the second man rested on his shoulder and the right hand of the third on the shoulder of the second. The eyes of the second and third men were shut. The three men were dressed in rags and wore dirty jippa-jappa baseball caps with long peaks. They said nothing and no noise came from them except the soft tapping of their sticks as they came slowly down the shadowed pavement towards the group of cars.

The three-blind men would not have been incongruous in Kingston, where there are many diseased people on the streets, but, in this quiet rich empty street, they made an unpleasant impression. And it was odd that they should all be Chinese negroes. This is not a common mixture of bloods.

In the cardroom, the sunburned hand reached out into the green pool of the centre table and gathered up the four cards. There was a quiet snap as the trick went to join the rest. 'Hundred honours,' said Strangways, 'and ninety below!' He looked at his watch and stood up. 'Back in twenty minutes. Your deal, Bill. Order some drinks. Usual for me. Don't bother to cook a hand for me while I'm gone. I always spot them.'

Bill Templar, the Brigadier, laughed shortly. He pinged the bell by his side and raked the cards in towards him. He said, 'Hurry up, blast you. You always let the cards go cold just as your partner's in the money.'

Strangways was already out of the door. The three men sat back resignedly in their chairs. The coloured steward came in and they ordered drinks for themselves and a whisky and water for Strangways.

There was this maddening interruption every evening at six-fifteen, about half way through their second rubber. At this time precisely, even if they were in the middle of a hand, Strangways had to go to his 'office' and 'make a call'. It was a damned nuisance. But Strangways was a vital part of their four and they put up with it. It was never explained what 'the call' was, and no one asked. Strangway's job was 'hush' and that was that. He was rarely away for more than twenty minutes and it was understood that he paid for his absence with a round of drinks.

The drinks came and the three men began to talk racing.

In fact, this was the most important moment in Strangways's day—the time of his duty radio contact with the powerful transmitter on the roof of the building in Regent's Park that is the headquarters of the Secret Service. Every day, at eighteen-thirty local time, unless he gave warning the day before that he would not be on the air—when he had business on one of the other islands in his territory, for instance, or was seriously ill—he would transmit his daily report and receive his orders. If he failed to come on the air precisely at six-thirty, there would be a second call, the 'Blue' call, at seven, and, finally, the 'Red' call at seventy-thirty. After this, if his transmitter remained silent, it was 'Emergency', and Section III, his controlling authority in London, would urgently get on the job of finding out what had happened to him.

Even a 'Blue' call means a bad mark for an agent unless his 'Reasons in Writing' are unanswerable. London's radio schedules round the world are desperately tight and their minute disruption by even one extra call is a dangerous nuisance. Strangways had never suffered the ignominy of a 'Blue' call, let alone a 'Red', and was as certain as could be that he never would do so. Every evening, at precisely six-fifteen, he left Queen's Club, got into his car and drove for ten minutes up into the foothills of the Blue Mountains to his neat bungalow with the fabulous view over Kingston harbour. At six twenty-five he walked through the hall to the office at the back. He unlocked the door and locked it again behind him. Miss Trueblood, who passed as his secretary, but was in fact his No. 2 and a former Chief Officer W.R.N.S., would already be sitting in front of the dials inside the dummy filing cabinet. She would have the earphones on and would be making first contact, tapping out his call-sign, WXN, on 14 megacycles. There would be a shorthand pad on her elegant knees. Strangways would drop into the chair beside her and pick up the other pair of headphones and, at exactly six twenty-eight, he would take over from her and wait for the sudden hollowness in the ether that meant that WWW in London was coming in to acknowledge.

It was an iron routine. Strangways was a man of iron routine. Unfortunately, strict patterns of behavior can be deadly if they are read by an enemy.

Strangways, a tall lean man with a black patch over the right eye and the sort of aquiline good looks you associate with the bridge of a destroyer, walked quickly across the mahogany panelled hallway of Queen's Club and pushed through the light mosquito-wired doors and ran down the three steps to the path.

There was nothing very much on his mind except the sensual pleasure of the clean fresh evening air and the memory of the finesse that had given him his three spades. There was this case, of course, the case he was working on, a curious and complicated affair that M had rather nonchalantly tossed over the air at him two weeks earlier. But it was going well. A chance lead into the Chinese community had paid off. Some odd angles had come to light—for the present the merest shadows of angles—but if they jelled, thought Strangways as he strode down the gravel path and into Richmond Road, he might find himself involved in something very odd indeed.

Strangways shrugged his shoulders. Of course it wouldn't turn out like that. The fantastic never materialized in his line of business. There would be some drab solution that had been embroidered by overheated imaginations and the usual hysteria of the Chinese.

Automatically, another part of Strangways's mind took in the three blind men. They were tapping slowly towards him down the sidewalk. They were about twenty yards away. He calculated that they would pass him a second or two before he reached his car. Out of shame for his own health and gratitude for it, Strangways felt for a coin. He ran his thumbnail down its edge to make sure it was a florin and not a penny. He took it out. He was parallel with the beggars. How odd, they were all Chigroes! How very odd! Strangways's hand went out. The coin clanged in the tin cup.

'Bless you, Master,' said the leading man. 'Bless you,' echoed the other two.

The car key was in Strangways's hand. Vaguely he registered the moment of silence as the tapping of the white sticks ceased. It was too late.

As Strangways had passed the last man, all three had swivelled. The back two had fanned out a step to have a clear field of fire. Three revolvers, ungainly with their sausage-shaped silencers, whipped out of holsters concealed among the rags. With disciplined precision the three men aimed at different points down Strangways's spine—one between the shoulders, one in the small of the back, one at the pelvis.

The three heavy coughs were almost one. Strangways's body was hurled forward as if it had been kicked. It lay absolutely still in the small puff of dust from the sidewalk.

It was six-seventeen. With a squeal of tyres, a dingy motor hearse with black plumes flying from the four corners of its roof took the T-intersection into Richmond Road and shot down towards the group on the pavement. The three men had just had time to pick up Strangways's body when the hearse slid to a stop abreast of them. The double doors at the back were open. So was the plain deal coffin inside. The three men manhandled the body through the doors and into the coffin. They climbed in. The lid was put on and the doors pulled shut. The three negroes sat down on three of the four little seats at the corners of the coffin and unhurriedly laid their white sticks beside them. Roomy black alpaca coats hung over the back of the seats. They put the coats on over their rags. Then they took off their baseball caps and reached down to the floor and picked up black top hats and put them on their heads.

The driver, who also was a Chinese negro, looked nervously over his shoulder.

'Go, man. Go!' said the biggest of the killers. He glanced down at the luminous dial of his wrist watch. It said six-twenty. Just three minutes for the job. Dead on time.

The hearse made a decorous U-turn and moved at a sedate speed up to the intersection. There it turned right and at thirty miles an hour it cruised genteelly up the tarmac highway towards the hills, its black plumes streaming the doleful signal of its burden and the three mourners sitting bolt upright with their arms crossed respectfully over their hearts.

'WXN calling WWW. . . . WXN calling WWW. . . . WXN . . . WXN . . . WXN . . .'

The centre finger of Mary Trueblood's right hand stabbed softly, elegantly, at the key. She lifted her left wrist. Six twenty-eight. He was a minute late. Mary Trueblood smiled at the thought of the little open Sunbeam tearing up the road towards her. Now, in a second, she would hear the quick step, then the key in the lock and he would be sitting beside her. There would be the apologetic smile as he reached for the earphones. 'Sorry Mary. Damned car wouldn't start.' Or, 'You'd think the blasted police knew my number by now. Stopped me at Halfway Tree.' Mary Trueblood took the second pair of earphones off their hook and put them on his chair to save him half a second.

'WXN calling WWW. . . . WXN calling WWW.' She tuned the dial a hair's breadth and tried again. Her watch said six twenty-nine. She began to worry. In a matter of seconds, London would be coming in. Suddenly she thought, God, what could she do if Strangways wasn't on time! It was useless for her to acknowledge London and pretend she was him—useless and dangerous. Radio Security would be monitoring the call, as they monitored every call from an agent. Those instruments which measured the minute peculiarities in an operator's 'fist' would at once detect it wasn't Strangways at the key. Mary Trueblood had been shown the forest of dials in the quiet room on the top floor at headquarters, had watched as the dancing hands registered the weight of each pulse, the speed of each cipher group, the stumble over a particular letter. The Controller had explained it all to her when she had joined the Carribbean station five years before—how a buzzer would sound and the contact be automatically broken if the wrong operator had come on the air. It was the basic protection against a Secret Service transmitter falling into enemy hands. And, if an agent had been captured and was being forced to contact London under torture, he had only to add a few hairbreadth peculiarities to his usual 'fist' and they would tell the story of his capture as clearly as if he had announced it *en clair.*

Now it had come! Now she was hearing the hollowness in the ether that meant London was coming in. Mary Trueblood glanced at her watch. Six-thirty. Panic! But now, at last, there were the footsteps in the hall. Thank God! In a second he would come in. She *must* protect him! Desperately she decided to take a chance and keep the circuit open.

'WWW calling WXN. . . . WWW calling WXN. . . . Can you hear me? . . . can you hear me?' London was coming over strong, searching for the Jamaica station.

The footsteps were at the door.

Coolly, confidently, she tapped back: 'Hear you loud and clear. . . . Hear you loud and clear. . . . Hear you . . .'

Behind her there was an explosion. Something hit her

on the ankle. She looked down. It was the lock of the door.

Mary Trueblood swivelled sharply on her chair. A man stood in the doorway. It wasn't Strangways. It was a big negro with yellowish skin and slanting eyes. There was a gun in his hand. It ended in a thick black cylinder.

Mary Trueblood opened her mouth to scream.

The man smiled broadly. Slowly, lovingly, he lifted the gun and shot her three times in and around the left breast.

The girl slumped sideways off her chair. The earphones slipped off her golden hair on to the floor. For perhaps a second the tiny chirrup of London sounded out into the room. Then it stopped. The buzzer at the Controller's desk in Radio Security had signalled that something was wrong on WXN.

The killer walked out of the door. He came back carrying a box with a coloured label on it that said PRESTO FIRE, and a big sugarsack marked TATE & LYLE. He put the box down on the floor and went to the body and roughly forced the sack over the head and down to the ankles. The feet stuck out. He bent them and crammed them in. He dragged the bulky sack out into the hall and came back. In the corner of the room the safe stood open, as he had been told it would, and the cipher books had been taken out and laid on the desk ready for work on the London signals. The man threw these and all the papers in the safe into the centre of the room. He tore down the curtains and added them to the pile. He topped it up with a couple of chairs. He opened the box of Presto firelighters and took out a handful and tucked them into the pile and lit them. Then he went out into the hall and lit similar bonfires in appropriate places. The tinder-dry furniture caught quickly and the flames began to lick up the panelling. The man went to the front door and opened it. Through the hibiscus hedge he could see the glint of the hearse. There was no noise except the zing of crickets and the soft tick-over of the car's engine. Up and down the road there was no other sign of life. The man went back into the smoke-filled hall and easily shouldered the sack and came out again, leaving the door open to make a draught. He walked swiftly down the path to the road. The back doors of the hearse were open. He handed in the sack and watched the two men force it into the coffin on top of Strangways's body. Then he climbed in and shut the doors and sat down and put on his top hat.

As the first flames showed in the upper windows of the bungalow, the hearse moved quietly from the sidewalk and went on its way up towards the Mona Reservoir. There the weighted coffin would slip down into its fifty-fathom grave and, in just forty-five minutes, the personnel and records of the Caribbean station of the Secret Service would have been utterly destroyed.

CHAPTER 2

Choice of Weapons

Three weeks later, in London, March came in like a rattlesnake.

From first light on March 1st, hail and icy sleet, with a Force 8 gale behind them, lashed at the city and went on lashing as the people streamed miserably to work, their legs whipped by the wet hems of their macintoshes and their faces blotching with the cold.

It was a filthy day and everybody said so—even M, who rarely admitted the existence of weather even in its extreme forms. When the old black Silver Wraith Rolls with the nondescript number-plate stopped outside the tall building in Regent's Park and he climbed stiffly out on to the pavement, hail hit him in the face like a whiff of small-shot. Instead of hurrying inside the building, he walked deliberately round the car to the window beside the chauffeur.

'Won't be needing the car again today, Smith. Take it away and go home. I'll use the tube this evening. No weather for driving a car. Worse than one of those PQ convoys.'

Ex-Leading Stoker Smith grinned gratefully. 'Aye-aye, sir. And thanks.' He watched the elderly erect figure walk round the bonnet of the Rolls and across the pavement and into the building. Just like the old boy. He'd always see the men right first. Smith clicked the gear lever into first and moved off, peering forward through the streaming windscreen. They didn't come like that any more.

M went up in the lift to the eighth floor and along the thick-carpeted corridor to his office. He shut the door behind him, took off his overcoat and scarf and hung them behind the door. He took out a large blue silk bandanna handkerchief and brusquely wiped it over his face. It was odd, but he wouldn't have done this in front of the porters or the liftman. He went over to his desk and sat down and bent towards the intercom. He pressed a switch. 'I'm in, Miss Moneypenny. The signals please, and anything else you've got. Then get me Sir James Molony. He'll be doing his rounds at St. Mary's about now. Tell the Chief of Staff I'll see 007 in half an hour. And let me have the Strangways file.' M waited for the metallic 'Yes, sir' and released the switch.

He sat back and reached for his pipe and began filling it thoughtfully. He didn't look up when his secretary came in with the stack of papers and he even ignored the half dozen pink Most Immediates on top of the signal file. If they had been vital he would have been called during the night.

A yellow light winked on the intercom. M picked up the black telephone from the row of four. 'That you, Sir James? Have you got five minutes?'

'Six, for you.' At the other end of the line the famous neurologist chuckled. 'Want me to certify one of Her Majesty's Ministers?'

'Not today.' M frowned irritably. The old Navy had respected governments. 'It's about that man of mine you've been handling. We won't bother about the name. This is an open line. I gather you let him out yesterday. Is he fit for duty?'

There was a pause on the other end. Now the voice

was professional, judicious. 'Physically he's as fit as a fiddle. Leg's healed up. Shouldn't be any after-effects. Yes, he's all right.' There was another pause. 'Just one thing, M. There's a lot of tension there, you know. You work these men of yours pretty hard. Can you give him something easy to start with? From what you've told me he's been having a tough time for some years now.'

M said gruffly, 'That's what he's paid for. It'll soon show if he's not up to the work. Won't be the first one that's cracked. From what you say, he sounds in perfectly good shape. It isn't as if he'd really been damaged like some of the patients I've sent you—men who've been properly put through the mangle.'

'Of course, if you put it like that. But pain's an odd thing. We know very little about it. You can't measure it—the difference in suffering between a woman having a baby and a man having a renal colic. And, thank God, the body seems to forget fairly quickly. But this man of yours has been in *real* pain, M. Don't think that just because nothing's been broken . . .'

'Quite, quite.' Bond had made a mistake and he had suffered for it. In any case M didn't like being lectured, even by one of the most famous doctors in the world, on how he should handle his agents. There had been a note of criticism in Sir James Molony's voice. M said abruptly, 'Ever hear of a man called Steincrohn—Dr. Peter Steincrohn?'

'No, who's he?'

'American doctor. Written a book my Washington people sent over for our library. This man talks about how much punishment the human body can put up with. Gives a list of the bits of the body an average man can do without. Matter of fact, I copied it out for future reference. Care to hear the list?' M dug into his coat pocket and put some letters and scraps of paper on the desk in front of him. With his left hand he selected a piece of paper and unfolded it. He wasn't put out by the silence on the other end of the line. 'Hullo, Sir James! Well, here they are: "Gall bladder, spleen, tonsils, appendix, one of his two kidneys, one of his two lungs, two of his four or five quarts of blood, two-fifths of his liver, most of his stomach, four of his twenty-three feet of intestines and half of his brain." ' M paused. When the silence continued at the other end, he said, 'Any comments, Sir James?'

There was a reluctant grunt at the other end of the telephone. 'I wonder he didn't add an arm and a leg, or all of them. I don't quite see what you're trying to prove.'

M gave a curt laugh. 'I'm not trying to prove anything, Sir James. It just struck me as an interesting list. All I'm trying to say is that my man seems to have got off pretty lightly compared with that sort of punishment. But,' M relented, 'don't let's argue about it.' He said in a milder voice, 'As a matter of fact I did have it in mind to let him have a bit of a breather. Something's come up in Jamaica.' M glanced at the streaming windows. 'It'll be more of a rest cure than anything. Two of my people, a man and a girl, have gone off together. Or that's what it looks like. Our friend can have a spell at being an inquiry agent—in the sunshine too. How's that?'

'Just the ticket. I wouldn't mind the job myself on a day like this.' But Sir James Molony was determined to get his message through. He persisted mildly, 'Don't think I wanted to interfere, M, but there are limits to a man's courage. I know you have to treat these men as if they were expendable, but presumably you don't want them to crack at the wrong moment. This one I've had here is tough. I'd say you'll get plenty more work out of him. But you know what Morgan has to say about courage in that book of his.'

'Don't recall.'

'He says that courage is a capital sum reduced by expenditure. I agree with him. All I'm trying to say is that this particular man seems to have been spending pretty hard since before the war. I wouldn't say he's over-drawn—not yet, but there are limits.'

'Just so.' M decided that was quite enough of that. Nowadays, softness was everywhere. 'That's why I'm sending him abroad. Holiday in Jamaica. Don't worry, Sir James. I'll take care of him. By the way, did you ever discover what the stuff was that Russian woman put into him?'

'Got the answer yesterday.' Sir James Molony also was glad the subject had been changed. The old man was as raw as the weather. Was there any chance that he had got his message across into what he described to himself as M's thick skull? 'Taken us three months. It was a bright chap at the School of Tropical Medicine who came up with it. The drug was *fugu* poison. The Japanese use it for committing suicide. It comes from the sex organs of the Japanese globefish. Trust the Russians to use something no one's ever heard of. They might just as well have used curare. It has much the same effect—paralysis of the central nervous system. *Fugu*'s scientific name is Tetrodotoxin. It's terrible stuff and very quick. One shot of it like your man got and in a matter of seconds the motor and respiratory muscles are paralysed. At first the chap sees double and then he can't keep his eyes open. Next he can't swallow. His head falls and he can't raise it. Dies of respiratory paralysis.'

'Lucky he got away with it.'

'Miracle. Thanks entirely to that Frenchman who was with him. Got your man on the floor and gave him artificial respiration as if he was drowning. Somehow kept his lungs going until the doctor came. Luckily the doctor had worked in South America. Diagnosed curare and treated him accordingly. But it was a chance in a million. By the same token, what happened to the Russian woman?'

M said shortly, 'Oh, she died. Well, many thanks, Sir James. And don't worry about your patient. I'll see he has an easy time of it. Goodbye.'

M hung up. His face was cold and blank. He pulled over the signal file and went quickly through it. On some of the signals he scribbled a comment. Occasionally he made a brief telephone call to one of the Sections. When he had finished he tossed the pile into

his *Out* basket and reached for his pipe and the tobacco
jar made out of the base of a fourteen-pounder shell.
Nothing remained in front of him except a buff folder
marked with the Top Secret red star. Across the centre
of the folder was written in block capitals: CARIB-
BEAN STATION, and underneath, in italics,
Strangways and Trueblood.

A light winked on the Intercom. M pressed down the
switch. 'Yes?'

'007's here, sir.'

'Send him in. And tell the Armourer to come up in
five minutes.'

M sat back. He put his pipe in his mouth and set a
match to it. Through the smoke he watched the door to
his secretary's office. His eyes were very bright and
watchful.

James Bond came through the door and shut it
behind him. He walked over to the chair across the desk
from M and sat down.

'Morning, 007.'

'Good morning, sir.'

There was silence in the room except for the rasping
of M's pipe. It seemed to be taking a lot of matches to
get it going. In the background the fingernails of the
sleet slashed against the two broad windows.

It was all just as Bond had remembered it through the
months of being shunted from hospital to hospital, the
weeks of dreary convalescence, the hard work of getting
his body back into shape. To him this represented
stepping back into life. Sitting here in this room opposite M was the symbol of normality he had longed
for. He looked across through the smoke clouds into the
shrewd grey eyes. They were watching him. What was
coming? A post-mortem on the shambles which had
been his last case? A curt relegation to one of the home
sections for a spell of desk work? Or some splendid new
assignment M had been keeping on ice while waiting for
Bond to get back to duty?

M threw the box of matches down on the red leather

desk. He leant back and clasped his hands behind his head.

'How do you feel? Glad to be back?'

'Very glad, sir. And I feel fine.'

'Any final thoughts about your last case? Haven't bothered you with it till you got well. You heard I ordered an inquiry. I believe the Chief of Staff took some evidence from you. Anything to add?'

M's voice was businesslike, cold. Bond didn't like it. Something unpleasant was coming. He said, 'No, sir. It was a mess. I blame myself for letting that woman get me. Shouldn't have happened.'

M took his hands from behind his neck and slowly leant forward and placed them flat on the desk in front of him. His eyes were hard. 'Just so.' The voice was velvet, dangerous. 'Your gun got stuck, if I recall. This Beretta of yours with the silencer. Something wrong there, 007. Can't afford that sort of mistake if you're to carry an 00 number. Would you prefer to drop it and go back to normal duties?'

Bond stiffened. His eyes looked resentfully into M's. The licence to kill for the Secret Service, the double-O prefix, was a great honour. It had been earned hardly. It brought Bond the only assignments he enjoyed, the dangerous ones. 'No, I wouldn't, sir.'

'Then we'll have to change your equipment. That was one of the findings of the Court of Inquiry. I agree with it. D'you understand?'

Bond said obstinately, 'I'm used to that gun, sir. I like working with it. What happened could have happened to anyone. With any kind of gun.'

'I don't agree. Nor did the Court of Inquiry. So that's final. The only question is what you're to use instead.' M bent forward to the intercom. 'Is the Armourer there? Send him in.'

M sat back. 'You may not know it, 007, but Major Boothroyd's the greatest small-arms expert in the world. He wouldn't be here if he wasn't. We'll hear what he has to say.'

The door opened. A short slim man with sandy hair came in and walked over to the desk and stood beside Bond's chair. Bond looked up into his face. He hadn't often seen the man before, but he remembered the very wide apart clear grey eyes that never seemed to flicker. With a non-committal glance down at Bond, the man stood relaxed, looking across at M. He said 'Good morning, sir,' in a flat, unemotional voice.

'Morning, Armourer. Now I want to ask you some questions.' M's voice was casual. 'First of all, what do you think of the Beretta, the .25?'

'Ladies' gun, sir.'

M raised ironic eyebrows at Bond. Bond smiled thinly.

'Really! And why do you say that?'

'No stopping power, sir. But it's easy to operate. A bit fancy-looking too, if you know what I mean, sir. Appeals to the ladies.'

'How would it be with a silencer?'

'Still less stopping power, sir. And I don't like silencers. They're heavy and get stuck in your clothing when you're in a hurry. I wouldn't recommend anyone to try a combination like that, sir. Not if they were meaning business.'

M said pleasantly to Bond, 'Any comment, 007?'

Bond shrugged his shoulders. 'I don't agree. I've used the .25 Beretta for fifteen years. Never had a stoppage and I haven't missed with it yet. Not a bad record for a gun. It just happens that I'm used to it and I can point it straight. I've used bigger guns when I've had to—the .45 Colt with the long barrel, for instance. But for close-up work and concealment I like the Beretta.' Bond paused. He felt he should give way somewhere. 'I'd agree about the silencer, sir. They're a nuisance. But sometimes you have to use them.'

'We've seen what happens when you do,' said M drily. 'And as for changing your gun, it's only a question of practice. You'll soon get the feel of a new one.' M allowed a trace of sympathy to enter his voice.

'Sorry, 007. But I've decided. Just stand up a moment. I want the Armourer to get a look at your build.'

Bond stood up and faced the other man. There was no warmth in the two pairs of eyes. Bond's showed irritation. Major Boothroyd's were indifferent, clinical. He walked round Bond. He said 'Excuse me' and felt Bond's biceps and forearms. He came back in front of him and said, 'Might I see your gun?'

Bond's hand went slowly into his coat. He handed over the taped Beretta with the sawn barrel. Boothroyd examined the gun and weighed it in his hand. He put it down on the desk. 'And your holster?'

Bond took off his coat and slipped off the chamois leather holster and harness. He put his coat on again.

With a glance at the lips of the holster, perhaps to see if they showed traces of snagging, Boothroyd tossed the holster down beside the gun with a motion that sneered. He looked across at M. 'I think we can do better than this, sir.' It was the sort of voice Bond's first expensive tailor had used.

Bond sat down. He just stopped himself gazing rudely at the ceiling. Instead he looked impassively across at M.

'Well, Armourer, what do you recommend?'

Major Boothroyd put on the expert's voice. 'As a matter of fact, sir,' he said modestly, 'I've just been testing most of the small automatics. Five thousand rounds each at twenty-five yards. Of all of them, I'd choose the Walther PPK 7.65 mm. It only came fourth after the Japanese M-14, the Russian Tokarev and the Sauer M-38. But I like its light trigger pull and the extension spur of the magazine gives a grip that should suit 007. It's a real stopping gun. Of course it's about a .32 calibre as compared with the Beretta's .25, but I wouldn't recommend anything lighter. And you can get ammunition for the Walther anywhere in the world. That gives it an edge on the Japanese and the Russian guns.'

M turned to Bond. 'Any comments?'

'It's a good gun, sir,' Bond admitted. 'Bit more bulky than the Beretta. How does the Armourer suggest I carry it?'

'Berns Martin Triple-draw holster,' said Major Boothroyd succinctly. 'Best worn inside the trouser band to the left. But it's all right below the shoulder. Stiff saddle leather. Holds the gun in with a spring. Should make for a quicker draw than that,' he gestured towards the desk. 'Three-fifths of a second to hit a man at twenty feet would be about right.'

'That's settled then.' M's voice was final. 'And what about something bigger?'

'There's only one gun for that, sir,' said Major Boothroyd stolidly. 'Smith & Wesson Centennial Airweight. Revolver. .38 calibre. Hammerless, so it won't catch in clothing. Overall length of six and a half inches and it only weighs thirteen ounces. To keep down the weight, the cylinder holds only five cartridges. But by the time they're gone,' Major Boothroyd allowed himself a wintry smile, 'somebody's been killed. Fires the .38 S & W Special. Very accurate cartridge indeed. With standard loading it has a muzzle velocity of eight hundred and sixty feet per second and muzzle energy of two hundred and sixty foot-pounds. There are various barrel lengths, three-and-a-half-inch, five-inch . . .'

'All right, all right.' M's voice was testy. 'Take it as read. If you say it's the best I'll believe you. So it's the Walther and the Smith & Wesson. Send up one of each to 007. With the harness. And arrange for him to fire them in. Starting today. He's got to be expert in a week. All right? Then thank you very much, Armourer. I won't detain you.'

'Thank you, sir,' said Major Boothroyd. He turned and marched stiffly out of the room.

There was a moment's silence. The sleet tore at the windows. M swivelled his chair and watched the streaming panes. Bond took the opportunity to glance at his watch. Ten o'clock. His eyes slid to the gun and holster on the desk. He thought of his fifteen years' marriage to the ugly bit of metal. He remembered the times its single word had saved his life—and the times when its threat alone had been enough. He thought of the days when he had literally dressed to kill—when he had dismantled the gun and oiled it and packed the bullets carefully into the springloaded magazine and tried the action once or twice, pumping the cartridges out on to the bedspread in some hotel bedroom somewhere round the world. Then the last wipe of a dry rag and the gun into the little holster and a pause in front of the mirror to see that nothing showed. And then out of the door and on his way to the rendezvous that was to end with either darkness or light. How many times had it saved his life? How many death sentences had it signed? Bond felt unreasonably sad. How could one have such ties with an inanimate object, an ugly one at that, and, he had to admit it, with a weapon that was not in the same class as the ones chosen by the Armourer? But he had the ties and M was going to cut them.

M swivelled back to face him. 'Sorry, James,' he said, and there was no sympathy in his voice. 'I know how you like that bit of iron. But I'm afraid it's got to go. Never give a weapon a second chance—any more than a man. I can't afford to gamble with the double-O section. They've got to be properly equipped. You understand that? A gun's more important than a hand or a foot in your job.'

Bond smiled thinly. 'I know, sir. I shan't argue. I'm just sorry to see it go.'

'All right then. We'll say no more about it. Now I've got some more news for you. There's a job come up. In Jamaica. Personnel problem. Or that's what it looks like. Routine investigation and report. The sunshine'll do you good and you can practise your new guns on the turtles or whatever they have down there. You can do with a bit of holiday. Like to take it on?'

Bond thought: He's got it in for me over the last job. Feels I let him down. Won't trust me with anything tough. Wants to see. Oh well! He said: 'Sounds rather like the soft life, sir. I've had almost too much of that lately. But if it's got to be done . . . If you say so, sir . . .'

'Yes,' said M. 'I say so.'

CHAPTER 3

Holiday Task

It was getting dark. Outside the weather was thickening. M reached over and switched on the green-shaded desklight. The centre of the room became a warm yellow pool in which the leather top of the desk glowed blood-red.

M pulled the thick file towards him. Bond noticed it for the first time. He read the reversed lettering without difficulty. What had Strangways been up to? Who was Trueblood?

M pressed a button on his desk. 'I'll get the Chief of Staff in on this,' he said. 'I know the bones of the case, but he can fill in the flesh. It's a drab little story, I'm afraid.'

The Chief of Staff came in. He was a colonel in the Sappers, a man of about Bond's age, but his hair was prematurely grey at the temples from the endless grind of work and responsibility. He was saved from a nervous breakdown by physical toughness and a sense of humour. He was Bond's best friend at headquarters. They smiled at each other.

'Bring up a chair, Chief of Staff. I've given 007 the Strangways case. Got to get the mess cleared up before we make a new appointment there. 007 can be acting Head of Station in the meantime. I want him to leave in a week. Would you fix that with the Colonial Office and the Governor? And now let's go over the case.' He turned to Bond. 'I think you knew Strangways, 007. See you worked with him on that treasure business about five years ago. What did you think of him?'

'Good man, sir. Bit highly strung. I'd have thought he'd have been relieved by now. Five years is a long time in the tropics.'

M ignored the comment. 'And his number two, this girl Trueblood, Mary Trueblood. Ever come across her?'

'No, sir.'

'I see she's got a good record. Chief Officer W.R.N.S. and then came to us. Nothing against her on her Confidential Record. Good-looker to judge from her photographs. That probably explains it. Would you say Strangways was a bit of a womanizer?'

'Could have been,' said Bond carefully, not wanting to say anything against Strangways, but remembering the dashing good looks. 'But what's happened to them, sir?'

'That's what we want to find out,' said M. 'They've gone, vanished into thin air. Both went on the same evening about three weeks ago. Left Strangways's bungalow burned to the ground—radio, codebooks, files. Nothing left but a few charred scraps. The girl left all her things intact. Must have taken only what she stood up in. Even her passport was in her room. But it would have been easy for Strangways to cook up two passports. He had plenty of blanks. He was Passport Control Officer for the island. Any number of planes they could have taken—to Florida or South America or one of the other islands in his area. Police are still checking the passenger lists. Nothing's come up yet, but they could have gone to ground for a day or two and then done a bunk. Dyed the girl's hair and so forth. Airport security doesn't amount to much in that part of the world. Isn't that so, Chief of Staff?'

'Yes, sir.' The Chief of Staff sounded dubious. 'But I still can't understand that last radio contact.' He turned to Bond. 'You see, they began to make their routine contact at eighteen-thirty Jamaican time. Someone, Radio Security thinks it was the girl, acknowledged our WWW and then went off the air. We tried to regain contact but there was obviously something fishy and we broke off. No answer to the Blue Call, or to the Red. So that was that. Next day Section III sent 258 down from Washington. By that time the police had taken over and the Governor had already made up his mind and was trying to get the case hushed up. It all seemed pretty obvious to him. Strangways has had occasional girl trouble down there. Can't blame the chap myself. It's a quiet station. Not much to occupy his time. The Governor jumped to the obvious conclusions. So, of course, did the local police. Sex and machete fights are about all they understand. 258 spent a week down there and couldn't turn up a scrap of contrary evidence. He reported accordingly and we sent him back to Washington. Since then the police have been scraping around rather ineffectually and getting nowhere.' The Chief of Staff paused. He looked apologetically at M. 'I know you're inclined to agree with the Governor, sir, but that radio contact sticks in my throat. I just can't see where it fits into the runaway-couple picture. And Strangways's friends at his club say he was perfectly normal. Left in the middle of a rubber of bridge—always did, when it was getting close to his deadline. Said he'd be back in twenty minutes. Ordered drinks all round—again just as he always did—and left the club dead on six-fifteen, exactly to schedule. Then he vanished into thin air. Even left his car in front of the club. Now, why should he set the rest of his bridge four looking for him if he wanted to skip with the girl? Why not leave in the morning, or better still, late at night, after they'd made their radio call and tidied up their lives? It doesn't make sense to me.'

M grunted non-committally. 'People in—er—love do stupid things,' he said gruffly. 'Act like lunatics sometimes. And anyway, what other explanation is there? Absolutely no trace of foul play—no reason for it that anyone can see. It's a quiet station down there. Same routines every month—an occasional communist trying to get into the island from Cuba, crooks from England thinking they can hide away just because Jamaica's so far from London. I don't suppose Strangways has had a big case since 007 was there.' He turned to Bond. 'On what you've heard, what do you think, 007? There's not much else to tell you.'

Bond was definite. 'I just can't see Strangways flying off the handle like that, sir. I daresay he was having an affair with the girl, though I wouldn't have thought he was a man to mix business with pleasure. But the Service was his whole life. He'd never have let it down. I can see him handing in his papers, and the girl doing the same, and then going off with her after you'd sent out reliefs. But I don't believe it was in him to leave us in the air like this. And from what you say of the girl, I'd say it would be much the same with her. Chief Officers W.R.N.S. don't go out of their senses.'

'Thank you, 007.' M's voice was controlled. 'These considerations had also crossed my mind. No one's been jumping to conclusions without weighing all the possibilities. Perhaps you can suggest another solution.'

M sat back and waited. He reached for his pipe and began filling it. The case bored him. He didn't like personnel problems, least of all messy ones like this. There were plenty of other worries waiting to be coped with round the world. It was only to give Bond the pretence of a job, mixed with a good rest, that he had decided to send him out to Jamaica to close the case. He put the pipe in his mouth and reached for the matches. 'Well?'

Bond wasn't going to be put off his stride. He had liked Strangways and he was impressed by the points the Chief of Staff had made. He said: 'Well, sir. For instance, what was the last case Strangeways was working on? Had he reported anything, or was there anything

Section III had asked him to look into. Anything at all in the last few months?'

'Nothing whatsoever.' M was definite. He took the pipe out of his mouth and cocked it at the Chief of Staff. 'Right?'

'Right, sir,' said the Chief of Staff. 'Only that damned business about the birds.'

'Oh that,' said M contemptuously. 'Some rot from the Zoo or somebody. Got wished on us by the Colonial Office. About six weeks ago, wasn't it?'

'That's right, sir. But it wasn't the Zoo. It was some people in America called the Audubon Society. They protect rare birds from extinction or something like that. Got on to our Ambassador in Washington, and the F.O. passed the buck to the Colonial Office. They shoved it on to us. Seems these bird people are pretty powerful in America. They even got an atom bombing range shifted on the West Coast because it interfered with some birds' nests.'

M snorted. 'Damned thing called a Whooping Crane. Read about it in the papers.'

Bond persisted. 'Could you tell me about it, sir? What did the Audubon people want us to do?'

M waved his pipe impatiently. He picked up the Strangways file and tossed it down in front of the Chief of Staff. 'You tell him, Chief of Staff,' he said wearily. 'It's all in there.'

The Chief of Staff took the file and riffled through the pages towards the back. He found what he wanted and bent the file in half. There was silence in the room while he ran his eye over three pages of typescript which Bond could see were headed with the blue and white cipher of the Colonial Office. Bond sat quietly, trying not to feel M's coiled impatience radiating across the desk.

The Chief of Staff slapped the file shut. He said, 'Well, this is the story as we passed it to Strangways on January 20th. He acknowledged receipt, but after that we heard nothing from him.' The Chief of Staff sat back in his chair. He looked at Bond. 'It seems there's a bird called a Roseate Spoonbill. There's a coloured photograph of it in here. Looks like a sort of pink stork with an ugly flat bill which it uses for digging for food in the mud. Not many years ago these birds were dying out. Just before the war there were only a few hundred left in the world, mostly in Florida and thereabouts. Then somebody reported a colony of them on an island called Crab Key between Jamaica and Cuba. It's British territory—a dependency of Jamaica. Used to be a guano island, but the quality of the guano was too low for the cost of digging it. When the birds were found there, it had been uninhabited for about fifty years. The Audubon people went there and ended up by leasing a corner as a sanctuary for these spoonbills. Put two wardens in charge and persuaded the airlines to stop flying over the island and disturbing the birds. The birds flourished and at the last count there were about five thousand of them on the island. Then came the war. The price of guano went up and some bright chap had the idea of buying the island and starting to work it again. He negotiated with the Jamaican Government and bought the place for ten thousand pounds with the condition that he didn't disturb the lease of the sanctuary. That was in 1943. Well, this man imported plenty of cheap labour and soon had the place working at a profit and it's gone on making a profit until recently. Then the price of guano took a dip and it's thought that he must be having a hard time making both ends meet.'

'Who is this man?'

'Chinaman, or rather half Chinese and half German. Got a daft name. Calls himself Doctor No—Doctor Julius No.'

'No? Spelt like Yes?'

'That's right.'

'Any facts about him?'

'Nothing except that he keeps very much to himself. Hasn't been seen since he made his deal with the Jamaican Government. And there's no traffic with the island. It's his and he keeps it private. Says he doesn't want people disturbing the guanay birds who turn out his guano. Seems reasonable. Well, nothing happened until just before Christmas when one of the Audubon wardens, a Barbadian, good solid chap apparently, arrived on the north shore of Jamaica in a canoe. He was very sick. He was terribly burned—died in a few days. Before he died he told some crazy story about their camp having been attacked by a dragon with flames coming out of its mouth. The dragon had killed his pal and burned up the camp and gone roaring off into the bird sanctuary belching fire among the birds and scaring them off God knows where. He had been badly burned but he'd escaped to the coast and stolen a canoe and sailed all one night to Jamaica. Poor chap was obviously off his rocker. And that was that, except that a routine report had to be sent off to the Audubon Society. And they weren't satisfied. Sent down two of their big brass in a Beechcraft from Miami to investigate. There's an airstrip on the island. This Chinaman's got a Grumman Amphibian for bringing in supplies . . .'

M interjected sourly, 'All these people seem to have a hell of a lot of money to throw about on their damned birds.'

Bond and the Chief of Staff exchanged smiles. M had been trying for years to get the Treasury to give him an Auster for the Caribbean Station.

The Chief of Staff continued: 'And the Beechcraft crashed on landing and killed the two Audubon men. Well, that aroused these bird people to a fury. They got a corvette from the U.S. Training Squadron in the Caribbean to make a call on Doctor No. That's how powerful these people are. Seems they've got quite a lobby in Washington. The captain of the corvette reported that he was received very civilly by Doctor No but was kept well away from the guano workings. He was taken to the airstrip and examined the remains of the plane. Smashed to pieces, but nothing suspicious—came in to land too fast probably. The bodies of the two men and the pilot had been reverently embalmed and packed in handsome coffins which were

handed over with quite a ceremony. The captain was
very impressed by Doctor No's courtesy. He asked to
see the wardens' camp and he was taken out there and
shown the remains of it. Doctor No's theory was that
the two men had gone mad because of the heat and the
loneliness, or any rate that one of them had gone mad
and burned down the camp with the other inside it. This
seemed possible to the captain when he'd seen what a
godforsaken bit of marsh the man had been living in for
ten years or more. There was nothing else to see and he
was politely steered back to his ship and sailed away.'
The Chief of Staff spread his hands. 'And that's the lot
except that the captain reported that he saw only a handful of roseate spoonbills. When his report got back to
the Audubon Society it was apparently the loss of their
blasted birds that infuriated these people most of all,
and ever since then they've been nagging at us to have
an inquiry into the whole business. Of course nobody at
the Colonial Office or in Jamaica's in the least interested. So in the end the whole fairy story was dumped
in our lap.' The Chief of Staff shrugged his shoulders
with finality. 'And that's how this pile of bumf,' he
waved the file, 'or at any rate the guts of it, got landed
on Strangways.'

   M looked morosely at Bond. 'See what I mean, 007?
Just the sort of mares' nest these old women's societies
are always stirring up. People start preserving
something—churches, old houses, decaying pictures,
birds—and there's always a hullabaloo of some sort.
The trouble is these sort of people get really worked up
about their damned birds or whatever it is. They get the
politicians involved. And somehow they all seem to
have stacks of money. God knows where it comes from.
Other old women, I suppose. And then there comes a
point when someone has to do something to keep them
quiet. Like this case. It gets shunted off on to me
because the place is British territory. At the same time
it's private land. Nobody wants to interfere officially.
So I'm supposed to do what? Send a submarine to the
island? For what? To find out what's happened to a

covey of pink storks.' M snorted. 'Anyway, you asked about Strangways's last case and that's it.' M leant forward belligerently. 'Any questions? I've got a busy day ahead.'

Bond grinned. He couldn't help it. M's occasional outbursts of rage were so splendid. And nothing set him going so well as any attempt to waste the time and energies and slim funds of the Secret Service. Bond got to his feet. 'Perhaps if I could have the file, sir,' he said placatingly. 'It just strikes me that four people seem to have died more or less because of these birds. Perhaps two more did—Strangways and the Trueblood girl. I agree it sounds ridiculous, but we've got nothing else to go on.'

'Take it, take it,' said M impatiently. 'And hurry up and get your holiday over. You may not have noticed it, but the rest of the world happens to be in a bit of a mess.'

Bond reached across and picked up the file. He also made to pick up his Beretta and the holster. 'No,' said M sharply. 'Leave that. And mind you've got the hang of the other two guns by the time I see you again.'

Bond looked across into M's eyes. For the first time in his life he hated the man. He knew perfectly well why M was being tough and mean. It was deferred punishment for having nearly got killed on his last job. Plus getting away from this filthy weather into the sunshine. M couldn't bear his men to have an easy time. In a way Bond felt sure he was being sent on this cushy assignment to humiliate him. The old bastard.

With the anger balling up inside him like cat's fur, Bond said, 'I'll see to it, sir,' and turned and walked out of the room.

CHAPTER 4

Reception Committee

The sixty-eight tons deadweight of the Super Constellation hurtled high above the green and brown chequerboard of Cuba and, with only another hundred miles to go, started its slow declining flight towards Jamaica.

Bond watched the big green turtle-backed island grow on the horizon and the water below him turn from the dark blue of the Cuba Deep to the azure and milk of the inshore shoals. Then they were over the North Shore, over its rash of millionaire hotels, and crossing the high mountains of the interior. The scattered dice of small-holdings showed on the slopes and in clearings in the jungle, and the setting sun flashed gold on the bright worms of tumbling rivers and streams. 'Xaymaca' the Arawak Indians had called it—'The Land of Hills and Rivers'. Bond's heart lifted with the beauty of one of the most fertile islands in the world.

The other side of the mountains was in deep violet shadow. Lights were already twinkling in the foothills and spangling the streets of Kingston, but, beyond, the

far arm of the harbour and the airport were still touched
with the sun against which the Port Royal lighthouse
blinked ineffectually. Now the Constellation was getting
its nose down into a wide sweep beyond the harbour.
There was a slight thump as the tricycle landing gear extended under the aircraft and locked into position, and
a shrill hydraulic whine as the brake flaps slid out of the
trailing edge of the wings. Slowly the great aircraft
turned in again towards the land and for a moment the
setting sun poured gold into the cabin. Then, the plane
had dipped below the level of the Blue Mountains and
was skimming down towards the single north-south run-
way. There was a glimpse of a road and telephone wires.
Then the concrete, scarred with black skid-marks, was
under the belly of the plane and there was the soft
double thump of a perfect landing and the roar of re-
versing props as they taxied in towards the low white
airport buildings.

The sticky fingers of the tropics brushed Bond's face
as he left the aircraft and walked over to Health and Im-
migration. He knew that by the time he had got through
Customs he would be sweating. He didn't mind. After
the rasping cold of London, the stuffy, velvet heat was
easily bearable.

Bond's passport described him as 'Import and Export
Merchant'.

'What company, sir?'

'Universal Export.'

'Are you here on business or pleasure, sir?'

'Pleasure.'

'I hope you enjoy your stay, sir.' The negro im-
migration officer handed Bond his passport with indifference.

'Thank you.'

Bond walked out into the Customs hall. At once he
saw the tall brown-skinned man against the barrier. He
was wearing the same old faded blue shirt and probably
the same khaki twill trousers he had been wearing when
Bond first met him five years before.

'Quarrel!'

From behind the barrier the Cayman Islander gave a broad grin. He lifted his right forearm across his eyes in the old salute of the West Indians. 'How you, cap'n?' he called delightedly.

'I'm fine,' said Bond. 'Just wait till I get my bag through. Got the car?'

'Sure, cap'n.'

The Customs officer who, like most men from the waterfront, knew Quarrel, chalked Bond's bag without opening it and Bond picked it up and went out through the barrier. Quarrel took it from him and held out his right hand. Bond took the warm dry calloused paw and looked into the dark grey eyes that showed descent from a Cromwellian soldier or a pirate of Morgan's time. 'You haven't changed, Quarrel,' he said affectionately. 'How's the turtle fishing?'

'Not so bad, cap'n, an' not so good. Much de same as always.' He looked critically at Bond. 'Yo been sick, or somepun?'

Bond was surprised. 'As a matter of fact I have. But I've been fit for weeks. What made you say that?'

Quarrel was embarrassed. 'Sorry, cap'n,' he said, thinking he might have offended Bond. 'Dere some pain lines in yo face since de las' time.'

'Oh well,' said Bond. 'It was nothing much. But I could do with a spell of your training. I'm not as fit as I ought to be.'

'Sho ting, cap'n.'

They were moving towards the exit when there came the sharp crack and flash of a press camera. A pretty Chinese girl in Jamaican dress was lowering her Speed Graphic. She came up to them. She said with synthetic charm, 'Thank you, gentlemen. I am from the *Daily Gleaner*.' She glanced down at a list in her hand. 'Mister Bond, isn't it? And how long will you be with us, Mister Bond?'

Bond was offhand. This was a bad start. 'In transit,' he said shortly. 'I think you'll find there were more interesting people on the plane.'

'Oh no, I'm sure not, Mister Bond. You look very important. And what hotel will you be staying at?'

Damn, thought Bond. He said 'Myrtle Bank' and moved on.

'Thank you, Mister Bond,' said the tinkling voice. 'I hope you'll enjoy . . .'

They were outside. As they walked towards the parking place Bond said, 'Ever seen that girl at the airport before?'

Quarrel reflected. 'Reck'n not, cap'n. But de *Gleaner* have plenty camera gals.'

Bond was vaguely worried. There was no earthly reason why his picture should be wanted by the Press. It was five years since his last adventures on the island, and anyway his name had been kept out of the papers.

They got to the car. It was a black Sunbeam Alpine. Bond looked sharply at it and then at the number plate. Strangways's car. What the hell? 'Where did you get this, Quarrel?'

'A.D.C. tell me fe to take him, cap'n. Him say hit de only spare car dey have. Why, cap'n? Him no good?'

'Oh, it's all right, Quarrel,' said Bond resignedly. 'Come on, let's get going.'

Bond got into the passenger seat. It was entirely his fault. He might have guessed at the chance of getting this car. But it would certainly put the finger on him and on what he was doing in Jamaica if anyone happened to be interested.

They moved off down the long cactus-fringed road towards the distant lights of Kingston. Normally, Bond would have sat and enjoyed the beauty of it all—the steady zing of the crickets, the rush of warm, scented air, the ceiling of stars, the necklace of yellow lights shimmering across the harbour—but now he was cursing his carelessness and knowing what he shouldn't have done.

What he *had* done was to send one signal through the Colonial Office to the Governor. In it he had first asked that the A.D.C. should get Quarrel over from the Cayman Islands for an indefinite period on a salary of ten pounds a week. Quarrel had been with Bond on his

last adventure in Jamaica. He was an invaluable
handyman with all the fine seaman's qualities of the
Cayman Islander, and he was a passport into the lower
strata of coloured life which would otherwise be closed
to Bond. Everybody loved him and he was a splendid
companion. Bond knew that Quarrel was vital if he was
to get anywhere on the Strangways case—whether it was
a case or just a scandal. Then Bond had asked for a
single room and shower at the Blue Hills Hotel, for the
loan of a car and for Quarrel to meet him with the car at
the airport. Most of this had been wrong. In particular
Bond should have taken a taxi to his hotel and made
contact with Quarrel later. Then he would have seen the
car and had a chance to change it.

As it was, reflected Bond, he might just as well have
advertised his visit and its purpose in the *Gleaner.* He
sighed. It was the mistakes one made at the beginning of
a case that were the worst. They were the irretrievable
ones, the ones that got you off on the wrong foot, that
gave the enemy the first game. But was there an enemy?
Wasn't he being overcautious? On an impulse Bond
turned in his seat. A hundred yards behind were two
dim sidelights. Most Jamaicans drive with their
headlights full on. Bond turned back. He said, 'Quarrel.
At the end of the Palisadoes, where the left fork goes to
Kingston and the right to Morant, I want you to turn
quickly down the Morant road and stop at once and
turn your lights off. Right? And now go like hell.'

'Okay, cap'n.' Quarrel's voice sounded pleased. He
put his foot down to the floorboards. The little car gave
a deep growl and tore off down the white road.

Now they were at the end of the straight. The car
skidded round the curve where the corner of the harbour bit into the land. Another five hundred yards and
they would be at the intersection. Bond looked back.
There was no sign of the other car. Here was the sign-
post. Quarrel did a racing change and hurled the car
round on a tight lock. He pulled in to the side and
dowsed his lights. Bond turned and waited. At once he

heard the roar of a big car at speed. Lights blazed on, looking for them. Then the car was past and tearing on towards Kingston. Bond had time to notice that it was a big American type taxicab and that there was no one in it but the driver. Then it was gone.

The dust settled slowly. They sat for ten minutes saying nothing. Then Bond told Quarrel to turn the car and take the Kingston road. He said, 'I think that car was interested in us, Quarrel. You don't drive an empty taxi back from the airport. It's an expensive run. Keep a watch out. He may find we've fooled him and be waiting for us.'

'Sho ting, cap'n,' said Quarrel happily. This was just the sort of life he had hoped for when he got Bond's message.

They came into the stream of Kingston traffic—buses, cars, horse-drawn carts, pannier-laden donkeys down from the hills, and the hand-drawn barrows selling violent coloured drinks. In the crush it was impossible to say if they were being followed. They turned off to the right and up towards the hills. There were many cars behind them. Any one of them could have been the American taxi. They drove for a quarter of an hour up to Halfway Tree and then on to the Junction Road, the main road across the island. Soon there was a neon sign of a green palm tree and underneath 'Blue Hills. THE hotel'. They drove in and up the drive lined with neatly rounded bushes of bougainvillaea.

A hundred yards higher up the road the black taxi waved the following drivers on and pulled in to the left. It made a U-turn in a break in the traffic and swept back down the hill towards Kingston.

The Blue Hills was a comfortable old-fashioned hotel with modern trimmings. Bond was welcomed with deference because his reservation had been made by King's House. He was shown to a finer corner room with a balcony looking out over the distant sweep of Kingston harbour. Thankfully he took off his London clothes, now moist with perspiration, and went into the

glass-fronted shower and turned the cold water full on
and stood under it for five minutes during which he
washed his hair to remove the last dirt of big-city life.
Then he pulled on a pair of Sea Island cotton shorts
and, with sensual pleasure at the warm soft air on his
nakedness, unpacked his things and rang for the waiter.

Bond ordered a double gin and tonic and one whole
green lime. When the drink came he cut the lime in half,
dropped the two squeezed halves into the long glass,
almost filled the glass with ice cubes and then poured in
the tonic. He took the drink out on to the balcony, and
sat and looked out across the spectacular view. He
thought how wonderful it was to be away from
headquarters, and from London, and from hospitals,
and to be here, at this moment, doing what he was doing
and knowing, as all his senses told him, that he was on a
good tough case again.

He sat for a while, luxuriously, letting the gin relax
him. He ordered another and drank it down. It was
seven-fifteen. He had arranged for Quarrel to pick him
up at seven-thirty. They were going to have dinner
together. Bond had asked Quarrel to suggest a place.
After a moment of embarrassment, Quarrel had said
that whenever he wanted to enjoy himself in Kingston
he went to a waterfront nightspot called The Joy Boat.
'Hit no great shakes, cap'n,' he had said apologetically,
'but da food an' drinks an' music is good and I got a
good fren' dere. Him owns de joint. Dey calls him
"Pus-Feller" seein' how him once fought wit' a big hoctopus.'

Bond smiled to himself at the way Quarrel, like most
West Indians, added an 'h' when it wasn't needed and
took it off when it was. He went into his room and
dressed in his old dark blue tropical worsted suit, a
sleeveless white cotton shirt and a black knitted tie,
looked in the glass to see that the Walther didn't show
under his armpit and went down and out to where the
car was waiting.

They swooped quietly down through the soft singing
dusk into Kingston and turned to the left along the har-

bour side. They passed one or two smart restaurants and night clubs from which came the throb and twang of calypso music. There was a stretch of private houses that dwindled into a poor-class shopping centre and then into shacks. Then, where the road curved away from the sea, there was a blaze of golden neon in the shape of a Spanish galleon above green lettering that said 'The Joy Boat'. They pulled into a parking place and Bond followed Quarrel through the gate into a small garden of palm trees growing out of lawn. At the end was the beach and the sea. Tables were dotted about under the palms, and in the centre was a small deserted cement dance floor to one side of which a calypso trio in sequined scarlet shirts was softly improvising on 'Take her to Jamaica where the rum comes from'.

Only half the tables were filled, mostly by coloured people. There was a sprinkling of British and American sailors with their girls. An immensely fat negro in a smart white dinner jacket left one of the tables and came to meet them.

'Hi, Mister Q. Long time no see. Nice table for two?'

'That's right, Pus-Feller. Closer to da kitchen dan da music.'

The big man chuckled. He led them down towards the sea and placed them at a quiet table under a palm tree that grew out of the base of the restaurant building. 'Drinks gemmun?'

Bond ordered his gin and tonic with a lime, and Quarrel a Red Stripe beer. They scanned the menu and both decided on broiled lobster followed by a rare steak with native vegetables.

The drinks came. The glasses were dripping with condensation. The small fact reminded Bond of other times in hot climates. A few yards away the sea lisped on the flat sand. The three-piece began playing 'Kitch'. Above them the palm fronds clashed softly in the night breeze. A gecko chuckled somewhere in the garden. Bond thought of the London he had left the day before. He said, 'I like this place, Quarrel.'

Quarrel was pleased. 'Him a good fren of mine, da

Pus-Feller. Him knows mostly what goes hon hin
Kingston case you got hany questions, cap'n. Him come
from da Caymans. Him an' me once share a boat. Then
him go hoff one day catching boobies' heggs hat Crab
Key. Went swimmin' to a rock for more heggs an' dis
big hoctopus get him. Dey mosly small fellers roun' here
but dey come bigger at da Crab seein' how its alongside
de Cuba Deep, da deepest waters roun' dese parts. Pus-
Feller have hisself a bad time wit dis hanimal. Bust one
lung cuttin' hisself free. Dat scare him an him sell me his
half of da boat an' come to Kingston. Dat were 'fore da
war. Now him rich man whiles I go hon fishin'.'
Quarrel chuckled at the quirk of fate.

'Crab Key,' said Bond. 'What sort of a place is that?'
Quarrel looked at him sharply. 'Dat a bad luck place
now, cap'n,' he said shortly. 'Chinee gemmun buy hit
durin' da war and bring in men and dig bird-dirt. Don'
let nobody land dere and don' let no one get hoff. We
gives it a wide bert'.'

'Why's that?'

'Him have plenty watchmen. An' guns—machine
guns. An' a radar. An' a spottin' plane. Frens o' mine
have landed dere and him never been seen again. Dat
Chinee keep him island plenty private. Tell da trut',
cap'n,' Quarrel was apologetic, 'dat Crab Key scare me
plenty.'

Bond said thoughtfully, 'Well, well.'

The food came. They ordered another round of
drinks and ate. While they ate, Bond gave Quarrel an
outline of the Strangways case. Quarrel listened
carefully, occasionally asking questions. He was particularly interested in the birds on Crab Key, and what
the watchmen had said, and how the plane was supposed to have crashed. Finally he pushed his plate away.
He wiped the back of his hand across his mouth. He
took out a cigarette and lit it. He leant forward.
'Cap'n,' he said softly, 'I no mind if hit was birds or
butterflies or bees. If dey was on Crab Key and da Commander was stickin' his nose into da business, yo kin bet
yo bottom dollar him been mashed. Him and him girl.

Da Chinee mash dem for sho.'

Bond looked carefully into the urgent grey eyes. 'What makes you so certain?'

Quarrel spread his hands. To him the answer was simple. 'Dat Chinee love him privacy. Him want be left alone. I know him kill ma frens order keep folk away from da Crab. Him a mos' powerful man. Him kill hanyone what hinterfere with him.'

'Why?'

'Don' rightly know, cap'n', said Quarrel indifferently. 'People dem want different tings in dis world. An what dem want sufficient dem gits.'

A glint of light caught the corner of Bond's eye. He turned quickly. The Chinese girl from the airport was standing in the near-by shadows. Now she was dressed in a tight-fitting sheath of black satin slashed up one side almost to her hip. She had a Leica with a flash attachment in one hand. The other hand was in a leather case at her side. The hand came out holding a flashbulb. The girl slipped the base into her mouth to wet it and improve the contact and made to screw it into the reflector.

'Get that girl,' said Bond quickly.

In two strides Quarrel was up with her. He held out his hand. 'Evenin', missy,' he said softly.

The girl smiled. She let the Leica hang on the thin strap round her neck. She took Quarrel's hand. Quarrel swung her round like a ballet dancer. Now he had her hand behind her back and she was in the crook of his arm.

She looked up at him angrily. 'Don't. You're hurting.'

Quarrel smiled down into the flashing dark eyes in the pale, almond-shaped face. 'Cap'n like you take a drink wit' we,' he said soothingly. He came back to the table, moving the girl along with him. He hooked a chair out with his foot and sat her down beside him, keeping the grip on her wrist behind her back. They sat bolt upright, like quarrelling lovers.

Bond looked into the pretty, angry little face. 'Good evening. What are you doing here? Why do you want another picture of me?'

'I'm doing the nightspots,' the Cupid's bow of a mouth parted persuasively. 'The first picture of you didn't come out. Tell this man to leave me alone.'

'So you work for the *Gleaner*? What's your name?'

'I won't tell you.'

Bond cocked an eyebrow at Quarrel.

Quarrel's eyes narrowed. His hand behind the girl's back turned slowly. The girl struggled like an eel, her teeth clenched on her lower lip. Quarrel went on twisting. Suddenly she said 'Ow!' sharply and gasped, 'I'll tell!' Quarrel eased his grip. The girl looked furiously at Bond: 'Annabel Chung.'

Bond said to Quarrel, 'Call the Pus-Feller.'

Quarrel picked up a fork with his free hand and clanged it against a glass. The big negro hurried up.

Bond looked up at him. 'Ever seen this girl before?'

'Yes, boss. She come here sometimes. She bein' a nuisance? Want for me to send her away?'

'No. We like her,' said Bond amiably, 'but she wants to take a studio portrait of me and I don't know if she's worth the money. Would you call up the *Gleaner* and ask if they've got a photographer called Annabel Chung? If she really is one of their people she ought to be good enough.'

'Sure, boss.' The man hurried away.

Bond smiled at the girl. 'Why didn't you ask that man to rescue you?'

The girl glowered at him.

'I'm sorry to have to exert pressure,' said Bond, 'but my export manager in London said that Kingston was full of shady characters. I'm sure you're not one of them, but I really can't understand why you're so anxious to get my picture. Tell me why.'

'What I told you,' said the girl sulkily. 'It's my job.'

Bond tried other questions. She didn't answer them.

The Pus-Feller came up. 'That's right, boss. Annabel

Chung. One of their freelance girls. They say she takes fine pictures. You'll be okay with her.' He looked bland. Studio portrait! Studio bed, more like.

'Thanks,' said Bond. The negro went away. Bond turned back to the girl. 'Freelance,' he said softly. 'That still doesn't explain who wanted my picture.' His face went cold. 'Now give!'

'No,' said the girl sullenly.

'All right, Quarrel. Go ahead.' Bond sat back. His instincts told him that this was the sixty-four thousand dollar question. If he could get the answer out of the girl he might be saved weeks of legwork.

Quarrel's right shoulder started to dip downwards. The girl squirmed towards him to ease the pressure, but he held her body away with his free hand. The girl's face strained towards Quarrel's. Suddenly she spat full in his eyes. Quarrel grinned and increased the twist. The girl's feet kicked wildly under the table. She hissed out words in Chinese. Sweat beaded on her forehead.

'Tell,' said Bond softly. 'Tell and it will stop and we'll be friends and have a drink.' He was getting worried. The girl's arm must be on the verge of breaking.

'——you.' Suddenly the girl's left hand flew up and into Quarrel's face. Bond was too slow to stop her. Something glinted and there was a sharp explosion. Bond snatched at her arm and dragged it back. Blood was streaming down Quarrel's cheek. Glass and metal tinkled on to the table. She had smashed the flashbulb on Quarrel's face. If she had been able to reach an eye it would have been blinded.

Quarrel's free hand went up and felt his cheek. He put it in front of his eyes and looked at the blood, 'Aha!' There was nothing but admiration and a feline pleasure in his voice. He said equably to Bond, 'We get nuthen out of dis gal, cap'n. She plenty tough. You want fe me to break she's arm?'

'Good God, no.' Bond let go the arm he was holding. 'Let her go.' He felt angry with himself for having hurt the girl and still failed. But he had learned something. Whoever was behind her held his people by a steel chain.

Quarrel brought the girl's right arm from behind her back. He still held on to the wrist. Now he opened the girl's hand. He looked into her eyes. His own were cruel. 'You mark me, Missy. Now I mark you.' He brought up his other hand and took the Mount of Venus, the soft lozenge of flesh in the palm below her thumb, between his thumb and forefinger. He began to squeeze it. Bond could see his knuckles go white with the pressure. The girl gave a yelp. She hammered at Quarrel's hand and then at his face. Quarrel grinned and squeezed harder. Suddenly he let go. The girl shot to her feet and backed way from the table, her bruised hand at her mouth. She took her hand down and hissed furiously, 'He'll get you, you bastards!' Then, her Leica dangling, she ran off through the trees.

Quarrel laughed shortly. He took a napkin and wiped it down his cheek and threw it on the ground and took up another. He said to Bond, 'She's Love Moun' be sore long after ma face done get healed. Dat a fine piece of a woman, de Love Moun'. When him fat like wit' dat girl you kin tell her'll be good in bed. You know dat, cap'n?'

'No,' said Bond. 'That's new to me.'

'Sho ting. Dat piece of da han' most hindicative. Don' you worry 'bout she,' he added, noticing the dubious expression on Bond's face. 'Hers got nuttin but a big bruise on she's Love Moun'. But boy, was dat a fat Love Moun'! I come back after dat gal sometime, see if ma teory is da troof.'

Appropriately the band started playing 'Don' touch me tomato'. Bond said, 'Quarrel, it's time you married and settled down. And you leave that girl alone or you'll get a knife between your ribs. Now come on. We'll get the check and go. It's three o'clock in the morning in London where I was yesterday. I need a night's sleep. You've got to start getting me into training. I think I'm going to need it. And it's about time you put some plaster on that cheek of yours. She's written her name and address on it.' .

Quarrel grunted reminiscently. He said with quiet pleasure, 'Dat were some tough baby.' He picked up a fork and clanged it against his glass.

CHAPTER 5

Facts and Figures

'He'll get you. . . . He'll get you. . . . He'll get you, you bastards.'

The words were still ringing in Bond's brain the next day as he sat on his balcony and ate a delicious breakfast and gazed out across the riot of tropical gardens to Kingston, five miles below him.

Now he was sure that Strangways and the girl had been killed. Someone had needed to stop them looking any further into his business, so he had killed them and destroyed the records of what they were investigating. The same person knew or suspected that the Secret Service would follow up Strangways's disappearance. Somehow he had known that Bond had been given the job. He had wanted a picture of Bond and he had wanted to know where Bond was staying. He would be keeping an eye on Bond to see if Bond picked up any of the leads that had led to Strangways's death. If Bond did so, Bond also would have to be eliminated. There would be a car smash or a street fight or some other innocent death. And how, Bond wondered, would this person react to their treatment of the Chung girl? If he was as ruthless as Bond supposed, that would be enough. It showed that Bond was on to something. Perhaps Strangways had made a preliminary report to London before he was killed. Perhaps someone had leaked. The enemy would be foolish to take chances. If he had any sense, after the Chung incident, he would deal with Bond and perhaps also with Quarrel without delay.

Bond lit his first cigarette of the day—the first Royal Blend he had smoked for five years—and let the smoke come out between his teeth in a luxurious hiss. That was his 'Enemy Appreciation'. Now, who was this enemy?

Well, there was only one candidate, and a pretty insubstantial one at that, Doctor No, Doctor Julius No, the German Chinese who owned Crab Key and made his money out of guano. There had been nothing on this man in Records and a signal to the F.B.I. had been negative. The affair of the roseate spoonbills and the trouble with the Audubon Society meant precisely nothing except, as M had said, that a lot of old women had got excited about some pink storks. All the same, four people had died because of these storks and, most significant of all to Bond, Quarrel was scared of Doctor No and his island. That was very odd indeed. Cayman Islanders, least of all Quarrel, did not scare easily. And why had Doctor No got this mania for privacy? Why did he go to such expense and trouble to keep people away from his guano island? Guano—bird dung. Who wanted the stuff? How valuable was it? Bond was due to call on the Governor at ten o'clock. After he had made his number he would get hold of the Colonial Secretary and try and find out all about the damned stuff and about Crab Key and, if possible, about Doctor No.

There was a double knock on the door. Bond got up and unlocked it. It was Quarrel, his left cheek decorated with a piratical cross of sticking-plaster. 'Mornin', cap'n. You said eight-tirty.'

'Yes, come on in, Quarrel. We've got a busy day. Had some breakfast?'

'Yes, tank you, cap'n. Salt fish an' ackee an' a tot of rum.'

'Good God,' said Bond. 'That's tough stuff to start the day on.'

'Mos' refreshin',' said Quarrel stolidly.

They sat down outside on the balcony. Bond offered Quarrel a cigarette and lit one himself. 'Now then,' he said. 'I'll be spending most of the day at King's House and perhaps at the Jamaica Institute. I shan't need you till tomorrow morning, but there are some things for you to do downtown. All right?'

'Okay, cap'n. Jes' yo say.'

'First of all, that car of ours is hot. We've got to get rid of it. Go down to Motta's or one of the other hire people and pick up the newest and best little self-drive car you can find, the one with the least mileage. Saloon. Take if for a month. Right? Then hunt around the waterfront and find two men who look as near as possible like us. One must be able to drive a car. Buy them both clothes, at least for their top halves, that look like ours. And the sort of hats we might wear. Say we want a car taken over to Montego tomorrow morning—by the Spanish Town, Ocho Rios road. To be left at Levy's garage there. Ring up Levy and tell him to expect it and to keep it for us. Right?'

Quarrel grinned. 'Yo want fox someone?'

'That's right. They'll get ten pounds each. Say I'm a rich American and I want my car to arrive in Montego Bay driven by a respectable couple of men. Make me out a bit mad. They must be here at six o'clock tomorrow morning. You'll be here with the other car. See they look the part and send them off in the Sunbeam with the roof down. Right?'

'Okay, cap'n.'

'What's happened to that house we had on the North Shore last time—Beau Desert at Morgan's Harbour? Do you know if it's let?'

'Couldn't say, cap'n. Hit's well away from the tourist

places and dey askin' a big rent for it.'

'Well, go to Graham Associates and see if you can rent it for a month, or another bungalow near by. I don't mind what you pay. Say it's for a rich American, Mr James. Get the keys and pay the rent and say I'll write and confirm. I can telephone them if they want more details.' Bond reached into his hip pocket and brought out a thick wad of notes. He handed half of it to Quarrel. 'Here's two hundred pounds. That should cover all this. Get in touch if you want some more. You know where I'll be.'

'Tanks, cap'n,' said Quarrel, awestruck by the big sum. He stowed it away inside his blue shirt and buttoned the shirt up to his neck. 'Anyting helse?'

'No, but take a lot of trouble about not being followed. Leave the car somewhere downtown and walk to these places. And watch out particularly for any Chinese near you.' Bond got up and they went to the door. 'See you tomorrow morning at six-fifteen and we'll get over to the North Coast. As far as I can see that's going to be our base for a while.'

Quarrel nodded. His face was enigmatic. He said 'Okay, cap'n' and went off down the corridor.

Half an hour later Bond went downstairs and took a taxi to King's House. He didn't sign the Governor's book in the cool hall. He was put in a waiting room for the quarter of an hour necessary to show him that he was unimportant. Then the A.D.C. came for him and took him up to the Governor's study on the first floor.

It was a large cool room smelling of cigar smoke. The Acting Governor, in a cream tussore suit and an inappropriate wing collar and spotted bow tie, was sitting at a broad mahogany desk on which there was nothing but the *Daily Gleaner,* the *Times Weekly* and a bowl of hibiscus blossoms. His hands lay flat on the desk in front of him. He was sixtyish with a red, rather petulant face and bright, bitter blue eyes. He didn't smile or get up. He said, 'Good morning, Mr—er—Bond. Please sit down.'

Bond took the chair across the desk from the Gover-

nor and sat down. He said, 'Good morning, sir,' and
waited. A friend at the Colonial Office had told him his
reception would be frigid. 'He's nearly at retiring age.
Only an interim appointment. We had to find an Acting
Governor to take over at short notice when Sir Hugh
Foot was promoted. Foot was a great success. This
man's not even trying to compete. He knows he's only
got the job for a few months while we find someone to
replace Foot. This man's been passed over for the
Governor Generalship of Rhodesia. Now all he wants is
to retire and get some directorships in the City. Last
thing he wants is any trouble in Jamaica. He keeps on
trying to close this Strangways case of yours. Won't like
you ferreting about.'

The Governor cleared his throat. He recognized that
Bond wasn't one of the servile ones. 'You wanted to see
me?'

'Just to make my number, sir,' said Bond equably.
'I'm here on the Strangways case. I think you had a
signal from the Secretary of State.' This was a reminder
that the people behind Bond were powerful people.
Bond didn't like attempts to squash him or his Service.

'I recall the signal. And what can I do for you? So far
as we're concerned here the case is closed.'

'In what way ''closed'', sir?'

The Governor said roughly, 'Strangways obviously
did a bunk with the girl. Unbalanced sort of fellow at
the best of times. Some of your—er—colleagues, don't
seem to be able to leave women alone.' The Governor
clearly included Bond. 'Had to bail the chap out of
various scandals before now. Doesn't do the Colony
any good Mr—er—Bond. Hope your people will be
sending us a rather better type of man to take his place.
That is,' he added coldly, 'if a Regional Control man is
really needed here. Personally I have every confidence
in our police.'

Bond smiled sympathetically. 'I'll report your views,
sir. I expect my Chief will like to discuss them with the
Minister of Defence and the Secretary of State.
Naturally, if you would like to take over these extra

duties it will be a saving in manpower so far as my Service is concerned. I'm sure the Jamaican Constabulary is most efficient.'

The Governor looked at Bond suspiciously. Perhaps he had better handle this man a bit more carefully. 'This is an informal discussion, Mr Bond. When I have decided on my views I will communicate them myself to the Secretary of State. In the meantime, is there anyone you wish to see on my staff?'

'I'd like to have a word with the Colonial Secretary, sir.'

'Really? And why, pray?'

'There's been some trouble on Crab Key. Something about a bird sanctuary. The case was passed to us by the Colonial Office. My Chief asked me to look into it while I'm here.'

The Governor looked relieved. 'Certainly, certainly. I'll see that Mr Pleydell-Smith receives you straight away. So you feel we can leave the Strangways case to sort itself out? They'll turn up before long, never fear.' He reached over and rang a bell. The A.D.C. came in. 'This gentleman would like to see the Colonial Secretary, A.D.C. Take him along, would you? I'll call Mr Pleydell-Smith myself and ask him to make himself available.' He got up and came round the desk. He held out his hand. 'Goodbye then, Mr Bond. And I'm so glad we see eye to eye. Crab Key, eh? Never been there myself, but I'm sure it would repay a visit.'

Bond shook hands. 'That was what I was thinking. Goodbye, sir.'

'Goodbye, goodbye.' The Governor watched Bond's back retreating out of the door and himself returned well satisfied to his desk. 'Young whippersnapper,' he said to the empty room. He sat down and said a few peremptory words down the telephone to the Colonial Secretary. Then he picked up the *Times Weekly* and turned to the Stock Exchange prices.

The Colonial Secretary was a youngish shaggy-haired man with bright, boyish eyes. He was one of those nervous pipe smokers who are constantly patting their pockets for matches, shaking the box to see how many are left in it, or knocking the dottle out of their pipes. After he had gone through this routine two or three times in his first ten minutes with Bond, Bond wondered if he ever got any smoke into his lungs at all.

After pumping energetically at Bond's hand and waving vaguely at a chair, Pleydell-Smith walked up and down the room scratching his temple with the stem of his pipe. 'Bond. Bond. Bond! Rings a bell. Now let me see. Yes, by jove! You were the chap who was mixed up in that treasure business here. By jove, yes! Four, five years ago. Found the file lying around only the other day. Splendid show. What a lark! I say, wish you'd start another bonfire like that here. Stir the place up a bit. All they think of nowadays is Federation and their bloody self-importance. Self-determination indeed! They can't even run a bus service. And the colour problem! My dear chap, there's far more colour problem between the straight-haired and the crinkly-haired Jamaicans than there is between me and my black cook. However,' Pleydell-Smith came to rest beside his desk. He sat down opposite Bond and draped one leg over the arm of his chair. Reaching for a tobacco jar with the arms of King's College, Cambridge, on it, he dug into it and started filling his pipe. 'I mean to say I don't want to bore you with all that. You go ahead and bore me. What's your problem? Glad to help. I bet it's more interesting than this muck,' he waved at the pile of papers in his *In* tray.

Bond grinned at him. This was more like it. He had found an ally, and an intelligent one at that. 'Well,' he said seriously. 'I'm here on the Strangways case. But first of all I want to ask you a question that may sound odd. Exactly how did you come to be looking at that other case of mine? You say you found the file lying about. How was that? Had someone asked for it? I don't want to be indiscreet, so don't answer if you don't want to. I'm just inquisitive.'

Pleydell-Smith cocked an eye at him. 'I suppose that's your job.' He reflected, gazing at the ceiling. 'Well, now

I come to think of it I saw it on my secretary's desk. She's a new girl. Said she was trying to get up to date with the files. Mark you,' the Colonial Secretary hastened to exonerate his girl, 'there were plenty of other files on her desk. It was just this one that caught my eye.'

'Oh, I see,' said Bond. 'It was like that.' He smiled apologetically. 'Sorry, but various people seem to be rather interested in me being here. What I really wanted to talk to you about was Crab Key. Anything you know about the place. And about this Chinaman, Doctor No, who bought it. And anything you can tell me about his guano business. Rather a tall order, I'm afraid, but any scraps will help.'

Pleydell-Smith laughed shortly through the stem of his pipe. He jerked the pipe out of his mouth and talked while he tamped down the burning tobacco with his matchbox. 'Bitten off a bit more than you can chew on guano. Talk to you for hours about it. Started in the Consular before I transferred to the Colonial Office. First job was in Peru. Had a lot to do with their people who administer the whole trade—*Compañía Administradora del Guano*. Nice people.' The pipe was going now and Pleydell-Smith threw his matchbox down on the table. 'As for the rest, it's just a question of getting the file.' He rang a bell. In a minute the door opened behind Bond. 'Miss Taro, the file on Crab Key, please. The one on the sale of the place and the other one on that warden fellow who turned up before Christmas. Miss Longfellow will know where to find them.'

A soft voice said, 'Yes, sir.' Bond heard the door close.

'Now then, guano.' Pleydell-Smith tilted his chair back. Bond prepared to be bored. 'As you know, it's bird dung. Comes from the rear end of two birds, the masked booby and the guanay. So far as Crab Key is concerned, it's only the guanay, otherwise known as the green cormorant, same bird as you find in England. The guanay is a machine for converting fish into guano. They mostly eat anchovies. Just to show you how much

fish they eat, they've found up to seventy anchovies inside one bird!' Pleydell-Smith took out his pipe and
pointed it impressively at Bond. 'The whole population
of Peru eats four thousand tons of fish a year. The sea
birds of the country eat five hundred thousand tons!'

Bond pursed his lips to show he was impressed.
'Really.'

'Well, now,' continued the Colonial Secretary, 'every
day each one of these hundreds of thousands of guanays
eat a pound or so of fish and deposit an ounce of guano
on the guanera—that's the guano island.'

Bond interrupted, 'Why don't they do it in the sea?'

'Don't know.' Pleydell-Smith took the question and
turned it over in his mind. 'Never occurred to me.
Anyway they don't. They do it on the land and they've
been doing it since before Genesis. That makes the hell
of a lot of bird dung—millions of tons of it on the
Pescadores and the other guanera. Then, around 1850
someone discovered it was the greatest natural fertilizer
in the world—stuffed with nitrates and phosphates and
what have you. And the ships and the men came to the
guaneras and simply ravaged them for twenty years or
more. It's a time known as the "Saturnalia" in Peru. It
was like the Klondyke. People fought over the muck, hi-
jacked each other's ships, shot the workers, sold phoney
maps of secret guano islands—anything you like. And
people made fortunes out of the stuff.'

'Where does Crab Key come in?' Bond wanted to get
down to cases.

'That was the only worthwhile guanera so far north.
It was worked too, God knows who by. But the stuff
had a low nitrate content. Water's not as rich round
here as it is down along the Humboldt Current. So the
fish aren't so rich in chemicals. So the guano isn't so
rich either. Crab Key got worked on and off when the
price was high enough, but the whole industry went
bust, with Crab Key and the other poor-quality deposits
in the van, when the Germans invented artificial
chemical manure. By this time Peru had realized that
she had squandered a fantastic capital asset and she set

about organizing the remains of the industry and protecting the guanera. She nationalized the industry and protected the birds, and slowly, very slowly, the supplies built up again. Then people found that there were snags about the German stuff, it impoverishes the soil, which guano doesn't do, and gradually the price of guano improved and the industry staggered back to its feet. Now it's going fine, except that Peru keeps most of the guano to herself, for her own agriculture. And that was where Crab Key came in again.'

'Ah.'

'Yes,' said Pleydell-Smith, patting his pockets for the matches, finding them on the desk, shaking them against his ear, and starting his pipe-filling routine, 'at the beginning of the war, this Chinaman, who must be a wily devil, by the way, got the idea that he could make a good thing out of the old guanera on Crab Key. The price was about fifty dollars a ton on this side of the Atlantic and he bought the island from us, for about ten thousand pounds as I recall it, brought in labour and got to work. Been working it ever since. Must have made a fortune. He ships direct to Europe, to Antwerp. They send him a ship once a month. He's installed the latest crushers and separators. Sweats his labour, I daresay. To make a decent profit, he'd have to. Particularly now. Last year I heard he was only getting about thirty-eight to forty dollars a ton c.i.f. Antwerp. God knows what he must pay his labour to make a profit at that price. I've never been able to find out. He runs that place like a fortress—sort of forced labour camp. No one ever gets off it. I've heard some funny rumours, but no one's ever complained. It's his island, of course, and he can do what he likes on it.'

Bond hunted for clues. 'Would it really be so valuable to him, this place? What do you suppose it's worth?'

Pleydell-Smith said, 'The guanay is the most valuable bird in the world. Each pair produces about two dollars' worth of guano in a year without any expense to the owner. Each female lays an average of three eggs and raises two young. Two broods a year. Say they're worth fifteen dollars a pair, and say there are one hundred thousand birds on Crab Key, which is a reasonable guess on the old figures we have. That makes his birds worth a million and a half dollars. Pretty valuable property. Add the value of the installations, say another million, and you've got a small fortune on that hideous little place. Which reminds me,' Pleydell-Smith pressed the bell, 'what the hell has happened to those files? You'll find all the dope you want in them.'

The door opened behind Bond.

Pleydell-Smith said irritably, 'Really, Miss Taro. What about those files?'

'Very sorry, sir,' said the soft voice. 'But we can't find them anywhere.'

'What do you mean "can't find them"? Who had them last?'

'Commander Strangways, sir.'

'Well, I remember distinctly him bringing them back to this room. What happened to them then?'

'Can't say, sir,' the voice was unemotional. 'The covers are there but there's nothing inside them.'

Bond turned in his chair. He glanced at the girl and turned back. He smiled grimly to himself. He knew where the files had gone. He also knew why the old file on himself had been out on the Secretary's desk. He also guessed how the particular significance of 'James Bond, Import and Export Merchant,' seemed to have leaked out of King's House, the only place where the significance was known.

Like Doctor No, like Miss Annabel Chung, the demure, efficient-looking little secretary in the horn-rimmed glasses was a Chinese.

CHAPTER 6

The Finger on the Trigger

The Colonial Secretary gave Bond lunch at Queen's Club. They sat in a corner of the elegant mahogany-panelled dining room with its four big ceiling fans and gossiped about Jamaica. By the time coffee came, Pleydell-Smith was delving well below the surface of the prosperous, peaceful island the world knows.

'It's like this.' He began his antics with the pipe. 'The Jamaican is a kindly lazy man with the virtues and vices of a child. He lives on a very rich island but he doesn't get rich from it. He doesn't know how to and he's too lazy. The British come and go and take the easy pickings, but for about two hundred years no Englishman has made a fortune out here. He doesn't stay long enough. He takes a fat cut and leaves. It's the Portuguese Jews who make the most. They came here with the British and they've stayed. But they're snobs and they spend too much of their fortunes on building fine houses and giving dances. They're the names that fill the social column in the *Gleaner* when the tourists have gone. They're in rum and tobacco and they represent the big British firms over here—motor cars, insurance and so forth. Then come the Syrians, very rich too, but not such good businessmen. They have most of the stores and some of the best hotels. They're not a very good risk. Get overstocked and have to have an occasional fire to get liquid again. Then there are the Indians with their usual flashy trade in soft goods and the like. They're not much of a lot. Finally there are the Chinese, solid, compact, discreet—the most powerful clique in Jamaica. They've got the bakeries and the laundries and the best food stores. They keep to themselves and keep their strain pure.' Pleydell-Smith laughed, 'Not that they don't take the black girls when they want them. You can see the result all over Kingston—Chigroes—Chinese negroes and negresses. The Chigroes are a tough, forgotten race. They look down on the negroes and the Chinese look down on them. One day they may become a nuisance. They've got some of the intelligence of the Chinese and most of the vices of the black man. The police have a lot of trouble with them.'

Bond said, 'That secretary of yours. Would she be one of them?'

'That's right. Bright girl and very efficient. Had her for about six months. She was far the best of the ones that answered our advertisement.'

'She looks bright,' said Bond non-committally. 'Are they organized, these people? Is there some head of the Chinese negro community?'

'Not yet. But someone'll get hold of them one of these days. They'd be a useful little pressure group.' Pleydell-Smith glanced at his watch. 'That reminds me. Must be getting along. Got to go and read the riot act about those files. Can't think what happened to them. I distinctly remember . . .' He broke off. 'However, main point is that I haven't been able to give you much dope about Crab Key and this doctor fellow. But I can tell you there wasn't much you'd have found out from the files. He seems to have been a pleasant spoken chap.

Very businesslike. Then there was that argument with the Audubon Society. I gather you know all about that. As for the place itself, there was nothing on the files but one or two prewar reports and a copy of the last ordnance survey. Godforsaken bloody place it sounds. Nothing but miles of mangrove swamps and a huge mountain of bird dung at one end. But you said you were going down to the Institute. Why don't I take you there and introduce you to the fellow who runs the map section?'

An hour later Bond was ensconced in a corner of a sombre room with the ordnance survey map of Crab Key, dated 1910, spread out on a table in front of him. He had a sheet of the Institute's writing-paper and had made a rough sketch-map and was jotting down the salient points.

The overall area of the island was about fifty square miles. Three-quarters of this, to the east, was swamp and shallow lake. From the lake a flat river meandered down to the sea and came out halfway along the south coast into a small sandy bay. Bond guessed that somewhere at the headwaters of the river would be a likely spot for the Audubon wardens to have chosen for their camp. To the west, the island rose steeply to a hill stated to be five hundred feet high and ended abruptly with what appeared to be a sheer drop to the sea. A dotted line led from this hill to a box in the corner of the map which contained the words 'Guano deposits. Last workings 1880'.

There was no sign of a road, or even of a track on the island, and no sign of a house. The relief map showed that the island looked rather like a swimming water rat—a flat spine rising sharply to the head—heading west. It appeared to be about thirty miles due north of Galina Point on the north shore of Jamaica and about sixty miles south of Cuba.

Little else could be gleaned from the map. Crab Key was surrounded by shoal water except below the western cliff where the nearest marking was five hundred fathoms. After that came the plunge into the Cuba Deep. Bond folded the map and handed it in to the librarian.

Suddenly he felt exhausted. It was only four o'clock, but it was roasting in Kingston and his shirt was sticking to him. Bond walked out of the Institute and found a taxi and went back up into the cool hills to his hotel. He was well satisfied with his day, but nothing else could be done on this side of the island. He would spend a quiet evening at his hotel and be ready to get up early next morning and be away.

Bond went to the reception desk to see if there was a message from Quarrel. 'No messages, sir,' said the girl. 'But a basket of fruit came from King's House. Just after lunch. The messenger took it up to your room.'

'What sort of a messenger?'

'Coloured man, sir. Said he was from the A.D.C.'s office.'

'Thank you.' Bond took his key and went up the stairs to the first floor. It was ridiculously improbable. His hand on the gun under his coat, Bond softly approached his door. He turned the key and kicked the door open. The empty room yawned at him. Bond shut and locked the door. On his dressing table was a large, ornate basket of fruit—tangerines, grapefruit, pink bananas, soursop, star-apples and even a couple of hothouse nectarines. Attached to a broad ribbon on the handle was a white envelope. Bond removed it and held it up to the light. He opened it. On a plain sheet of expensive white writing paper was typed 'With the Compliments of His Excellency the Governor'.

Bond snorted. He stood looking at the fruit. He bent his ear to it and listened. He then took the basket by the handle and tipped its contents out on to the floor. The fruit bounced and rolled over the coconut matting. There was nothing but fruit in the basket. Bond grinned at his precautions. There was a last possibility. He picked up one of the nectarines, the most likely for a greedy man to choose first, and took it into the bathroom. He dropped it in the washbasin and went back to the bedroom and, after inspecting the lock, unlocked the wardrobe. Gingerly he lifted out his suitcase and stood it in the middle of the room. He knelt down and looked for the traces of talcum powder he had dusted round the two locks. They were smeared and there were minute scratches round the keyholes. Bond sourly examined the marks. These people were not as careful as some others he had had to deal with. He unlocked the case and stood it up on end. There were four innocent copper studs in the welting at the front right-hand corner of the lid. Bond prised at the top one of these studs with his nail and it eased out. He took hold of it and pulled out three feet of thick steel wire and put it on the floor beside him. This wire threaded through small wire loops inside the lid and sewed the case shut. Bond lifted the lid and verified that nothing had been disturbed. From his 'tool case' he took out a jeweller's glass and went back into the bathroom and switched on the light over the shaving mirror. He screwed the glass into his eye and gingerly picked the nectarine out of the washbasin and revolved it slowly between finger and thumb.

Bond stopped turning the nectarine. He had come to a minute pinhole, its edges faintly discoloured brown. It was in the crevice of the fruit, invisible except under a magnifying glass. Bond put the nectarine carefully down in the washbasin. He stood for a moment and looked thoughtfully into his eyes in the mirror.

So it *was* war! Well, well. How very interesting. Bond felt the slight tautening of the skin at the base of his stomach. He smiled thinly at his reflection in the mirror. So his instincts and his reasoning had been correct. Strangways and the girl had been murdered and their records destroyed because they had got too hot on the trail. Then Bond had come on the scene and, thanks to Miss Taro, they had been waiting for him. Miss Chung, and perhaps the taxi driver, had picked up the scent. He had been traced to the Blue Hills hotel. The first shot had been fired. There would be others. And whose finger was on the trigger? Who had got him so accurately in his sights? Bond's mind was made up. The evidence was nil. But he was certain of it. This was long range fire, from Crab Key. The man behind the gun was Doctor No.

Bond walked back into the bedroom. One by one he picked up the fruit and took each piece back to the bathroom and examined it through his glass. The pin-prick was always there, concealed in the stalk-hole or a crevice. Bond rang down and asked for a cardboard box and paper and string. He packed the fruit carefully in the box and picked up the telephone and called King's House. He asked for the Colonial Secretary. 'That you, Pleydell-Smith? James Bond speaking. Sorry to bother you. Got a bit of a problem. Is there a public analyst in Kingston? I see. Well, I've got something I want analysed. If I sent the box down to you, would you be very kind and pass it on to this chap? I don't want my name to come into this. All right? I'll explain later. When you get his report would you sent me a short telegram telling me the answer? I'll be at Beau Desert, over at Morgan's Harbour, for the next week or so. Be glad if you'd keep that to yourself too. Sorry to be so damned mysterious. I'll explain everything when I see you next. I expect you'll get a clue when you see what the analyst has to say. And by the way, tell him to handle the specimens carefully, would you. Warn him there's more in them than meets the eye. Very many thanks. Lucky I met you this morning. Goodbye.'

Bond addressed the parcel and went down and paid a taxi to deliver it at once to King's House. It was six o'clock. He went back to his room and had a shower and changed and ordered his first drink. He was about to take it out on the balcony when the telephone rang. It was Quarrel.

'Everyting fixed, cap'n.'

'Everything? That's wonderful. That house all right?'

'Everyting okay.' Quarrel repeated, his voice careful. 'See yo as yo done said, cap'n.'

'Fine,' said Bond. He was impressed with Quarrel's

efficiency and a sense of security. He put down the telephone and went out on to the balcony.

The sun was just setting. The wave of violet shadow was creeping down towards the town and the harbour. When it hits the town, thought Bond, the lights will go on. It happened as he had expected. Above him there was the noise of a plane. It came into sight, a Super Constellation, the same flight that Bond had been on the night before. Bond watched it sweep out over the sea and then turn and come in to land at the Palisadoes airport. What a long way he had come since that moment, only twenty-four hours before, when the door of the plane had clanged open and the loudspeaker had said, 'This is Kingston, Jamaica. Will passengers please remain seated until the aircraft has been cleared by the Health Authorities.'

Should he tell M how the picture had changed? Should he make a report to the Governor? Bond thought of the Governor and dismissed that idea. But what about M? Bond had his own cipher. He could easily send M a signal through the Colonial Office. What would he say to M? That Doctor No had sent him some poisoned fruit? But he didn't even know that it was poisoned, or, for the matter of that, that it had come from Doctor No. Bond could see M's face as he read the signal. He saw him press down the lever on the intercom: 'Chief of Staff, 007's gone round the bend. Says someone's been trying to feed him a poisoned banana. Fellow's lost his nerve. Been in hospital too long. Better call him home.'

Bond smiled to himself. He got up and rang down for another drink. It wouldn't be quite like that, of course. But still . . . No, he'd wait until he had something more to show. Of course if something went badly wrong, and he hadn't sent a warning, he'd be in trouble. It was up to him to see that nothing did go wrong.

Bond drank his second drink and thought over the details of his plan. Then he went down and had dinner in the half-deserted dining-room and read the *Hand-*

book of the West Indies. By nine o'clock he was half
asleep. He went back to his room and packed his bag
ready for the morning. He telephoned down and
arranged to be called at five-thirty. Then he bolted the
door on the inside, and also shut and bolted the slatted
jalousies across the windows. It would mean a hot,
stuffy night. That couldn't be helped. Bond climbed
naked under the single cotton sheet and turned over on
his left side and slipped his right hand on to the butt of
the Walther PPK under the pillow. In five minutes he
was asleep.

The next thing Bond knew was that it was three
o'clock in the morning. He knew it was three o'clock
because the luminous dial of his watch was close to his
face. He lay absolutely still. There was not a sound in
the room. He strained his ears. Outside, too, it was
deathly quiet. Far in the distance a dog started to bark.
Other dogs joined in and there was a brief hysterical
chorus which stopped as suddenly as it had begun. Then
it was quite quiet again. The moon coming through the
slats in the jalousies threw black and white bars across
the corner of the room next to his bed. It was as if he
was lying in a cage. What had woken him up? Bond
moved softly, preparing to slip out of bed.

Bond stopped moving. He stopped as dead as a live
man can.

Something had stirred on his right ankle. Now it was
moving up the inside of his shin. Bond could feel the
hairs on his leg being parted. It was an insect of some
sort. A very big one. It was long, five or six inches—as
long as his hand. He could feel dozens of tiny feet
lightly touching his skin. What was it?

Then Bond heard something he had never heard
before—the sound of the hair on his head rasping up on
the pillow. Bond analysed the noise. It couldn't be! It
simply couldn't! Yes, his hair was standing on end.
Bond could even feel the cool air reaching his scalp between the hairs. How extraordinary! How very extraordinary! He had always thought it was a figure of
speech. But why? Why was it happening to him?

The thing on his leg moved. Suddenly Bond realized that he was afraid, terrified. His instincts, even before they had communicated with his brain, had told his body that he had a centipede on him.

Bond lay frozen. He had once seen a tropical centipede in a bottle of spirit on the shelf in a museum. It had been pale brown and very flat and five or six inches long—about the length of this one. On either side of the blunt head there had been curved poison claws. The label on the bottle had said that its poison was mortal if it hit an artery. Bond had looked curiously at the corkscrew of dead cuticle and had moved on.

The centipede had reached his knee. It was starting up his thigh. Whatever happened he mustn't move, mustn't even tremble. Bond's whole consciousness had drained down to the two rows of softly creeping feet. Now they had reached his flank. God, it was turning down towards his groin! Bond set his teeth. Supposing it liked the warmth there! Supposing it tried to crawl into the crevices! Could he stand it? Supposing it chose that place to bite? Bond could feel it questing amongst the first hairs. It tickled. The skin on Bond's belly fluttered. There was nothing he could do to control it. But now the thing was turning up and along his stomach. Its feet were gripping tighter to prevent it falling. Now it was at his heart. If it bit there, surely it would kill him. The centipede trampled steadily on through the thin hairs on Bond's right breast up to his collar bone. It stopped. What was it doing? Bond could feel the blunt head questing blindly to and fro. What was it looking for? Was there room between his skin and the sheet for it to get through? Dare he lift the sheet an inch to help it. No. Never! The animal was at the base of his jugular. Perhaps it was intrigued by the heavy pulse there. Christ, if only he could control the pumping of his blood. Damn you! Bond tried to communicate with the centipede. It's nothing. It's not dangerous, that pulse. It means you no harm. Get on out into the fresh air!

As if the beast had heard, it moved on up the column of the neck and into the stubble on Bond's chin. Now it

was at the corner of his mouth, tickling madly. On it
went, up along the nose. Now he could feel its whole
weight and length. Softly Bond closed his eyes. Two by
two the pairs of feet, moving alternately, trampled
across his right eyelid. When it got off his eye, should he
take a chance and shake it off—rely on its feet slipping
in his sweat? No for God's sake! The grip of the feet
was endless. He might shake one lot off, but not the
rest.

With incredible deliberation the huge insect ambled
across Bond's forehead. It stopped below the hair.
What the hell was it doing now? Bond could feel it nuz-
zling at his skin. It was drinking! Drinking the beads of
salt sweat. Bond was sure of it. For minutes it hardly
moved. Bond felt weak with the tension. He could feel
the sweat pouring off the rest of his body on to the
sheet. In a second his limbs would start to tremble. He
could feel it coming on. He would start to shake with an
ague of fear. Could he control it, could he? Bond lay
and waited, the breath coming softly through his open,
snarling mouth.

The centipede started to move again. It walked into
the forest of hair. Bond could feel the roots being
pushed aside as it forced its way along. Would it like it
there? Would it settle down? How did centipedes sleep?
Curled up or at full length? The tiny millipedes he had
known as a child, the ones that always seemed to find
their way up the plughole into the empty bath, curled up
when you touched them. Now it had come to where his
head lay against the sheet. Would it walk out on to the
pillow or would it stay on in the warm forest? The centipede stopped. Out! OUT! Bond's nerves screamed at
it.

The centipede stirred. Slowly it walked out of his hair
on to the pillow.

Bond waited a second. Now he could hear the rows of
feet picking softly at the cotton. It was a tiny scraping
noise, like soft fingernails.

With a crash that shook the room Bond's body
jackknifed out of bed and on to the floor.

At once Bond was on his feet and at the door. He turned on the light. He found he was shaking uncontrollably. He staggered to the bed. There it was, crawling out of sight over the edge of the pillow. Bond's first instinct was to twitch the pillow on to the floor. He controlled himself, waiting for his nerves to quieten. Then softly, deliberately, he picked up the pillow by one corner and walked into the middle of the room and dropped it. The centipede came out from under the pillow. It started to snake swiftly away across the matting. Now Bond was uninterested. He looked round for something to kill it with. Slowly he went and picked up a shoe and came back. The danger was past. His mind was now wondering how the centipede had got into his bed. He lifted the shoe and slowly, almost carelessly, smashed it down. He heard the crack of the hard carapace.

Bond lifted the shoe.

The centipede was whipping from side to side in its agony—five inches of grey-brown, shiny death. Bond hit it again. It burst open, yellowly.

Bond dropped the shoe and ran for the bathroom and was violently sick.

CHAPTER 7

Night Passage

'By the way, Quarrel—' Bond dared a bus with 'Brown Bomber' painted above its windshield. The bus pulled over and roared on down the hill towards Kingston sounding a furious chord on its triple wind-horn to restore the driver's ego—'what do you know about centipedes?'

'Centipedes, cap'n?' Quarrel squinted sideways for a clue to the question. Bond's expression was casual. 'Well, we got some bad ones here in Jamaica. Tree, fo, five inches long. Dey kills folks. Dey mos'ly lives in de old houses in Kingston. Dey loves de rotten wood an' de mouldy places. Dey hoperates mos'ly at night. Why, cap'n? Yo seen one?'

Bond dodged the question. He had also not told Quarrel about the fruit. Quarrel was a tough man, but there was no reason to sow the seeds of fear. 'Would you expect to find one in a modern house, for instance? In your shoe, or in a drawer, or in your bed?'

'Nossir.' Quarrel's voice was definite. 'Not hunless dem put dere a purpose. Dese hinsecks love de holes and

68

de crannies. Dey not love de clean places. Dey dirty-livin' hinsecks. Mebbe yo find dem in de bush, under logs an' stones. But never in de bright places.'

'I see.' Bond changed the subject. 'By the way, did those two men get off all right in the Sunbeam?'

'Sho ting, cap'n. Dey plenty happy wid de job. An' dey look plently like yo an' me, cap'n.' Quarrel chuckled. He glanced at Bond and said hesitantly, 'I fears dey weren't very good citizens, cap'n. Had to find de two men wheres I could. Me, I'm a beggarman, cap'n. An' fo you, cap'n, I get a misrable no-good whiteman from Betsy's.'

'Who's Betsy?'

'She done run de lousiest brothel in town, cap'n,' Quarrel spat emphatically out of the window. 'Dis whiteman, he does de bookkeepin'.'

Bond laughed. 'So long as he can drive a car. I only hope they get to Montego all right.'

'Don' yo worry,' Quarrel misunderstood Bond's concern. 'I say I tell de police dey stole de car if dey don'.'

They were at the saddleback at Stony Hill where the Junction Road dives down through fifty S-bends towards the North Coast. Bond put the little Austin A.30 into second gear and let it coast. The sun was coming up over the Blue Mountain peak and dusty shafts of gold lanced into the plunging valley. There were few people on the road—an occasional man going off to his precipitous small-holding on the flank of a hill, his three-foot steel cutlass dangling from his right hand, chewing at his breakfast, a foot of raw sugar cane held in his left, or a woman sauntering up the road with a covered basket of fruit or vegetables for Stony Hill market, her shoes on her head, to be donned when she got near the village. It was a savage, peaceful scene that had hardly changed, except for the surface of the road, for two hundred years or more. Bond almost smelled the dung of the mule train in which he would have been riding over from Port Royal to visit the garrison at Morgan's Harbour in 1750.

Quarrel interrupted his thoughts. 'Cap'n,' he said

apologetically, 'beggin' yo pardon, but kin yo tell me what yo have in mind for we? I'se bin puzzlin' an' Ah caint seem to figger hout yo game.'

'I've hardly figured it out myself, Quarrel.' Bond changed up into top and dawdled through the cool, beautiful glades of Castleton Gardens. 'I told you I'm here because Commander Strangways and his secretary have disappeared. Most people think they've gone off together. I think they've been murdered.'

'Dat so?' said Quarrel unemotionally. 'Who yo tink done hit?'

'I've come to agree with you. I think Doctor No, that Chinaman on Crab Key, had it done. Strangways was poking his nose into this man's affairs—something to do with the bird sanctuary. Doctor No has this mania for privacy. You were telling me so yourself. Seems he'll do anything to stop people climbing over his wall. Mark you, it's not more than a guess about Doctor No. But some funny things happened in the last twenty-four hours. That's why I sent the Sunbeam over to Montego, to lay a false scent. And that's why we're going to hide out at Beau Desert for a few days.'

'Den what, cap'n?'

'First of all I want you to get me absolutely fit—the way you trained me the last time I was here. Remember?'

'Sho, cap'n. Ah kin do dat ting.'

'And then I was thinking you and me might go and take a look at Crab Key.'

Quarrel whistled. The whistle ended on a downward note.

'Just sniff around. We needn't get too close to Doctor No's end. I want to take a look at this bird sanctuary. See for myself what happened to the wardens' camp. If we find anything wrong, we'll get away again and come back by the front door—with some soldiers to help. Have a full-dress inquiry. Can't do that until we've got something to go on. What do you think?'

Quarrel dug into his hip pocket for a cigarette. He made a fuss about lighting it. He blew a cloud of smoke through his nostrils and watched it whip out of the window. He said, 'Cap'n, Ah tink yo'se plumb crazy to trespass hon dat island.' Quarrel had wound himself up. He paused. There was no comment. He looked sideways at the quiet profile. He said more quietly, in am embarrassed voice, 'Jess one ting, cap'n. Ah have some folks back in da Caymans. Would yo consider takin' hout a life hinsurance hon me afore we sail?'

Bond glanced affectionately at the strong brown face. It had a deep cleft of worry between the eyes. 'Of course, Quarrel. I'll fix it at Port Maria tomorrow. We'll make it big, say five thousand pounds. Now then, how shall we go? Canoe?'

'Dat's right, cap'n.' Quarrel's voice was reluctant. 'We need a calm sea an' a light wind. Come him on de Noreasterly Trades. Mus' be a dark night. Dey startin' right now. By end of da week we git da secon' moon quarter. Where you reckon to land, cap'n?'

'South shore near the mouth of the river. Then we'll go up the river to the lake. I'm sure that's where the wardens' camp was. So as to have fresh water and be able to get down to the sea to fish.'

Quarrel grunted without enthusiasm. 'How long we stayin', cap'n? Caint take a whole lot of food wit us. Bread, cheese, salt pork. No tobacco—caint risk da smoke an' light. Dat's mighty rough country, cap'n. Marsh an' mangrove.'

Bond said: 'Better plan for three days. Weather may break and stop us getting off for a night or two. Couple of good hunting knives. I'll take a gun. You never can tell.'

'No, sir,' said Quarrel emphatically. He relapsed into a brooding silence which lasted until they got to Port Maria.

They went through the little town and on round the headland to Morgan's Harbour. It was just as Bond remembered—the sugar-loaf of the Isle of Surprise rising out of the calm bay, the canoes drawn up beside the mounds of empty conch shells, the distant boom of the surf on the reef which had so nearly been his grave.

Bond, his mind full of memories, took the car down the little side road and through the cane fields in the middle of which the gaunt ruin of the old Great House of Beau Desert Plantation stood up like a stranded galleon.

They came to the gate leading to the bungalow. Quarrel got out and opened the gate, and Bond drove through and pulled up in the yard behind the white single-storeyed house. It was very quiet. Bond walked round the house and across the lawn to the edge of the sea. Yes, there it was, the stretch of deep, silent water—the submarine path he had taken to the Isle of Surprise. It sometimes came back to him in nightmares. Bond stood looking at it and thinking of Solitaire, the girl he had brought back, torn and bleeding, from that sea. He had carried her across the lawn to the house. What had happened to her? Where was she? Brusquely Bond turned and walked back into the house, driving the phantoms away from him.

It was eight-thirty. Bond unpacked his few things and changed into sandals and shorts. Soon there was the delicious smell of coffee and frying bacon. They ate their breakfast while Bond fixed his training routine— up at seven, swim a quarter of a mile, breakfast, an hour's sunbathing, run a mile, swim again, lunch, sleep, sunbathe, swim a mile, hot bath and massage, dinner and asleep by nine.

After breakfast the routine began.

Nothing interrupted the grinding week except a brief story in the *Daily Gleaner* and a telegram from Pleydell-Smith. The *Gleaner* said that a Sunbeam Talbot, H. 2473, had been involved in a fatal accident on the Devil's Racecourse, a stretch of winding road between Spanish Town and Ocho Rios—on the Kingston–Montego route. A runaway lorry, whose driver was being traced, had crashed into the Sunbeam as it came round a bend. Both vehicles had left the road and hurtled into the ravine below. The two occupants of the Sunbeam, Ben Gibbons of Harbour Street, and Josiah Smith, no address, had been killed. A Mr Bond, an English visitor, who had been lent the car, was asked to contact the nearest police station.

Bond burned that copy of the *Gleaner*. He didn't want to upset Quarrel.

With only one day to go, the telegram came from Pleydell-Smith. It said:

EACH OBJECT CONTAINED ENOUGH CYANIDE TO KILL A HORSE STOP SUGGEST YOU CHANGE YOUR GROCER STOP GOOD LUCK SMITH

Bond also burned the telegram.

Quarrel hired a canoe and they spent three days sailing it. It was a clumsy shell cut out of a single giant cotton tree. It had two thin thwarts, two heavy paddles and a small sail of dirty canvas. It was a blunt instrument. Quarrel was pleased with it.

'Seven, eight hours, cap'n,' he said. 'Den we bring down de sail an' use de paddles. Less target for de radar to see.'

The weather held. The forecast from Kingston radio was good. The nights were black as sin. The two men got in their stores. Bond fitted himself out with cheap black canvas jeans and a dark blue shirt and rope-soled shoes.

The last evening came. Bond was glad he was on his way. He had only once been out of the training camp— to get the stores and arrange Quarrel's insurance—and he was chafing to get out of the stable and on to the track. He admitted to himself that this adventure excited him. It had the right ingredients—physical exertion, mystery, and a ruthless enemy. He had a good companion. His cause was just. There might also be the satisfaction of throwing the 'holiday in the sun' back in M's teeth. That had rankled. Bond didn't like being coddled.

The sun blazed beautifully into its grave.

Bond went into his bedroom and took out his two guns and looked at them. Neither was a part of him as the Beretta had been—an extension of his right hand—but he already knew them as better weapons. Which should he take? Bond picked up each in turn, hefting them in his hand. It had to be the heavier Smith & Wesson. There would be no close shooting, if there was any shooting, on Crab Key. Heavy, long-range stuff—if anything. The brutal, stumpy revolver had an extra twenty-five yards over the Walther. Bond fitted the holster into the waistband of his jeans and clipped in the gun. He put twenty spare rounds in his pocket. Was it over-insurance to take all this metal on what might only be a tropical picnic?

Bond went to the icebox and took a pint of Canadian Club Blended Rye and some ice and soda-water and went and sat in the garden and watched the last light flame and die.

The shadows crept from behind the house and marched across the lawn and enveloped him. The Undertaker's Wind that blows at night from the centre of the island, clattered softly in the tops of the palm trees. The frogs began to tinkle among the shrubs. The fireflies, the 'blink-a-blinks', as Quarrel called them, came out and began flashing their sexual morse. For a moment the melancholy of the tropical dusk caught at Bond's heart. He picked up the bottle and looked at it. He had drunk a quarter of it. He poured another big slug into his glass and added some ice. What was he drinking for? Because of the thirty miles of black sea he had to cross tonight? Because he was going into the unknown? Because of Doctor No?

Quarrel came up from the beach. 'Time, cap'n.'

Bond swallowed his drink and followed the Cayman Islander down to the canoe. It was rocking quietly in the water, its bows on the sand. Quarrel went aft and Bond climbed into the space between the forward thwart and the bows. The sail, wrapped round the short mast, was at his back. Bond took up his paddle and pushed off, and they turned slowly and headed out for the break in the softly creaming waves that was the passage through the reef. They paddled easily, in unison, the paddles

turning in their hands so that they did not leave the
water on the forward stroke. The small waves slapped
softly against the bows. Otherwise they made no noise.
It was dark. Nobody saw them go. They just left the
land and went off across the sea.

Bond's only duty was to keep paddling. Quarrel did
the steering. At the opening through the reef there was a
swirl and suck of conflicting currents and they were in
amongst the jagged niggerheads and coral trees, bared
like fangs by the swell. Bond could feel the strength of
Quarrel's great sweeps with the paddle as the heavy
craft wallowed and plunged. Again and again Bond's
own paddle thudded against rock, and once he had to
hold on as the canoe hit a buried mass of brain coral and
slid off again. Then they were through, and far below
the boat there were indigo patches of sand and around
them the solid oily feel of deep water.

'Okay, cap'n,' said Quarrel softly. Bond shipped his
paddle and got down off one knee and sat with his back
to the thwart. He heard the scratching of Quarrel's nails
against canvas as he unwrapped the sail and then the
sharp flap as it caught the breeze. The canoe
straightened and began to move. It tilted slowly. There
was a soft hiss under the bows. A handful of spray
tossed up into Bond's face. The wind of their movement
was cool and would soon get cold. Bond hunched up his
knees and put his arms round them. The wood was
already beginning to bite into his buttocks and his back.
It crossed his mind that it was going to be the hell of a
long and uncomfortable night.

In the darkness ahead Bond could just make out the
rim of the world. Then came a layer of black haze above
which the stars began, first sparsely and then merging
into a dense bright carpet. The Milky Way soared
overhead. How many stars? Bond tried counting a
finger's length and was soon past the hundred. The stars
lit the sea into a faint grey road and then arched away
over the tip of the mast towards the black silhouette of
Jamaica. Bond looked back. Behind the hunched figure
of Quarrel there was a faraway cluster of lights which

would be Port Maria. Already they were a couple of miles out. Soon they would be a tenth of the way, then a quarter, then a half. That would be around midnight when Bond would take over. Bond sighed and put his head down to his knees and closed his eyes.

He must have slept because he was awakened by the clonk of a paddle against the boat. He lifted his arm to show that he had heard and glanced at the luminous blaze of his watch. Twelve-fifteen. Stiffly he unbent his legs and turned and scrambled over the thwart.

'Sorry, Quarrel,' he said, and it was odd to hear his voice. 'You ought to have shaken me up before.'

'Hit don signify, cap'n,' said Quarrel with a grey glint of teeth. 'Do yo good to sleep.'

Gingerly they slipped past each other and Bond settled in the stern and picked up the paddle. The sail was secured to a bent nail beside him. It was flapping. Bond brought the bows into the wind and edged them round so that the North Star was directly over Quarrel's head in the bows. For a time this would be fun. There was something to do.

There was no change in the night except that it seemed darker and emptier. The pulse of the sleeping sea seemed slower. The heavy swell was longer and the troughs deeper. They were running through a patch of phosphorus that winked at the bows and dripped jewels when Bond lifted the paddle out of the water. How safe it was, slipping through the night in this ridiculously vulnerable little boat. How kind and soft the sea could be. A covey of flying fish broke the surface in front of the bows and scattered like shrapnel. Some kept going for a time beside the canoe, flying as much as twenty yards before they dived into the wall of the swell. Was some bigger fish after them or did they think the canoe was a fish, or were they just playing? Bond thought of what was going on in the hundreds of fathoms below the boat, the big fish, the shark and barracuda and tarpon and sailfish quietly cruising, the shoals of kingfish and mackerel and bonito and, far below in the grey twilight of the great depths, the phosphorus jellied boneless things that were never seen, the fifty-foot squids, with eyes a foot wide, that streamed along like zeppelins, the last real monsters of the sea, whose size was only known from the fragments found inside whales. What would happen if a wave caught the canoe broadside and capsized them? How long would they last? Bond took an ounce more pains with his steering and put the thought aside.

One o'clock, two o'clock, three, four. Quarrel awoke and stretched. He called softly to Bond, 'Ah smells land, cap'n.' Soon there was a thickening of the darkness ahead. The low shadow slowly took on the shape of a huge swimming rat. A pale moon rose slowly behind them. Now the island showed distinctly, a couple of miles away, and there was the distant grumble of surf.

They changed places. Quarrel brought down the sail and they took up the paddles. For at least another mile, thought Bond, they would be invisible in the troughs of the waves. Not even radar would distinguish them from the crests. It was the last mile they would have to hurry over with the dawn not far off.

Now he too could smell the land. It had no particular scent. It was just something new in the nose after hours of clean sea. He could make out the white fringe of surf. The swell subsided and the waves became choppier. 'Now, cap'n,' called Quarrel, and Bond, the sweat already dropping off his chin, dug deeper and more often. God, it was hard work! The hulking log of wood which had sped along so well under the sail now seemed hardly to move. The wave at the bows was only a ripple. Bond's shoulders were aching like fire. The one knee he was resting on was beginning to bruise. His hands were cramped on the clumsy shaft of a paddle made of lead.

It was incredible, but they were coming up with the reef. Patches of sand showed deep under the boat. Now the surf was a roar. They followed along the edge of the reef, looking for an opening. A hundred yards inside the reef, breaking the sandline, was the shimmer of water running inland. The river! So the landfall had been all right. The wall of surf broke up. There was a patch of black oily current swelling over hidden coral heads. The nose of the canoe turned towards it and into it. There was a turmoil of water and a series of grating thuds, and then a sudden rush forward into peace and the canoe was moving slowly across a smooth mirror towards the shore.

Quarrel steered the boat towards the lee of a rocky promontory where the beach ended. Bond wondered why the beach didn't shine white under the thin moon. When they grounded and Bond climbed stiffly out he understood why. The beach was black. The sand was soft and wonderful to the feet but it must have been formed out of volcanic rock, pounded over the centuries, and Bond's naked feet on it looked like white crabs.

They made haste. Quarrel took three short lengths of thick bamboo out of the boat and laid them up the flat beach. They heaved the nose of the canoe on to the first and pushed the boat up the rollers. After each yard of progress, Bond picked up the back roller and brought it to the front. Slowly the canoe moved up the sand until at last it was over the black tideline and among the rocks and turtle grass and low sea-grape bushes. They pushed it another twenty yards inland into the beginning of the mangrove. There they covered it with dried seaweed and bits of driftwood from the tideline. Then Quarrel cut lengths of screwpalm and went back over their tracks, sweeping and tidying.

It was still dark, but the breath of grey in the east would soon be turning to pearl. It was five o'clock. They were dead tired. They exchanged a few words and Quarrel went off among the rocks on the promontory. Bond scooped out a depression in the fine dry sand under a thick bush of sea-grape. There were a few hermit crabs beside his bed. He picked up as many as he could find and hurled them into the mangrove. Then, not caring what other animals or insects might come to his smell and his warmth, he lay down full length in the sand and rested his head on his arm.

He was at once asleep.

CHAPTER 8

The Elegant Venus

Bond awoke lazily. The feel of the sand reminded him where he was. He glanced at his watch. Ten o'clock. The sun through the round thick leaves of the sea-grape was already hot. A larger shadow moved across the dappled sand in front of his face. Quarrel? Bond shifted his head and peered through the fringe of leaves and grass that concealed him from the beach. He stiffened. His heart missed a beat and then began pounding so that he had to breathe deeply to quieten it. His eyes, as he stared through the blades of grass, were fierce slits.

It was a naked girl, with her back to him. She was not quite naked. She wore a broad leather belt around her waist with a hunting knife in a leather sheath at her right hip. The belt made her nakedness extraordinarily erotic. She stood not more than five yards away on the tideline looking down at something in her hand. She stood in the classical relaxed pose of the nude, all the weight on the right leg and the left knee bent and turning slightly inwards, the head to one side as she examined the things in her hand.

It was a beautiful back. The skin was a very light uniform *café au lait* with the sheen of dull satin. The gentle curve of the backbone was deeply indented, suggesting more powerful muscles than is usual in a woman, and the behind was almost as firm and rounded as a boy's. The legs were straight and beautiful and no pinkness showed under the slightly lifted left heel. She was not a coloured girl.

Her hair was ash blonde. It was cut to the shoulders and hung there and along the side of her bent cheek in thick wet strands. A green diving mask was pushed back above her forehead, and the green rubber thong bound her hair at the back.

The whole scene, the empty beach, the green and blue sea, the naked girl with the strands of fair hair, reminded Bond of something. He searched his mind. Yes, she was Botticelli's Venus, seen from behind.

How had she got there? What was she doing? Bond looked up and down the beach. It was not black, he now saw, but a deep chocolate brown. To the right he could see as far as the river mouth, perhaps five hundred yards away. The beach was empty and featureless except for a scattering of small pinkish objects. There were a lot of them, shells of some sort Bond supposed, and they looked decorative against the dark brown background. He looked to the left, to where, twenty yards away, the rocks of the small headland began. Yes, there was a yard or two of groove in the sand where a canoe had been drawn up into the shelter of the rocks. It must have been a light one or she couldn't have drawn it up alone. Perhaps the girl wasn't alone. But there was only one set of footprints leading down from the rocks to the sea and another set coming out of the sea and up the beach to where she now stood on the tideline. Did she live here, or had she too sailed over from Jamaica that night? Hell of a thing for a girl to do. Anyway, what in God's name *was* she doing here?

As if to answer him, the girl made a throwaway

gesture of the right hand and scattered a dozen shells on the sand beside her. They were violet pink and seemed to Bond to be the same as he had noticed on the beach. The girl looked down into her left hand and began to whistle softly to herself. There was a happy note of triumph in the whistle. She was whistling 'Marion', a plaintive little calypso that has now been cleaned up and made famous outside Jamaica. It had always been one of Bond's favourites. It went:

> All day, all night, Marion,
> Sittin' by the seaside siftin' sand . . .

The girl broke off to stretch her arms out in a deep yawn. Bond smiled to himself. He wet his lips and took up the refrain:

> 'The water from her eyes could sail a boat,
> The hair on her head could tie a goat . . .'

The hands flew down and across her chest. The muscles of her behind bunched with tension. She was listening, her head, still hidden by the curtain of hair, cocked to one side.

Hesitantly she began again. The whistle trembled and died. At the first note of Bond's echo, the girl whirled round. She didn't cover her body with the two classical gestures. One hand flew downwards, but the other, instead of hiding her breasts, went up to her face, covering it below the eyes, now wide with fear. 'Who's that?' The words came out in a terrified whisper.

Bond got to his feet and stepped out through the sea-grape. He stopped on the edge of the grass. He held his hands open at his sides to show they were empty. He smiled cheerfully at her. 'It's only me. I'm another trespasser. Don't be frightened.'

The girl dropped her hand down from her face. It went to the knife at her belt. Bond watched the fingers curl round the hilt. He looked up at her face. Now he realized why her hand had instinctively gone to it. It was

a beautiful face, with wide-apart deep blue eyes under
lashes paled by the sun. The mouth was wide and when
she stopped pursing the lips with tension they would be
full. It was a serious face and the jawline was determined—the face of a girl who fends for herself. And
once, reflected Bond, she had failed to fend. For the
nose was badly broken, smashed crooked like a boxer's.
Bond stiffened with revolt at what had happened to this
supremely beautiful girl. No wonder this was her shame
and not the beautiful firm breasts that now jutted
towards him without concealment.

The eyes examined him fiercely. 'Who are you? What
are you doing here?' There was the slight lilt of a
Jamaican accent. The voice was sharp and accustomed
to being obeyed.

'I'm an Englishman. I'm interested in birds.'

'Oh,' the voice was doubtful. The hand still rested on
the knife. 'How long have you been watching me? How
did you get here?'

'Ten minutes, but no more answers until you tell me
who *you* are.'

'I'm no one in particular. I come from Jamaica. I
collect shells.'

'I came in a canoe. Did you?'

'Yes. Where is your canoe?'

'I've got a friend with me. We've hidden it in the
mangroves.'

'There are no marks of a canoe landing.'

'We're careful. We covered them up. Not like you.'
Bond gestured towards the rocks. 'You ought to take
more trouble. Did you use a sail? Right up to the reef?'

'Of course. Why not? I always do.'

'Then they'll know you're here. They've got radar.'

'They've never caught me yet.' The girl took her hand
away from her knife. She reached up and stripped off
the diving mask and stood swinging it. She seemed to
think she had the measure of Bond. She said, with some
of the sharpness gone from her voice, 'What's your
name?'

'Bond. James Bond. What's yours?'

She reflected. 'Rider.'

'What Rider?'

'Honeychile.'

Bond smiled.

'What's so funny about it?'

'Nothing. Honeychile Rider. It's a pretty name.'

She unbent. 'People call me "Honey".'

'Well, I'm glad to meet you.'

The prosaic phrase seemed to remind her of her nakedness. She blushed. She said uncertainly, 'I must get dressed.' She looked down at the scattered shells around her feet. She obviously wanted to pick them up. Perhaps she realized that the movement might be still more revealing than her present pose. She said sharply, 'You're not to touch those while I'm gone.'

Bond smiled at the childish challenge. 'Don't worry, I'll look after them.'

The girl looked at him doubtfully and then turned and walked stiff-legged over to the rocks and disappeared behind them.

Bond walked the few steps down the beach and bent and picked up one of the shells. It was alive and the two halves were shut tight. It appeared to be some kind of a cockle, rather deeply ribbed and coloured a mauve-pink. Along both edges of the hinge, thin horns stood out, about half a dozen to each side. It didn't seem to Bond a very distinguished shell. He replaced it carefully with the others.

He stood looking down at the shells and wondering. Was she really collecting them? It certainly looked like it. But what a risk to take to get them—the voyage over alone in the canoe and then back again. And she seemed to realize that this was a dangerous place. 'They've never caught me yet.' What an extraordinary girl. Bond's heart warmed and his senses stirred as he thought of her. Already, as he had found so often when people had deformities, he had almost forgotten her broken nose. It had somehow slipped away behind his memory of her eyes and her mouth and her amazingly beautiful body. Her imperious attitude and her quality of attack were exciting. The way she had reached for her knife to defend herself! She was like an animal whose cubs are threatened. Where did she live? Who were her parents? There was something uncared for about her—a dog that nobody wants to pet. Who was she?

Bond heard her footsteps riffling the sand. He turned to look at her. She was dressed almost in rags—a faded brown shirt with torn sleeves and a knee-length patched brown cotton skirt held in place by the leather belt with the knife. She had a canvas knapsack slung over one shoulder. She looked like a principal girl dressed as Man Friday.

She came up with him and at once went down on one knee and began picking up the live shells and stowing them in the knapsack.

Bond said, 'Are those rare?'

She sat back on her haunches and looked up at him. She surveyed his face. Apparently she was satisfied. 'You promise you won't tell anybody? Swear?'

'I promise,' said Bond.

'Well then, yes, they are rare. Very. You can get five dollars for a perfect specimen. In Miami. That's where I deal with. They're called *Venus elegans*—The Elegant Venus.' Her eyes sparkled up at him with excitement. 'This morning I found what I wanted. The bed where they live,' she waved towards the sea. 'You wouldn't find it though,' she added with sudden carefulness. 'It's very deep and hidden away. I doubt if you could dive that deep. And anyway,' she looked happy, 'I'm going to clear the whole bed today. You'd only get the imperfect ones if you came back here.'

Bond laughed. 'I promise I won't steal any. I really don't know anything about shells. Cross my heart.'

She stood up, her work completed. 'What about these birds of yours? What sort are they? Are they valuable too? I won't tell either if you tell me. I only collect shells.'

'They're called roseate spoonbills,' said Bond. 'Sort of pink stork with a flat beak. Ever seen any?'

'Oh, *those*,' she said scornfully. 'There used to be

thousands of them here. But you won't find many now. They scared them all away.' She sat down on the sand and put her arms round her knees, proud of her superior knowledge and now certain that she had nothing to fear from this man.

Bond sat down a yard away. He stretched out and turned towards her, resting on his elbow. He wanted to preserve the picnic atmosphere and try to find out more about this queer, beautiful girl. He said, easily, 'Oh, really. What happened? Who did it?'

She shrugged impatiently. 'The people here did it. I don't know who they are. There's a Chinaman. He doesn't like birds or something. He's got a dragon. He sent the dragon after the birds and scared them away. The dragon burned up their nesting places. There used to be two men who lived with the birds and looked after them. They got scared away too, or killed or something.'

It all seemed quite natural to her. She gave the facts indifferently, staring out to sea.

Bond said, 'This dragon. What kind is he? Have you ever seen him?'

'Yes, I've seen him.' She screwed up her eyes and made a wry face as if she was swallowing bitter medicine. She looked earnestly at Bond to make him share her feelings. 'I've been coming here for about a year, looking for shells and exploring. I only found these,' she waved at the beach, 'about a month ago. On my last trip. But I've found plenty of other good ones. Just before Christmas I thought I'd explore the river. I went up it to the top, where the birdmen had their camp. It was all broken up. It was getting late and I decided to spend the night there. In the middle of the night I woke up. The dragon was coming by only a few chains away from me. It had two great glaring eyes and a long snout. It had sort of short wings and a pointed tail. It was all black and gold.' She frowned at the expression on Bond's face. 'There was a full moon. I could see it quite clearly. It went by me. It was making a sort of roaring noise. It went over the marsh and came to some thick mangrove and it simply climbed over the bushes and went on. A whole flock of birds got up in front of it and suddenly a lot of fire came out of its mouth and it burned a lot of them up and all the trees they'd been roosting in. It was horrible. The most horrible thing I've ever seen.'

The girl leant sideways and peered at Bond's face. She sat up straight again and stared obstinately out to sea. 'I can see you don't believe me,' she said in a furious, tense voice. 'You're one of these city people. You don't believe anything. Ugh,' she shuddered with dislike of him.

Bond said reasonably, 'Honey, there just aren't such things as dragons in the world. You saw something that looked very like a dragon. I'm just wondering what it was.'

'How do you know there aren't such things as dragons?' Now he had made her really angry. 'Nobody lives on this end of the island. One could easily have survived here. Anyway, what do you think you know about animals and things? I've lived with snakes and things since I was a child. Alone. Have you ever seen a praying mantis eat her husband after they've made love? Have you ever seen the mongoose dance? Or an octopus dance? How long is a humming bird's tongue? Have you ever had a pet snake that wore a bell round its neck and rang it to wake you? Have you seen a scorpion get sunstroke and kill itself with its own sting? Have you seen the carpet of flowers under the sea at night? Do you know that a John Crow can smell a dead lizard a mile away . . . ?' The girl had fired these questions like scornful jabs with a rapier. Now she stopped, out of breath. She said hopelessly, 'Oh, you're just city folk like all the rest.'

Bond said, 'Honey, now look here. You know these things. I can't help it that I live in towns. I'd like to know about your things too. I just haven't had that sort of life. I know other things instead. Like . . .' Bond searched his mind. He couldn't think of anything as interesting as hers. He finished lamely, 'Like for instance that this Chinaman is going to be more interested in your visit this time. This time he's going to try and stop you getting away.' He paused and added, 'And me for the matter of that.'

She turned and looked at him with interest. 'Oh. Why? But then it doesn't really matter. One just hides during the day and gets away at night. He's sent dogs after me and even a plane. He hasn't got me yet.' She examined Bond with a new interest. 'Is it you he's after?'

'Well, yes,' admitted Bond. 'I'm afraid it is. You see we dropped the sail about two miles out so that their radar wouldn't pick us up. I think the Chinaman may have been expecting a visit from me. Your sail will have been reported and I'd bet anything he'll think your canoe was mine. I'd better go and wake my friend up and we'll talk it over. You'll like him. He's a Cayman Islander, name of Quarrel.'

The girl said, 'Well, I'm sorry if . . .' the sentence trailed away. Apologies wouldn't come easy to someone so much on the defensive. 'But after all I couldn't know, could I?' She searched his face.

Bond smiled into the questing blue eyes. He said reassuringly, 'Of course you couldn't. It's just bad luck—bad luck for you too. I don't suppose he minds too much about a solitary girl who collects shells. You can be sure they've had a good look at your footprints and found clues like that'—he waved at the scattered shells on the beach. 'But I'm afraid he'd take a different view of me. Now he'll try and hunt me down with everything he's got. I'm only afraid he may get you into the net in the process. Anyway,' Bond grinned reassuringly, 'we'll see what Quarrel has to say. You stay here.'

Bond got to his feet. He walked along the promontory and cast about him. Quarrel had hidden himself well. It took Bond five minutes to find him. He was lying in a grassy depression between two big rocks, half covered by a board of grey driftwood. He was still fast asleep, the brown head, stern in sleep, cradled on his forearm. Bond whistled softly and smiled as the eyes sprang wide open like an animal's. Quarrel saw Bond and scrambled to his feet, almost guiltily. He rubbed his big hands over his face as if he was washing it.

'Mornin', cap'n,' he said. 'Guess Ah been down deep. Dat China girl come to me.'

Bond smiled. 'I got something different,' he said. They sat down and Bond told him about Honeychile Rider and her shells and the fix they were in. 'And now it's eleven o'clock,' Bond added. 'And we've got to make a new plan.'

Quarrel scratched his head. He looked sideways at Bond. 'Yo don' plan we jess ditch dis girl?' he asked hopefully. 'Ain't nuttin to do wit me . . .' Suddenly he stopped. His head swivelled round and pointed like a dog's. He held up a hand for silence, listening intently.

Bond held his breath. In the distance, to the eastwards, there was a faint droning.

Quarrel jumped to his feet. 'Quick, cap'n,' he said urgently. 'Dey's a comin'.'

CHAPTER 9

Close Shaves

Ten minutes later the bay was empty and immaculate. Small waves curled lazily in across the mirrored water inside the reef and flopped exhausted on the dark sand where the mauve shells glittered like shed toenails. The heap of discarded shells had gone and there was no longer any trace of footprints. Quarrel had cut branches of mangrove and had walked backwards sweeping carefully as he went. Where he had swept, the sand was of a different texture from the rest of the beach, but not too different as to be noticed from outside the reef. The girl's canoe had been pulled deeper among the rocks and covered with seaweed and driftwood.

Quarrel had gone back to the headland. Bond and the girl lay a few feet apart under the bush of sea-grape where Bond had slept, and gazed silently out across the water to the corner of the headland round which the boat would come.

The boat was perhaps a quarter of a mile away. From the slow pulse of the twin diesels Bond guessed that

every cranny of the coastline was being searched for
signs of them. It sounded a powerful boat. A big cabin
cruiser, perhaps. What crew would it have? Who would
be in command of the search? Doctor No? Unlikely. He
would not trouble himself with this kind of police work.

From the west a wedge of cormorants appeared,
flying low over the sea beyond the reef. Bond watched
them. They were the first evidence he had seen of the
guanay colony at the other end of the island. These, according to Pleydell-Smith's description, would be scouts
looking for the silver flash of the anchovy near the surface. Sure enough, as he watched, they began to back-
pedal in the air and then go into shallow dives, hitting
the water like shrapnel. Almost at once a fresh file appeared from the west, then another and another that
merged into a long stream and then into a solid black
river of birds. For minutes they darkened the skyline
and then they were down on the water, covering several
acres of it, screeching and fighting and plunging their
heads below the surface, cropping at the solid field of
anchovy like piranha fish feasting on a drowned horse.

Bond felt a gentle nudge from the girl. She gestured
with her head. 'The Chinaman's hens getting their
corn.'

Bond examined the happy, beautiful face. She had
seemed quite unconcerned by the arrival of the search
party. To her it was only the game of hide-and-seek she
had played before. Bond hoped she wasn't going to get
a shock.

The iron thud of the diesels was getting louder. The
boat must be just behind the headland. Bond took a last
look round the peaceful bay and then fixed his eyes,
through the leaves and grass, on the point of the
headland inside the reef.

The knife of white bows appeared. It was followed by
ten yards of empty polished deck, glass windshields, a
low raked cabin with a siren and blunt radio mast, the
glimpse of a man inside at the wheel, then the long flat
well of the stern and a drooping red ensign. Converted
M.T.B., British Government surplus?

Bond's eyes went to the two men standing in the
stern. They were pale-skinned negroes. They wore neat
khaki ducks and shirts, broad belts, and deep visored
baseball caps of yellow straw. They were standing side
by side, bracing themselves against the slow swell. One
of them was holding a long black loud-hailer with a wire
attached. The other was manning a machine gun on a
tripod. It looked to Bond like a Spandau.

The man with the loud-hailer let it fall so that it
swung on a strap round his neck. He picked up a pair of
binoculars and began inching them along the beach. The
low murmur of his comments just reached Bond above
the glutinous flutter of the diesels.

Bond watched the eyes of the binoculars begin with
the headland and then sweep the sand. The twin eyes
paused among the rocks and moved on. They came
back. The murmur of comment rose to a jabber. The
man handed the glasses to the machine gunner who took
a quick glance through them and gave them back. The
scanner shouted something to the helmsman. The cabin
cruiser stopped and backed up. Now she lay outside the
reef exactly opposite Bond and the girl. The scanner
again levelled the binoculars at the rocks where the girl's
canoe lay hidden. Again the excited jabber came across
the water. Again the glasses were passed to the machine
gunner who glanced through. This time he nodded
decisively.

Bond thought: now we've had it. These men know
their job.

Bond watched the machine gunner pull the bolt back
to load. The double click came to him over the bubbling
of the diesels.

The scanner lifted his loud-hailer and switched it on.
The twanging echo of the amplifier moaned and
screeched across the water. The man brought it up to his
lips. The voice roared across the bay.

'Okay, folks! Come on out and you won't get hurt.'

It was an educated voice. There was a trace of
American accent.

'Now then, folks,' the voice thundered, 'make it

quick! We've seen where you came ashore. We've spotted the boat under the driftwood. We ain't fools an' we ain't fooling. Take it easy. Just walk out with your hands up. You'll be okay.'

Silence fell. The waves lapped softly on the beach. Bond could hear the girl breathing. The thin screeching of the cormorants came to them muted across the mile of sea. The diesels bubbled unevenly as the swell covered the exhaust pipe and then opened it again.

Softly Bond reached over to the girl and tugged at her sleeve. 'Come close,' he whispered. 'Smaller target.' He felt her warmth nearer to him. Her cheek brushed against his forearm. He whispered, 'Burrow into the sand. Wriggle. Every inch'll help.' He began to worm his body carefully deeper into the depression they had scooped out for themselves. He felt her do the same. He peered out. Now his eyes were only just above the skyline of the top of the beach.

The man was lifting his loud-hailer. The voice roared. 'Okay, folks! Just so as you'll know this thing isn't for show.' He lifted his thumb. The machine gunner trained his gun into the tops of the mangroves behind the beach. There came the swift rattling roar Bond had last heard coming from the German lines in the Ardennes. The bullets made the same old sound of frightened pigeons whistling overhead. Then there was silence.

In the distance Bond watched the black cloud of cormorants take to the air and begin circling. His eyes went back to the boat. The machine gunner was feeling the barrel of his gun to see if it had warmed. The two men exchanged some words. The scanner picked up his loud-hailer.

' 'Kay, folks,' he said harshly. 'You've been warned. This is it.'

Bond watched the snout of the Spandau swing and depress. The man was going to start with the canoe among the rocks. Bond whispered to the girl, 'All right, Honey. Stick it. Keep right down. It won't last long.' He felt her hand squeeze his arm. He thought: poor little bitch, she's in this because of me. He leant to the right to cover her head and pushed his face deep into the sand.

This time the crash of noise was terrific. The bullets howled into the corner of the headland. Fragments of splintered rock whined over the beach like hornets. Ricochets twanged and buzzed off into the hinterland. Behind it all there was the steady road-drill hammer of the gun.

There was a pause. New magazine, thought Bond. Now it's us. He could feel the girl clutching at him. Her body was trembling along his flank. Bond reached out an arm and pressed her to him.

The roar of the gun began again. The bullets came zipping along the tideline towards them. There was a succession of quick close thuds. The bush above them was being torn to shreds. 'Zwip. Zwip. Zwip.' It was as if the thong of a steel whip was cutting the bush to pieces. Bits scattered around them, slowly covering them. Bond could smell the cooler air that meant they were now lying in the open. Were they hidden by the leaves and debris? The bullets marched away along the shoreline. In less than a minute the racket stopped.

The silence sang. The girl whimpered softly. Bond hushed her and held her tighter.

The loud-hailer boomed. 'Okay, folks. If you still got ears, we'll be along soon to pick up the bits. And we'll be bringing the dogs. 'Bye for now.'

The slow thud of the diesel quickened. The engine accelerated into a hasty roar and through the fallen leaves Bond watched the stern of the launch settle lower in the water as it made off to the west. Within minutes it was out of earshot.

Bond cautiously raised his head. The bay was serene, the beach unmarked. All was as before except for the stench of cordite and the sour smell of blasted rock. Bond pulled the girl to her feet. There were tear streaks down her face. She looked at him aghast. She said solemnly, 'That was horrible. What did they do it for? We might have been killed.'

Bond thought, this girl has always had to fend for

herself, but only against nature. She knows the world of
animals and insects and fishes and she's got the better of
it. But it's been a small world, bounded by the sun and
the moon and the seasons. She doesn't know the big
world of the smoke-filled room, of the bullion broker's
parlour, of the corridors and waiting rooms of government offices, of careful meetings on park seats—she
doesn't know about the struggle for big power and big
money by the big men. She doesn't know that she's been
swept out of her rock pool into the dirty waters.

He said, 'It's all right, Honey. They're just a lot of
bad men who are frightened of us. We can manage
them.' Bond put his arm round her shoulders, 'And you
were wonderful. As brave as anything. Come on now,
we'll look for Quarrel and make some plans. Anyway,
it's time we had something to eat. What do you eat on
these expeditions?'

They turned and walked up the beach to the
headland. After a minute she said in a controlled voice,
'Oh, there's stacks of food about. Sea urchins mostly.
And there are wild bananas and things. I eat and sleep
for two days before I come out here. I don't need
anything.'

Bond held her more closely. He dropped his arm as
Quarrel appeared on the skyline. Quarrel scrambled
down among the rocks. He stopped, looking down.
They came up with him. The girl's canoe was sawn
almost in half by the bullets. The girl gave a cry. She
looked desperately at Bond, 'My boat! How am I to get
back?'

'Don' you worry, missy,' Quarrel appreciated the loss
of a canoe better than Bond. He guessed it might be
most of the girl's capital. 'Cap'n fix you up wit' anudder. An' yo come back wit' we. Us got a fine boat in de
mangrove. Hit not get broke. Ah's bin to see him.'
Quarrel looked at Bond. Now his face was worried. 'But
cap'n, yo sees what I means about dese folk. Dey
mighty tough men an' dey means business. Dese dogs
dey speak of. Dose is policehouns—Pinschers dey's
called. Big bastards. Mah frens tell me as der's a pack of

twenty or moh. We better make plans quick—an' good.'

'All right, Quarrel. But first we must have something to eat. And I'm damned if I'm going to be scared off the island before I've had a good look. We'll take Honey with us.' He turned to the girl. 'Is that all right with you, Honey? You'll be all right with us. Then we'll sail home together.'

The girl looked doubtfully at him. 'I guess there's no alternative. I mean, I'd love to go with you if I won't be in the way. I really don't want anything to eat. But will you take me home as soon as you can? I don't want to see any more of those people. How long are you going to be looking at these birds?'

Bond said evasively, 'Not long. I've got to find out what happened to them and why. Then we'll be off.' He looked at his watch. 'It's twelve now. You wait here. Have a bath or something. Don't walk about leaving footprints. Come on, Quarrel, we'd better get that boat hidden.'

It was one o'clock before they were ready. Bond and Quarrel filled the canoe with stones and sand until it sank in a pool among the mangroves. They smeared over their footprints. The bullets had left so much litter behind the shoreline that they could do most of their walking on broken leaves and twigs. They ate some of their rations—avidly, the girl reluctantly—and climbed across the rocks and into the shallow water off-shore. Then they trudged along the shallows towards the river mouth three hundred yards away down the beach.

It was very hot. A harsh, banking wind had sprung up from the north-east. Quarrel said this wind blew daily the year round. It was vital to the guanera. It dried the guano. The glare from the sea and from the shiny green leaves of the mangroves was dazzling. Bond was glad he had taken trouble to get his skin hardened to the sun.

There was a sandy bar at the river mouth and a long deep stagnant pool. They could either get wet or strip. Bond said to the girl, 'Honey, we can't be shy on this trip. We'll keep our shirts on because of the sun. Wear

what's sensible and walk behind us.' Without waiting
for her reply the two men took off their trousers.
Quarrel rolled them and packed them in the knapsack
with the provisions and Bond's gun. They waded into
the pool, Quarrel in front, then Bond, then the girl. The
water came up to Bond's waist. A big silver fish leaped
out of the pool and fell back with a splash. There were
arrows on the surface where others fled out of their
way. 'Tarpon,' commented Quarrel.

The pool converged into a narrow neck over which
the mangroves touched. For a time they waded through
a cool tunnel, and then the river broadened into a deep
sluggish channel that meandered ahead among the giant
spiderlegs of the mangroves. The bottom was muddy
and at each step their feet sank inches into slime. Small
fish or shrimps wriggled and fled from under their feet,
and every now and then they had to stoop to brush away
leeches before they got hold. But otherwise it was easy
going and quiet and cool among the bushes and, at least
to Bond, it was a blessing to be out of the sun.

Soon, as they got away from the sea, it began to smell
bad with the bad egg, sulphuretted hydrogen smell of
marsh gas. The mosquitoes and sandflies began to find
them. They liked Bond's fresh body. Quarrel told him
to dip himself in the river water. 'Dem like dere meat
wid salt on him,' he explained cheerfully. Bond took off
his shirt and did as he was told. Then it was better and
after a while Bond's nostrils even got used to the marsh
gas, except when Quarrel's feet disturbed some aged
pocket in the mud and a vintage bubble wobbled up
from the bottom and burst stinking under his nose.

The mangroves became fewer and sparser and the
river slowly opened out. The water grew shallower and
the bottom firmer. Soon they came round a bend and
into the open. Honey said, 'Better watch out now. We'll
be easier to see. It goes on like this for about a mile.
Then the river gets narrower until the lake. Then there's
the sandspit the birdmen lived on.'

They stopped in the shadow of the mangrove tunnel
and looked out. The river meandered sluggishly away

from them towards the centre of the island. Its banks, fringed with low bamboo and sea-grape, would give only half shelter. From its western bank the ground rose slowly and then sharply up to the sugar-loaf about two miles away which was the guanera. Round the base of the mountain there was a scattering of Quonset huts. A zigzag of silver ran down the hillside to the huts—a Decauderville Track, Bond guessed, to bring the guano from the diggings down to the crusher and separator. The summit of the sugar-loaf was white, as if with snow. From the peak flew a smoky flag of guano dust. Bond could see the black dots of cormorants against the white background. They were landing and taking off like bees at a hive.

Bond stood and gazed at the distant glittering mountain of bird dung. So this was the kingdom of Doctor No! Bond thought he had never seen a more god-forsaken landscape in his life.

He examined the ground between the river and the mountain. It seemed to be the usual grey dead coral broken, where there was a pocket of earth, by low scrub and screwpalm. No doubt a road or a track led down the mountainside to the central lake and the marshes. It looked bad stuff to cross unless there was. Bond noticed that all the vegetation was bent to the westwards. He imagined living the year round with that hot wind constantly scouring the island, the smell of the marsh gas and the guano. No penal colony could have a worse site than this.

Bond looked to the east. There the mangroves in the marshland seemed more hospitable. They marched away in a solid green carpet until they lost their outline in the dancing heat haze on the horizon. Over them a thick froth of birds tossed and settled and tossed again. Their steady scream carried over on the harsh wind.

Quarrel's voice broke in on Bond's thoughts. 'Dey's a comin', cap'n.'

Bond followed Quarrel's eyes. A big lorry was racing down from the huts, dust streaming from its wheels. Bond followed it for ten minutes until it disappeared amongst the mangroves at the head of the river. He listened. The baying of dogs came down on the wind.

Quarrel said, 'Dey'll come down de ribber, cap'n. Dem'll know we caint move 'cept up de ribber, assumin' we ain't dead. Dey'll surely come down de ribber to de beach and look for de pieces. Den mos' likely de boat come wit' a dinghy an' take de men and dogs off. Least-ways, dat's what Ah'd do in dere place.'

Honey said, 'That's what they do when they look for me. It's quite all right. You cut a piece of bamboo and when they get near you go under the water and breathe through the bamboo till they've gone by.'

Bond smiled at Quarrel. He said, 'Supposing you get the bamboo while I find a good mangrove clump.'

Quarrel nodded dubiously. He started off upstream towards the bamboo thickets. Bond turned back into the mangrove tunnel.

Bond had avoided looking at the girl. She said impatiently, 'You needn't be so careful of looking at me. It's no good minding those things at a time like this. You said so yourself.'

Bond turned and looked at her. Her tattered shirt came down to the waterline. There was a glimpse of pale wavering limbs below. The beautiful face smiled at him. In the mangroves the broken nose seemed appropriate in its animalness.

Bond looked at her slowly. She understood. He turned and went on downstream and she followed him.

Bond found what he wanted, a crack in the wall of mangrove that seemed to go deeper. He said, 'Don't break a branch.' He bent his head and waded in. The channel went in ten yards. The mud under their feet became deeper and softer. Then there was a solid wall of roots and they could go no farther. The brown water flowed slowly through a wide, quiet pool. Bond stopped. The girl came close to him. 'This is real hide and seek,' she said tremulously.

'Yes, isn't it.' Bond was thinking of his gun. He was wondering how well it would shoot after a bath in the river—how many dogs and men he could get if they

were found. He felt a wave of disquiet. It had been a
bad break coming across this girl. In combat, like it or
not, a girl is your extra heart. The enemy has two targets
against your one.

Bond remembered his thirst. He scooped up some
water. It was brackish and tasted of earth. It was all
right. He drank some more. The girl put out her hand
and stopped him. 'Don't drink too much. Wash your
mouth out and spit. You could get fever.'

Bond looked at her quietly. He did as she told him.

Quarrel whistled from somewhere in the main stream.
Bond answered and waded out towards him. They came
back along the channel. Quarrel splashed the mangrove
roots with water where their bodies might have brushed
against them. 'Kill da smell of us,' he explained briefly.
He produced his handful of bamboo lengths and began
whittling and cutting them. Bond looked to his gun and
the spare ammunition. They stood still in the pool so as
not to stir up more mud.

The sunlight dappled down through the thick roof of
leaves. The shrimps nibbled softly at their feet. Tension
built up in the hot, crouching silence.

It was almost a relief to hear the baying of the dogs.

CHAPTER 10

Dragon Spoor

The search party was coming fast down the river. The two men in bathing trunks and tall waders were having to run to keep up with the dogs. They were big Chinese negroes wearing shoulder holsters across their naked sweating chests. Occasionally they exchanged shouts that were mostly swear-words. Ahead of them the pack of big Dobermann Pinschers swam and floundered through the water, baying excitedly. They had a scent and they quested frenziedly, the diamond-shaped ears erect on the smooth, serpentine heads.

'May be a —ing crocodile,' yelled the leading man through the hubbub. He was carrying a short whip which he occasionally cracked like a whipper-in on the hunting field.

The other man converged towards him. He shouted excitedly, 'For my money it's the —ing limey! Bet ya he's lying up in the mangrove. Mind he doesn't give us a —ing ambush.' The man took the gun out of its holster and put it under his armpit and kept his hand on the butt.

They were coming out of the open river into the mangrove tunnel. The first man had a whistle. It stuck out of his broad face like a cigar butt. He blew a shrill blast. When the dogs swept on he laid about him with the whip. The dogs checked, whimpering as the slow current forced them to disobey orders. The two men took their guns and waded slowly downstream through the straggly legs of the mangroves.

The leading man came to the narrow break that Bond had found. He grasped a dog by the collar and swung it into the channel. The dog snorted eagerly and paddled forward. The man's eyes squinted at the mangrove roots on either side of the channel to see if they were scratched.

The dog and the man came into the small enclosed pool at the end of the channel. The man looked round disgustedly. He caught the dog by the collar and pulled him back. The dog was reluctant to leave the place. The man lashed down into the water with his whip.

The second man had been waiting at the entrance to the little channel. The first man came out. He shook his head and they went on downstream, the dogs, now less excited, streaming ahead.

Slowly the noise of the hunt grew less and vanished.

For another five minutes nothing moved in the mangrove pool, then, in one corner among the roots, a thin periscope of bamboo rose slowly out of the water. Bond's face emerged, the forehead streaked with wet hair, like the face of a surfacing corpse. In his right hand under the water the gun was ready. He listened intently. There was dead silence, not a sound. Or was there? What was that soft swish out in the main stream? Was someone wading very quietly along in the wake of the hunt? Bond reached out on either side of him and softly touched the other two bodies that lay among the roots on the edge of the pool. As the two faces surfaced he put his finger to his lips. It was too late. Quarrel had coughed and spat. Bond made a grimace and nodded urgently towards the main stream. They all listened. There was dead silence. Then the soft swishing began

again. Whoever it was was coming into the side-
channel. The tubes of bamboo went back into the three
mouths and the heads softly submerged again.

Underwater, Bond rested his head in the mud,
pinched his nostrils with his left hand and pursed his lips
round the tube. He knew the pool had been examined
once already. He had felt the disturbance of the swimming dog. That time they had not been found. Would
they get away with it again? This time there would have
been less chance for the stirred mud to seep away out of
the pool. If this searcher saw the darker brown stain,
would he shoot into it or stab into it? What weapons
would he have? Bond decided that he wouldn't take
chances. At the first movement in the water near him he
would get to his feet and shoot and hope for the best.

Bond lay and focused all his senses. What hell this
controlled breathing was and how maddening the soft
nibbling of the shrimps! It was lucky none of them had
a sore on their bodies or the damned things would have
eaten into it. But it had been a bright idea of the girl's.
Without it the dogs would have got to them wherever
they had hidden.

Suddenly Bond cringed. A rubber boot had stepped
on his shin and slid off. Would the man think it was a
branch? Bond couldn't chance it. With one surge of
motion he hurled himself upwards, spitting out the
length of bamboo.

Bond caught a quick impression of a huge body
standing almost on top of him and of a swirling rifle
butt. He lifted his left arm to protect his head and felt
the jarring blow on his forearm. At the same time his
right hand lunged forward and as the muzzle of his gun
touched the glistening right breast below the hairless
aureole he pulled the trigger.

The kick of the explosion, pent up against the man's
body, almost broke Bond's wrist, but the man crashed
back like a chopped tree into the water. Bond caught a
glimpse of a huge rent in his side as he went under. The
rubber waders thrashed once and the head, a Chinese
negroid head, broke the surface, its eyes turned up and

water pouring from its silently yelling mouth. Then the head went under again and there was nothing but muddy froth and a slowly widening red stain that began to seep away downstream.

Bond shook himself. He turned. Quarrel and the girl were standing behind him, water streaming from their bodies. Quarrel was grinning from ear to ear, but the girl's knuckles were at her mouth and her eyes were staring horror-struck at the reddened water.

Bond said curtly, 'I'm sorry, Honey. It had to be done. He was right on top of us. Come on, let's get going.' He took her roughly by the arm and thrust her away from the place and out into the main stream, only stopping when they had reached the open river at the beginning of the mangrove tunnel.

The landscape was empty again. Bond glanced at his watch. It had stopped at three o'clock. He looked at the westering sun. It might be four o'clock now. How much farther had they to go? Bond suddenly felt tired. Now he'd torn it. Even if the shot hadn't been heard—and it would have been well muffled by the man's body and by the mangroves—the man would be missed when the others rendezvoused, if Quarrel's guess was right, at the river mouth to be taken off to the launch. Would they come back up the river to look for the missing man? Probably not. It would be getting dark before they knew for certain that he was missing. They'd send out a search party in the morning. The dogs would soon get to the body. Then what?

The girl tugged at his sleeve. She said angrily, 'It's time you told me what all this is about! Why's everybody trying to kill each other? And who are you? I don't believe all this story about birds. You don't take a revolver after birds.'

Bond looked down into the angry, wide-apart eyes. 'I'm sorry, Honey. I'm afraid I've got you into a bit of a mess. I'll tell you all about it this evening when we get to the camp. It's just bad luck you being mixed up with me like this. I've got a bit of a war on with these people. They seem to want to kill me. Now I'm only interested in seeing us all off the island without anyone else getting hurt. I've got enough to go on now so that next time I can come back by the front door.'

'What do you mean? Are you some sort of a policeman? Are you trying to send this Chinaman to prison?'

'That's about it,' Bond smiled down at her. 'At least you're on the side of the angels. And now you tell me something. How much farther to the camp?'

'Oh, about an hour.'

'Is it a good place to hide? Could they find us there easily?'

'They'd have to come across the lake or up the river. It'll be all right so long as they don't send their dragon after us. He can go through the water. I've seen him do it.'

'Oh well,' said Bond diplomatically, 'let's hope he's got a sore tail or something.'

The girl snorted. 'All right, Mr Know-all,' she said angrily. 'Just you wait.'

Quarrel splashed out of the mangroves. He was carrying a rifle. he said apologetically. 'No harm 'n havin' anudder gun, cap'n. Looks like us may need hit.'

Bond took it. It was a U.S. Army Remington Carbine, .300. These people certainly had the right equipment. He handed it back.

Quarrel echoed his thoughts. 'Dese is sly folks, cap'n. Dat man mus' of come sneakin' down soffly behind de udders to ketch us comin' out after de dawgs had passed. He sho is a sly mongoose, dat Doctor feller.'

Bond said thoughtfully, 'He must be quite a man.' He shrugged away his thoughts. 'Now let's get going. Honey says there's another hour to the camp. Better keep to the left bank so as to get what cover we can from the hill. For all we know they've got glasses trained on the river.' Bond handed his gun to Quarrel who stowed it in the sodden knapsack. They moved off again with Quarrel in the lead and Bond and the girl walking together.

They got some shade from the bamboo and bushes

along the western bank, but now they had to face the full force of the scorching wind. They splashed water over their arms and faces to cool the burn. Bond's eyes were bloodshot with the glare and his arm ached intolerably where the gun butt had struck. And he was not looking forward to his dinner of soaking bread and cheese and salt pork. How long would they be able to sleep? He hadn't had much last night. It looked like the same ration again. And what about the girl? She had had none. He and Quarrel would have to keep watch and watch. And then tomorrow. Off into the mangrove again and work their way slowly back to the canoe across the eastern end of the island. It looked like that. And sail the following night. Bond thought of hacking a way for five miles through solid mangroves. What a prospect! Bond trudged on, thinking of M's 'holiday in the sunshine'. He'd certainly give something for M to be sharing it with him now.

The river grew narrower until it was only a stream between the bamboo clumps. Then it widened out into a flat marshy estuary beyond which five square miles of shallow lake swept away to the other side of the island in a ruffled blue-grey mirror. Beyond, there was the shimmer of the airstrip and the glint of the sun on a single hangar. The girl told them to keep to the east and they worked their way slowly along inside the fringe of bushes.

Suddenly Quarrel stopped, his face pointing like a gun-dog's at the marshy ground in front of him. Two deep parallel grooves were cut into the mud, with a fainter groove in the centre. They were the tracks of something that had come down from the hill and gone across the marsh towards the lake.

The girl said indifferently, 'That's where the dragon's been.'

Quarrel turned the whites of his eyes towards her.

Bond walked slowly along the tracks. The outside ones were quite smooth with an indented curve. They could have been made by wheels, but they were vast—at least two feet across. The centre track was of the same shape but only three inches across, about the width of a motor tyre. The tracks were without a trace of tread, and they were fairly fresh. They marched along in a dead straight line and the bushes they crossed were squashed flat as if a tank had gone over them.

Bond couldn't imagine what kind of vehicle, if it was a vehicle, had made them. When the girl nudged him and whispered fiercely 'I told you so,' he could only say thoughtfully, 'Well, Honey, if it isn't a dragon, it's something else I've never seen before.'

Farther on, she tugged urgently at his sleeve. 'Look,' she whispered. She pointed forward to a big clump of bushes beside which the tracks ran. They were leafless and blackened. In the centre there showed the charred remains of birds' nests. 'He breathed on them,' she said excitedly.

Bond walked up to the bushes and examined them. 'He certainly did,' he admitted. Why had this particular clump been burned? It was all very odd.

The tracks swerved out towards the lake and disappeared into the water. Bond would have liked to follow them but there was no question of leaving cover. They trudged on, wrapped in their different thoughts.

Slowly the day began to die behind the sugar-loaf, and at last the girl pointed ahead through the bushes and Bond could see a long spit of sand running out into the lake. There were thick bushes of sea-grape along its spine and, halfway, perhaps a hundred yards from the shore, the remains of a thatched hut. It looked a reasonably attractive place to spend the night and it was well protected by the water on both sides. The wind had died and the water was soft and inviting. How heavenly it was going to be to take off their filthy shirts and wash in the lake, and, after the hours of squelching through the mud and stench of the river and the marsh, be able to lie down on the hard dry sand!

The sun blazed yellowly and sank behind the mountain. The day was still alive at the eastern tip of the island, but the black shadow of the sugar-loaf was slowly marching across the lake and would soon reach out and kill that too. The frogs started up, louder than in Jamaica, until the thick dusk was shrill with them. Across the lake a giant bull frog began to drum. The eerie sound was something between a tom-tom and an ape's roar. It sent out short messages that were suddenly throttled. Soon it fell silent. It had found what it had sent for.

They reached the neck of the sandspit and filed out along a narrow track. They came to the clearing with the smashed remains of the wattle hut. The big mysterious tracks led out of the water on both sides and through the clearing and over the near-by bushes as if the thing, whatever it was, had stampeded the place. Many of the bushes were burned or charred. There were the remains of a fireplace made of lumps of coral and a few scattered cooking pots and empty tins. They searched in the debris and Quarrel unearthed a couple of unopened tins of Heinz pork and beans. The girl found a crumpled sleeping-bag. Bond found a small leather purse containing five one-dollar notes, three Jamaica pounds and some silver. The two men had certainly left in a hurry.

They left the place and moved farther along to a small sandy clearing. Through the bushes they could see lights winking across the water from the mountain, perhaps two miles away. To the eastwards there was nothing but the soft black sheen of water under the darkening sky.

Bond said, 'As long as we don't show a light we should be fine here. The first thing is to have a good wash. Honey, you take the rest of the sandspit and we'll have the landward end. See you for dinner in about half an hour.'

The girl laughed. 'Will you be dressing?'

'Certainly,' said Bond. 'Trousers.'

Quarrel said, 'Cap'n, while dere's henough light I'll get dese tins open and get tings fixed for de night.' He rummaged in the knapsack. 'Here's yo trousers and yo gun. De bread don't feel so good but hit only wet. Hit eat okay an' mebbe hit dry hout come de mornin'.

Guess we'd better eat de tins tonight an' keep de cheese an' pork. Dose tins is heavy an' we got plenty footin' tomorrow.'

Bond said, 'All right, Quarrel. I'll leave the menu to you.' He took the gun and the damp trousers and walked down into the shallow water and back the way they had come. He found a hard dry stretch of sand and took off his shirt and stepped back into the water and lay down. The water was soft but disgustingly warm. He dug up handfuls of sand and scrubbed himself with it, using it as soap. Then he lay and luxuriated in the silence and the loneliness.

The stars began to shine palely, the stars that had brought them to the island last night, a year ago, the stars that would take them away again tomorrow night, a year away. What a trip! But at least it had already paid off. Now he had enough evidence, and witnesses, to go back to the Governor and get a full-dress inquiry going into the activities of Doctor No. One didn't use machine guns on people, even on trespassers. And, by the same token, what was this thing of Doctor No's that had trespassed on the leasehold of the Audubon Society, the thing that had smashed their property and had possibly killed one of their wardens? That would have to be investigated too. And what would he find when he came back to the island through the front door, in a destroyer, perhaps, and with a detachment of marines? What would be the answer to the riddle of Doctor No? What was he hiding? What did he fear? Why was privacy so important to him that he would murder, again and again, for it? Who *was* Doctor No?

Bond heard splashing away to his right. He thought of the girl. And who, for the matter of that, was Honeychile Rider? That, he decided, as he climbed out on to dry land, was at least something that he ought to be able to find out before the night was over.

Bond pulled on his clammy trousers and sat down on the sand and dismantled his gun. He did it by touch, using his shirt to dry each part and each cartridge. Then he reassembled the gun and clicked the trigger round the empty cylinder. The sound was healthy. It would be days before it rusted. He loaded it and tucked it into the holster inside the waistband of his trousers and got up and walked back to the clearing.

The shadow of Honey reached up and pulled him down beside her. 'Come on,' she said, 'we're starving. I got one of the cooking pots and cleaned it out and we poured the beans into it. There's about two full handfuls each and a cricket ball of bread. And I'm not feeling guilty about eating your food because you made me work far harder than I would if I'd been alone. Here, hold out your hand.'

Bond smiled at the authority in her voice. He could just make out her silhouette in the dusk. Her head looked sleeker. He wondered what her hair looked like when it was combed and dry. What would she be like when she was wearing clean clothes over that beautiful golden body? He could see her coming into a room or across the lawn at Beau Desert. She would be a beautiful, ravishing, Ugly Duckling. Why had she never had the broken nose mended? It was an easy operation. Then she would be the most beautiful girl in Jamaica.

Her shoulder brushed against him. Bond reached out and put his hand down in her lap, open. She picked up his hand and Bond felt the cold mess of beans being poured into it.

Suddenly he smelled her warm animal smell. It was so sensually thrilling that his body swayed against her and for a moment his eyes closed.

She gave a short laugh in which there was shyness and satisfaction and tenderness. She said 'There,' maternally, and carried his laden hand away from her and back to him.

CHAPTER 11

Amidst the Alien Cane

It would be around eight o'clock, Bond thought. Apart from the background tinkle of the frogs it was very quiet. In the far corner of the clearing he could see the dark outline of Quarrel. There was the soft clink of metal as he dismantled and dried the Remington.

Through the bushes the distant yellow lights from the guanera made festive pathways across the dark surface of the lake. The ugly wind had gone and the hideous scenery lay drowned in darkness. It was cool. Bond's clothes had dried on him. The three big handfuls of food had warmed his stomach. He felt comfortable and drowsy and at peace. Tomorrow was a long way off and presented no problems except a great deal of physical exercise. Life suddenly felt easy and good.

The girl lay beside him in the sleeping-bag. She was lying on her back with her head cradled in her hands, looking up at the roof of stars. He could just make out the pale pool of her face. She said, 'James. You promised to tell me what this is all about. Come on. I shan't go to sleep until you do.'

Bond laughed. 'I'll tell if you'll tell. I want to know what you're all about.'

'I don't mind. I've got no secrets. But you first.'

'All right then.' Bond pulled his knees up to his chin and put his arms round them. 'It's like this. I'm a sort of policeman. They send me out from London when there's something odd going on somewhere in the world that isn't anybody else's business. Well, not long ago one of the Governor's staff in Kingston, a man called Strangways, friend of mine, disappeared. His secretary, who was a pretty girl, did too. Most people thought they'd run away together. I didn't. I . . .'

Bond told the story in simple terms, with good men and bad men, like an adventure story out of a book. He ended, 'So you see, Honey, it's just a question of getting back to Jamaica tomorrow night, all three of us in the canoe, and then the Governor will listen to us and send over a lot of soldiers to get this Chinaman to own up. I expect that'll mean he'll go to prison. He'll know that too and that's why he's trying to stop us. That's all. Now it's your turn.'

The girl said, 'You seem to live a very exciting life. Your wife can't like you being away so much. Doesn't she worry about you getting hurt?'

'I'm not married. The only people who worry about me getting hurt are my insurance company.'

She probed, 'But I suppose you have girls.'

'Not permanent ones.'

'Oh.'

There was a pause. Quarrel came over to them. 'Cap'n, Ah'll take de fust watch if dat suits. Be out on de point of de sandspit. Ah'll come call you around midnight. Den mebbe yo take on till five and den we all git goin'. Need to get well away from dis place afore it's light.'

'Suits me,' said Bond. 'Wake me if you see anything. Gun all right?'

'Him's jess fine,' said Quarrel happily. He said, 'Sleep well, missy,' with a hint of meaning, and melted noiselessly away into the shadows.

'I like Quarrel,' said the girl. She paused, then, 'Do you really want to know about me? It's not as exciting as your story.'

'Of course I do. And don't leave anything out.'

'There's nothing to leave out. You could get my whole life on to the back of a postcard. To begin with I've never been out of Jamaica. I've lived all my life at a place called Beau Desert on the North Coast near Morgan's Harbour.'

Bond laughed. 'That's odd. So do I. At least for the moment. I didn't notice you about. Do you live up a tree?'

'Oh, I suppose you've taken the beach house. I never go near the place. I live in the Great House.'

'But there's nothing left of it. It's a ruin in the middle of the cane fields.'

'I live in the cellars. I've lived there since I was five. It was burned down then and my parents were killed. I can't remember anything about them so you needn't say you're sorry. At first I lived there with my black nanny. She died when I was fifteen. For the last five years I've lived there alone.'

'Good heavens.' Bond was appalled. 'But wasn't there anyone else to look after you? Didn't your parents leave any money?'

'Not a penny.' There was no bitterness in the girl's voice—pride if anything. 'You see the Riders were one of the old Jamaican families. The first one had been given the Beau Desert lands by Cromwell for having been one of the people who signed King Charles's death warrant. He built the Great House and my family lived in it on and off ever since. But then sugar collapsed and I suppose the place was badly run, and by the time my father inherited it there was nothing but debts—mortgages and things like that. So when my father and mother died the property was sold up. I didn't mind. I was too young. Nanny must have been wonderful. They wanted people to adopt me, the clergyman and the legal people did, but Nanny collected the sticks of furniture that hadn't been burned and we settled down in the ruins and after a bit no one came and interfered with us. She did a bit of sewing and laundry in the village and grew a few plantains and bananas and things and there was a big breadfruit tree up against the old house. We ate what the Jamaicans eat. And there was the sugar cane all round us and she made a fishpot which we used to go and take up every day. It was all right. We had enough to eat. Somehow she taught me to read and write. There was a pile of old books left from the fire. There was an encyclopedia. I started with A when I was about eight. I've got as far as the middle of T.' She said defensively, 'I bet I know more than you do about a lot of things.'

'I bet you do.' Bond was lost in the picture of the little flaxen-haired girl pattering about the ruins with the obstinate old negress watching over her and calling her in to do the lessons that must have been just as much a riddle to the old woman. 'Your nanny must have been a wonderful person.'

'She was a darling.' It was a flat statement. 'I thought I'd die when she did. It wasn't such fun after that. Before, I'd led a child's life; then I suddenly had to grow up and do everything for myself. And men tried to catch me and hurt me. They said they wanted to make love to me.' She paused. 'I used to be pretty then.'

Bond said seriously, 'You're one of the most beautiful girls I've ever seen.'

'With this nose? Don't be silly.'

'You don't understand.' Bond tried to find words that she would believe. 'Of course anyone can see your nose is broken. But since this morning I've hardly noticed it. When you look at a person you look into their eyes or at their mouth. That's where the expressions are. A broken nose isn't any more significant than a crooked ear. Noses and ears are bits of face-furniture. Some are prettier than others, but they're not nearly as important as the rest. They're part of the background of the face. If you had a beautiful nose as well as the rest of you you'd be the most beautiful girl in Jamaica.'

'Do you mean that?' her voice was urgent. 'Do you think I could be beautiful? I know some of me's all right, but when I look in the glass I hardly see anything except my broken nose. I'm sure it's like that with other people who are, who are—well—sort of deformed.'

Bond said impatiently, 'You're not deformed! Don't talk such nonsense. And anyway you can have it put right by a simple operation. You've only got to get over to America and it would be done in a week.'

She said angrily, 'How do you expect me to do that? I've got about fifteen pounds under a stone in my cellar. I've got three skirts and three shirts and a knife and a fishpot. I know all about these operations. The doctor at Port Maria found out for me. He's a nice man. He wrote to America. Do you know, to have it properly done it would cost me about five hundred pounds, what with the fare to New York and the hospital and everything?' Her voice became hopeless. 'How do you expect me to find that amount of money?'

Bond had already made up his mind what would have to be done about that. Now he merely said tenderly, 'Well, I expect there are ways. But anyway, go on with your story. It's very exciting—far more interesting than mine. You'd got to where your nanny died. What happened then?'

The girl began again reluctantly.

'Well, it's your fault for interrupting. And you mustn't talk about things you don't understand. I suppose people tell you you're good-looking. I expect you get all the girls you want. Well you wouldn't if you had a squint or a hare-lip or something. As a matter of fact,' he could hear the smile in her voice, 'I think I shall go to the obeahman when we get back and get him to put a spell on you and give you something like that.' She added lamely, 'Then we should be more alike.'

Bond reached out. His hand brushed against her. 'I've got other plans,' he said. 'But come on. I want to hear the rest of the story.'

'Oh well,' the girl sighed, 'I'll have to go back a bit. You see all the property is in cane and the old house stands in the middle of it. Well, about twice a year they cut the cane and send it off to the mill. And when they do that all the animals and insects and so on that live in the cane fields go into a panic and most of them have their houses destroyed and get killed. At cutting time some of them took to coming to the ruins of the house and hiding. My nanny was terrified of them to begin with, the mongooses and the snakes and the scorpions and so on, but I made a couple of the cellar rooms into sort of homes for them. I wasn't frightened of them and they never hurt me. They seemed to understand that I was looking after them. They must have told their friends or something because after a bit it was quite natural for them all to come trooping into their rooms and set-tling down there until the young cane had started to grow again. Then they all filed out and went back to living in the fields. I gave them what food we could spare when they were staying with us and they behaved very well except for making a bit of a smell and sometimes fighting amongst each other. But they all got quite tame with me, and their children did, too, and I could do anything with them. Of course the cane-cutters found out about this and saw me walking about with snakes round my neck and so forth, and they got frightened of me and thought I was obeah. So they left us absolutely alone.' She paused. 'That's where I found out so much about animals and insects. I used to spend a lot of time in the sea finding out about those people too. It was the same with birds. If you find out what all these people like to eat and what they're afraid of, and if you spend all your time with them you can make friends.' She looked up at him. 'You miss a lot not knowing about these things.'

'I'm afraid I do,' said Bond truthfully. 'I expect they're much nicer and more interesting than humans.'

'I don't know about that,' said the girl thoughtfully. 'I don't know many human people. Most of the ones I have met have been hateful. But I suppose they can be interesting too.' She paused. 'I hadn't ever really thought of liking them like I like the animals. Except for

Nanny, of course. Until . . .' She broke off with a shy laugh. 'Well, anyway we all lived happily together until I was fifteen and Nanny died and then things got difficult. There was a man called Mander. A horrible man. He was the white overseer for the people who own the property. He kept coming to see me. He wanted me to move up to his house near Port Maria. I hated him and I used to hide when I heard his horse coming through the cane. One night he came on foot and I didn't hear him. He was drunk. He came into the cellar and fought with me because I wouldn't do what he wanted me to do. You know, the things people in love do.'

'Yes, I know.'

'I tried to kill him with my knife, but he was very strong and he hit me as hard as he could in the face and broke my nose. He knocked me unconscious and then I think he did things to me. I mean I know he did. Next day I wanted to kill myself when I saw my face and when I found what he had done. I thought I would have a baby. I would certainly have killed myself if I'd had a baby by that man. Anyway I didn't, so that was that. I went to the doctor and he did what he could for my nose and didn't charge me anything. I didn't tell him about the rest. I was too ashamed. The man didn't come back. I waited and did nothing until the next cane-cutting. I'd got my plan. I was waiting for the Black Widow spiders to come in for shelter. One day they came. I caught the biggest of the females and shut her in a box with nothing to eat. They're the bad ones, the females. Then I waited for a dark night without any moon. I took the box with the spider in it and walked and walked until I came to the man's house. It was very dark and I was frightened of the duppies I might meet on the road but I didn't see any. I waited in his garden in the bushes and watched him go up to bed. Then I climbed a tree and got on to his balcony. I waited there until I heard him snoring and then I crept through the window. He was lying naked on the bed under the mosquito net. I lifted the edge and opened the box and shook the spider out on to his stomach. Then I went away and came home.'

'God Almighty!' said Bond reverently. 'What happened to him?'

She said happily, 'He took a week to die. It must have hurt terribly. They do, you know. The obeahmen say there's nothing like it.' She paused. When Bond made no comment, she said anxiously, 'You don't think I did wrong, do you?'

'It's not a thing to make a habit of,' said Bond mildly. 'But I can't say I blame you the way it was. So what happened then?'

'Well then I just settled down again,' her voice was matter-of-fact. 'I had to concentrate on getting enough food, and of course all I wanted to do was save up money to get my nose made good again.' She said persuasively, 'It really was quite a pretty nose before. Do you think the doctors can put it back to how it was?'

'They can make it any shape you like,' said Bond definitely. 'What did you make money at?'

'It was the encyclopedia. It told me that people collect seashells. That one could sell the rare ones. I talked to the local schoolmaster, without telling him my secret of course, and he found out that there's an American magazine called *Nautilus* for shell collectors. I had just enough money to subscribe to it and I began looking for the shells that people said they wanted in the advertisements. I wrote to a dealer in Miami and he started buying from me. It was thrilling. Of course I made some awful mistakes to begin with. I thought people would like the prettiest shells, but they don't. Very often they want the ugliest. And then when I found rare ones I cleaned them and polished them to make them look better. That's wrong too. They want shells just as they come out of the sea, with the animal in and all. So I got some formalin from the doctor and put it into the live shells to stop them smelling and sent them off to this man in Miami. I only got it right about a year ago and I've already made fifteen pounds. I'd worked out that now I knew how they wanted them, and if I was lucky, I ought to make at least fifty pounds a year. Then in ten years I would be able to go to America and have the operation. And then,' she giggled delightedly, 'I had a terrific stroke of luck. I went over to Crab Key. I'd been there before, but this was just before Christmas, and I found these purple shells. They didn't look very exciting, but I sent one or two to Miami and the man wrote back at once and said he could take as many as I could get at five dollars each for the whole ones. He said that I must keep the place where they live a dead secret as otherwise we'd what he called "spoil the market" and the price would get cheaper. It's just like having one's private gold mine. Now I may be able to save up the money in five years. That's why I was so suspicious of you when I found you on my beach. I thought you'd come to steal my shells.'

'You gave me a bit of a shock. I thought you must be Doctor No's girl friend.'

'Thanks very much.'

'But when you've had the operation, what are you going to do then? You can't go on living alone in a cellar all your life.'

'I thought I'd be a call girl.' She said it as she might have said 'nurse' or 'secretary'.

'Oh, what do you mean by that?' Perhaps she had picked up the expression without understanding it.

'One of those girls who has a beautiful flat and lovely clothes. You know what I mean,' she said impatiently. 'People ring them up and come and make love to them and pay them for it. They get a hundred dollars for each time in New York. That's where I thought I'd start. Of course,' she admitted, 'I might have to do it for less to begin with. Until I learned to do it really well. How much do you pay the untrained ones?'

Bond laughed. 'I really can't remember. It's quite a long time since I had one.'

She sighed. 'Yes, I suppose you can have as many women as you want for nothing. I suppose it's only the ugly men that pay. But that can't be helped. Any kind of job in the big towns must be dreadful. At least you can earn much more being a call girl. Then I can come back to Jamaica and buy Beau Desert. I'd be rich enough to find a nice husband and have some children. Now that I've found these Venus shells I've worked out that I might be back in Jamaica by the time I'm thirty. Won't that be lovely?'

'I like the last part of the plan. But I'm not so sure of the first. Anyway, where did you find out about these call girls? Were they under C in the encyclopedia?'

'Of course not. Don't be silly. There was a big case about them in New York about two years ago. There was a rich playboy called Jelke. He had a whole string of girls. There was a lot about the case in the *Gleaner*. They gave all the prices and everything. And anyway, there are thousands of those sort of girls in Kingston, only of course not such good ones. They only get about five shillings and they have nowhere to go and do it except the bush. My nanny told me about them. She said I mustn't grow up like them or I'd be very unhappy. I can see that for only five shillings. But for a hundred dollars . . . !'

Bond said, 'You wouldn't be able to keep all of that. You'd have to have a sort of manager to get the men, and then you'd have to bribe the police to leave you alone. And you could easily go to prison if something went wrong. I really don't think you'd like the work. I'll tell you what, with all you know about animals and insects and so on you could get a wonderful job looking after them in one of the American zoos. Or what about the Jamaica Institute? I'm sure you'd like that better. You'd be just as likely to meet a nice husband. Anyway you mustn't think of being a call girl any more. You've got a beautiful body. You must keep it for the men you love.'

'That's what people say in books,' she said doubtfully. 'The trouble is there aren't any men to love at Beau Desert.' She said, 'You're the first Englishman I've ever talked to. I liked you from the beginning. I don't mind telling you these things at all. I suppose there are plenty of other people I should like if I could get away.'

'Of course there are. Hundreds. And you're a wonderful girl. I thought so directly I saw you.'

'Saw my behind, you mean.' The voice was getting
drowsy, but it was full of pleasure.

Bond laughed. 'Well, it was a wonderful behind. And
the other side was wonderful too.' Bond's body began
to stir with the memory of how she had been. He said
gruffly, 'Now come on, Honey. It's time to go to sleep.
There'll be plenty of time to talk when we get back to
Jamaica.'

'Will there?' she said sleepily. 'Promise?'

'Promise.'

He heard her stir in the sleeping-bag. He looked
down. He could just make out the pale profile turned
towards him. She gave the deep sigh of a child before it
falls asleep.

There was silence in the clearing. It was getting cold.
Bond put his head down on his hunched knees. He knew
it was no good trying to get to sleep. His mind was full
of the day and of this extraordinary Girl Tarzan who
had come into his life. It was as if some beautiful animal
had attached itself to him. There would be no dropping
the leash until he had solved her problems for her. He
knew it. Of course there would be no difficulty about
most of them. He could fix the operation—even, with
the help of friends, find a proper job and a home for
her. He had the money. He would buy her dresses, have
her hair done, get her started in the big world. It would
be fun. But what about the other side? What about the
physical desire he felt for her? One could not make love
to a child. But was she a child? There was nothing
childish about her body or her personality. She was fully
grown and highly intelligent in her fashion, and far
more capable of taking care of herself than any girl of
twenty Bond had ever met.

Bond's thoughts were interrupted by a tug at his
sleeve. The small voice said, 'Why don't you go to
sleep? Are you cold?'

'No, I'm fine.'

'It's nice and warm in the sleeping-bag. Would you
like to come in? There's plenty of room.'

'No thank you, Honey. I'll be all right.'

There was a pause, then, almost in a whisper, 'If you're thinking . . . I mean—you don't have to make love to me . . . We could go to sleep back to front, you know, like spoons.'

'Honey, darling, you go to sleep. It'd be lovely to be like that, but not tonight. Anyway I'll have to take over from Quarrel soon.'

'Yes, I see.' The voice was grudging. 'Perhaps when we get back to Jamaica.'

'Perhaps.'

'Promise. I won't go to sleep until you promise.'

Bond said desperately, 'Of course I promise. Now go to sleep, Honeychile.'

The voice whispered triumphantly, 'Now you owe me slave-time. You've promised. Good night, darling James.'

'Good night, darling Honey.'

CHAPTER 12

The Thing

The grip on Bond's shoulder was urgent. He was instantly on his feet.

Quarrel whispered fiercely, 'Somepn comin' across de water, cap'n! It de dragon fo sho!'

The girl woke up. She said anxiously, 'What's happened?'

Bond said, 'Stay there, Honey! Don't move. I'll be back.' He broke through the bushes on the side away from the mountain and ran along the sand with Quarrel at his elbow.

They came to the tip of the sandspit, twenty yards from the clearing. They stopped under cover of the final bushes. Bond parted them and looked through.

What was it? Half a mile away, coming across the lake, was a shapeless thing with two glaring orange eyes with black pupils. From between these, where the mouth might be, fluttered a yard of blue flame. The grey luminescence of the stars showed some kind of a domed head above two short batlike wings. The thing was making a low moaning roar that overlaid another noise, a deep rhythmic thud. It was coming towards them at about ten miles an hour, throwing up a creamy wake.

Quarrel whispered, 'Gawd, cap'n! What's dat fearful ting?'

Bond stood up. He said shortly, 'Don't know exactly. Some sort of a tractor affair dressed up to frighten. It's running on a diesel engine, so you can forget about dragons. Now let's see,' Bond spoke half to himself. 'No good running away. The thing's too fast for us and we know it can go over mangroves and swamp. Have to fight it here. What'll its weak spots be? The drivers. Of course they'll have protection. We don't know how much. Quarrel, you start firing at that dome on top when it gets to two hundred yards. Aim carefully and keep on firing. I'll go for its headlights when it gets to fifty yards. It's not running on tracks. Must have some kind of giant tyres, aeroplane tyres probably. I'll go for them too. Stay here. I'll go ten yards along. They may start firing back and we've got to keep the bullets away from the girl. Okay?' Bond reached out and squeezed the big shoulder. 'And don't worry too much. Forget about dragons. It's just some gadget of Doctor No's. We'll kill the drivers and capture the damn thing and ride it down to the coast. Save us shoe-leather. Right?'

Quarrel laughed shortly. 'Okay, cap'n. Since yo says so. But Ah sho hopes de Almighty knows he's no dragon too!'

Bond ran down the sand. He broke through the bushes until he had a clear field of fire. He called softly, 'Honey!'

'Yes, James.' There was relief in the near-by voice.

'Make a hole in the sand like we did on the beach. Behind the thickest roots. Get into it and lie down. There may be some shooting. Don't worry about dragons. This is just a painted up motor car with some of Doctor No's men in it. Don't be frightened. I'm quite close.'

'All right, James. Be careful.' The voice was high with fright.

Bond knelt on one knee in the leaves and sand and peered out.

Now the thing was only about three hundred yards away and its yellow headlights were lighting up the sandpit. Blue flames were still fluttering from the mouth. They were coming from a long snout mocked-up with gaping jaws and gold paint to look like a dragon's mouth. Flame-thrower! That would explain the burned bushes and the warden's story. The blue flames would be coming from some kind of an after-burner. The apparatus was now in neutral. What would its range be when the compression was unleashed?

Bond had to admit that the thing was an awesome sight as it moaned forward through the shallow lake. It was obviously designed to terrify. It would have frightened him but for the earthly thud of the diesel. Against native intruders it would be devastating. But how vulnerable would it be to people with guns who didn't panic?

He was answered at once. There came the crack of Quarrel's Remington. A spark flew off the domed cabin and there was a dull clang. Quarrel fired another single shot and then a burst. The bullets hammered ineffect-ually against the cabin. There was not even a check in speed. The thing rolled on, swerving slightly to make for the source of the gunfire. Bond cradled the Smith & Wesson on his forearm and took careful aim. The deep cough of his gun sounded above the rattle of the Remington. One of the headlamps shattered and went out. He fired four shots at the other and got it with the fifth and last round in the cylinder. The thing didn't care. It rolled straight on towards Quarrel's hiding place. Bond reloaded and began firing at the huge bulge of the tyres under the bogus black and gold wings. The range was now only thirty yards and he could have sworn that he hit the nearest wheel again and again. No effect. Solid rubber? The first breath of fear stirred Bond's skin.

He reloaded. Was the damn thing vulnerable from the rear? Should he dash out into the lake and try and board it? He took a step forward through the bushes. Then he froze, incapable of movement.

Suddenly, from the dribbling snout, a yellow-tipped bolt of blue flame had howled out towards Quarrel's hiding place. There was a single puff of orange and red flame from the bushes to Bond's right and one unearthly scream, immediately choked. Satisfied, the searing tongue of fire licked back into the snout. The thing turned on its axis and stopped dead. Now the blue hole of its mouth aimed straight at Bond.

Bond stood and waited for his unspeakable end. He looked into the blue jaws of death and saw the glowing red filament of the firer deep inside the big tube. He thought of Quarrel's body—there was no time to think of Quarrel—and imagined the blackened, smoking figure lying in the melted sand. Soon he, too, would flame like a torch. The single scream would be wrung from him and his limbs would jerk into the dancing pose of burned bodies. Then it would be Honey's turn. Christ, what had he led them into! Why had he been so insane as to take on this man with his devastating armoury. Why hadn't he been warned by the long finger that had pointed at him in Jamaica? Bond set his teeth. Hurry up, you bastards. Get it over.

There came the twang of a loud-hailer. A voice howled metallically, 'Come on out, Limey. And the doll. Quick, or you'll fry in hell like your pal.' To rub in the command, the bolt of flame spat briefly towards him. Bond stepped back from the searing heat. He felt the girl's body against his back. She said hysterically, 'I had to come. I had to come.'

Bond said, 'It's all right, Honey. Keep behind me.'

He had made up his mind. There was no alternative. Even if death was to come later it couldn't be worse than this kind of death. Bond reached for the girl's hand and drew her after him out on to the sand.

The voice howled. 'Stop there. Good boy. And drop the peashooter. No tricks or the crabs'll be getting a cooked breakfast.'

Bond dropped his gun. So much for the Smith &

Wesson. The Beretta would have been just as good against this thing. The girl whimpered. Bond squeezed her hand. 'Stick it, Honey,' he said. 'We'll get out of this somehow'. Bond sneered at himself for the lie.

There was the clang of an iron door being opened. From the back of the dome a man dropped into the water and walked towards them. There was a gun in his hand. He kept out of the line of fire of the flame-thrower. The fluttering blue flame lit up his sweating face. He was a Chinese negro, a big man, clad only in trousers. Something dangled from his left hand. When he came closer, Bond saw it was handcuffs.

The man stopped a few yards away. He said, 'Hold out your hands. Wrists together. Then walk towards me. You first, Limey. Slowly or you get an extra navel.'

Bond did as he was told. When he was within sweat-smell of the man, the man put his gun between his teeth and reached out and snapped the handcuffs on Bond's wrists. Bond looked into the face, gunmetal-coloured from the blue flames. It was a brutal, squinting face. It sneered at him. 'Dumb bastard,' said the man.

Bond turned his back on the man and started walking away. He was going to see Quarrel's body. He had to say goodbye to it. There was the roar of a gun. A bullet kicked up sand close to his feet. Bond stopped and turned slowly round. 'Don't be nervous,' he said. 'I'm going to take a look at the man you've just murdered. I'll be back.'

The man lowered his gun. He laughed harshly. 'Okay. Enjoy yourself. Sorry we ain't got a wreath. Come back quick or we give the doll a toastin'. Two minutes.'

Bond walked on towards the smoking clump of bushes. He got there and looked down. His eyes and mouth winced. Yes, it had been just as he had visualized. Worse. He said softly, 'I'm sorry Quarrel.' He kicked into the ground and scooped up a handful of cool sand between his manacled hands and poured it over the remains of the eyes. Then he walked slowly back and stood beside the girl.

The man waved them forward with his gun. They walked round the back of the machine. There was a small square door. A voice from inside said, 'Get in and sit on the floor. Don't touch anything or you get your fingers broke.'

They scrambled into the iron box. It stank of sweat and oil. There was just room for them to sit with their knees hunched up. The man with the gun followed them in and banged the door. He switched on a light and sat down on an iron tractor seat beside the driver. He said, 'Okay, Sam. Let's get goin'. You can put out the fire. It's light enough to steer by.'

There was a row of dials and switches on the instrument panel. The driver reached forward and pulled down a couple of the switches. He put the machine into gear and peered out through a narrow slit in the iron wall in front of him. Bond felt the machine turn. There came a faster beat from the engine and they moved off.

The girl's shoulder pressed against his. 'Where are they taking us?' The whisper trembled.

Bond turned his head and looked at her. It was the first time he had been able to see her hair when it was dry. Now it was disarrayed by sleep, but it was no longer a bunch of rats' tails. It hung heavily straight down to her shoulders, where it curled softly inwards. It was of the palest ash blonde and shone almost silver under the electric light. She looked up at him. The skin round her eyes and at the corners of her mouth was white with fear.

Bond shrugged with an indifference he didn't feel. He whispered, 'Oh, I expect we're going to see Doctor No. Don't worry too much, Honey. These men are just little gangsters. It'll be different with him. When we get to him don't you say anything, I'll talk for both of us.' He pressed her shoulder. 'I like the way you do your hair. I'm glad you don't cut it too short.'

Some of the tension went out of her face. 'How can you think of things like that?' She half smiled at him. 'But I'm glad you like it. I wash it in coconut oil once a week.' At the memory of her other life her eyes grew bright with tears. She bent her head down to her manacled hands to hide her tears. She whispered almost to herself, 'I'll try to be brave. It'll be all right as long as you're there.'

Bond shifted so that he was right up against her. He brought his handcuffed hands close up to his eyes and examined them. They were the American police model. He contracted his left hand, the thinner of the two, and tried to pull it through the squat ring of steel. Even the sweat on his skin was no help. It was hopeless.

The two men sat on their iron seats with their backs to them, indifferent. They knew they had total command. There wasn't room for Bond to give any trouble. Bond couldn't stand up or get enough momentum into his hands to do any damage to the backs of their heads with his handcuffs. If Bond somehow managed to open the hatch and drop into the water, where would that get him? They would at once feel the fresh air on their backs and stop the machine, and either burn him in the water or pick him up. It annoyed Bond that they didn't worry about him, that they knew he was utterly in their power. He also didn't like the idea that these men were intelligent enough to know that he presented no threat. Stupider men would have sat over him with a gun out, would have trussed him and the girl with inexpert thoroughness, might even have knocked them unconscious. These two knew their business. They were professionals, or had been trained to be professionals.

The two men didn't talk to each other. There was no nervous chatter about how clever they had been, about their destination, about how tired they were. They just drove the machine quietly, efficiently along, finishing their competent job.

Bond still had no idea what this contraption was. Under the black and gold paint and the rest of the fancy dress it was some sort of a tractor, but of a kind he had never seen or heard of. The wheels, with their vast smooth rubber tyres, were nearly twice as tall as himself. He had seen no trade name on the tyres, it had been too dark, but they were certainly either solid or filled

with porous rubber. At the rear there had been a small
trailing wheel for stability. An iron fin, painted black
and gold, had been added to help the dragon effect. The
high mudguards had been extended into short
backswept wings. A long metal dragon's head had been
added to the front of the radiator and the headlamps
had been given black centres to make 'eyes'. That was
all there was to it, except that the cabin had been
covered with an armoured dome and the flame-thrower
added. It was, as Bond had thought, a tractor dressed
up to frighten and burn—though why it had a flame-
thrower instead of a machine gun he couldn't imagine.
It was clearly the only sort of vehicle that could travel
the island. Its huge wide wheels would ride over
mangrove and swamp and across the shallow lake. It
would negotiate the rough coral uplands and, since its
threat would be at night, the heat in the iron cabin
would remain at least tolerable.

Bond was impressed. He was always impressed by
professionalism. Doctor No was obviously a man who
took immense pains. Soon Bond would be meeting him.
Soon he would be up against the secret of Doctor No.
And then what? Bond smiled grimly to himself. He
wouldn't be allowed to get away with his knowledge. He
would certainly be killed unless he could escape or talk
his way out. And what about the girl? Could Bond
prove her innocence and have her spared? Conceivably,
but she would never be let off the island. She would
have to stay there for the rest of her life, as the mistress
or wife of one of the men, or Doctor No himself if she
appealed to him.

Bond's thoughts were interrupted by rougher going
under the wheels. They had crossed the lake and were on
the track that led up the mountain to the huts. The cabin
tilted and the machine began to climb. In five minutes
they would be there.

The co-driver glanced over his shoulder at Bond and
the girl. Bond smiled cheerfully up at him. He said,
'You'll get a medal for this.'

The brown and yellow eyes looked impassively into

his. The purple, blubbery lips parted in a sneer in which there was slow hate: 'Shut your —ing mouth.' The man turned back.

The girl nudged him and whispered, 'Why are they so rude? Why do they hate us so much?'

Bond grinned down at her, 'I expect it's because we made them afraid. Perhaps they're still afraid. That's because we don't seem to be frightened of them. We must keep them that way.'

The girl pressed against him. 'I'll try.'

Now the climb was getting steeper. Grey light showed through the slots in the armour. Dawn was coming up. Outside, another day of brazen heat and ugly wind and the smell of marsh gas would be beginning. Bond thought of Quarrel, the brave giant who would not be seeing it, with whom they should now be setting off for the long trek through the mangrove swamps. He remembered the life insurance. Quarrel had smelled his death. Yet he had followed Bond unquestioningly. His faith in Bond had been stronger than his fear. And Bond had let him down. Would Bond also be the death of the girl?

The driver reached forward to the dashboard. From the front of the machine there sounded the brief howl of a police siren. It meandered into a dying moan. After a minute the machine stopped, idling in neutral. The man pressed a switch and took a microphone off a hook beside him. He spoke into it and Bond could hear the echoing voice of the loud-hailer outside. 'Okay. Got the Limey and the girl. Other man's dead. That's the lot. Open up.'

Bond heard a door being pulled sideways on iron rollers. The driver put in the clutch and they rolled slowly forward a few yards and stopped. The man switched off the engine. There was a clang as the iron hatch was opened from the outside. A gush of fresh air and a flood of brighter light came into the cabin. Hands took hold of Bond and dragged him roughly out backwards on to a cement floor. Bond stood up. He felt the prod of a gun in his side. A voice said, 'Stay where you are. No tricks.' Bond looked at the man. He was another Chinese negro, from the same stable as the others. The yellow eyes examined him curiously. Bond turned away indifferently. Another man was prodding the girl with his gun. Bond said sharply, 'Leave the girl alone.' He walked over and stood beside her. The two men seemed surprised. They stood, pointing their guns indecisively.

Bond looked around him. They were in one of the Quonset huts he had seen from the river. It was a garage and workshop. The 'dragon' had been halted over an examination pit in the concrete. A dismantled outboard motor lay on one of the benches. Strips of white sodium lighting ran along the ceiling. There was a smell of oil and exhaust smoke. The driver and his mate were examining the machine. Now they sauntered up.

One of the guards said, 'Passed the message along. The word is to send them through. Everything go okay?'

The co-driver, who seemed to be the senior man present, said, 'Sure. Bit of gunfire. Lights gone. May be some holes in the tyres. Get the boys crackin'—full overhaul. I'll put these two through and go get myself some shuteye.' He turned to Bond. 'Okay, git moving,' he gestured down the long hut.

Bond said, 'Get moving yourself. Mind your manners. And tell those apes to take their guns off us. They might let one off by mistake. They look dumb enough.'

The man came closer. The other three closed up behind him. Hate shone redly in their eyes. The leading man lifted a clenched fist as big as a small ham and held it under Bond's nose. He was controlling himself with an effort. He said tensely, 'Listen, mister. Sometimes us boys is allowed to join in the fun at the end. I'm just praying this'll be one of those times. Once we made it last a whole week. An, Jees, if I get you . . .' He broke off. His eyes were alight with cruelty. He looked past Bond at the girl. The eyes became mouths that licked their lips. He wiped his hands down the sides of his trousers. The tip of his tongue showed pinkly between the purple lips. He turned to the other three. 'What say, fellers?'

The three men were also looking at the girl. They nodded dumbly, like children in front of a Christmas tree.

Bond longed to run berserk among them, laying into their faces with his manacled wrists, accepting their bloody revenge. But for the girl he would have done it. Now all he had achieved with his brave words was to get her frightened. He said, 'All right, all right. You're four and we're two and we've got our hands tied. Come on. We won't hurt you. Just don't push us around too much. Doctor No might not be pleased.'

At the name, the men's faces changed. Three pairs of eyes looked whitely from Bond to the leader. For a minute the leader stared suspiciously at Bond, wondering, trying to fathom whether perhaps Bond had got some edge on their boss. His mouth opened to say something. He thought better of it. He said lamely, 'Okay, okay. We was just kiddin'.' He turned to the men for confirmation. 'Right?'

'Sure! Sure thing.' It was a ragged mumble. The men looked away.

The leader said gruffly, 'This way, mister.' He walked off down the long hut.

Bond took the girl's wrist and followed. He was impressed with the weight of Doctor No's name. That was something to remember if they had any more dealings with the staff.

The man came to a rough wooden door at the end of the hut. There was a bellpush beside it. He rang twice and waited. There came a click and the door opened to reveal ten yards of carpeted rock passage with another door, smarter and cream-painted, at the end.

The man stood aside. 'Straight ahead, mister. Knock on the door. The receptionist'll take over.' There was no irony in his voice and his eyes were impassive.

Bond led the girl into the passage. He heard the door shut behind them. He stopped and looked down at her. He said, 'Now what?'

She smiled tremulously. 'It's nice to feel carpet under one's feet.'

Bond squeezed her wrist. He walked forward to the cream-painted door and knocked.

The door opened. Bond went through with the girl at his heels. When he stopped dead in his tracks, he didn't feel the girl bump into him. He just stood and stared.

CHAPTER 13

Mink-Lined Prison

It was the sort of reception room the largest American corporations have on the President's floor in their New York skyscrapers. It was of pleasant proportions, about twenty feet square. The floor was close-carpeted in the thickest wine-red Wilton and the walls and ceiling were painted a soft dove grey. Colour lithograph reproductions of Degas ballet sketches were well hung in groups on the walls and the lighting was by tall modern standard lamps with dark green silk shades in a fashionable barrel design.

To Bond's right was a broad mahogany desk with a green leather top, handsome matching desk furniture and the most expensive type of intercom. Two tall antique chairs waited for visitors. On the other side of the room was a refectory-type table with shiny magazines and two more chairs. On both the desk and the table were tall vases of freshly cut hibiscus. The air was fresh and cool and held a slight, expensive fragrance.

There were two women in the room. Behind the desk,

with pen poised over a printed form, sat an efficient-looking Chinese girl with hornrimmed spectacles below a bang of black hair cut short. Her eyes and mouth wore the standard receptionist's smile of welcome—bright, helpful, inquisitive.

Holding the door through which they had come, and waiting for them to move farther into the room so that she could close it, stood an older, rather matronly woman of about forty-five. She also had Chinese blood. Her appearance, wholesome, bosomy, eager, was almost excessively gracious. Her square cut pince-nez gleamed with the hostess's desire to make them feel at home.

Both women were dressed in spotless white, with white stockings and white suede brogues, like assistants in the most expensive American beauty-parlours. There was something soft and colourless about their skins as if they rarely went out of doors.

While Bond took in the scene, the woman at the door twittered conventional phrases of welcome as if they had been caught in a storm and had arrived late at a party.

'You poor dears. We simply didn't know when to expect you. We kept on being told you were on your way. First it was teatime yesterday, then dinner, and it was only half an hour ago we heard you would only be here in time for breakfast. You must be famished. Come along now and help Sister Rose fill in your forms and then I'll pack you both straight off to bed. You must be tired out.'

Clucking softly, she closed the door and ushered them forward to the desk. She got them seated in the chairs and rattled on, 'Now I'm Sister Lily and this is Sister Rose. She just wants to ask you a few questions. Now, let me see, a cigarette?' She picked up a tooled leather box. She opened it and put it on the desk in front of them. It had three compartments. She pointed with a little finger, 'Those are American, and those are Players, and those are Turkish.' She picked up an expensive desk-lighter and waited.

Bond reached out his manacled hands to take a Turkish cigarette.

Sister Lily gave a squeak of dismay. 'Oh, but really.' She sounded genuinely embarrassed. 'Sister Rose, the key, quickly. I've said again and again that patients are never to be brought in like that.' There was impatience and distaste in her voice. 'Really, that outside staff! It's time they had a talking to.'

Sister Rose was just as much put out. Hastily she scrabbled in a drawer and handed a key across to Sister Lily who, with much cooing and tut-tutting, unlocked the two pairs of handcuffs and walked behind the desk and dropped them as if they were dirty bandages into the wastepaper basket.

'Thank you.' Bond was unable to think of any way to handle the situation except to fall in with what was happening on the stage. He reached out and took a cigarette and lit it. He glanced at Honeychile Rider who sat looking dazed and nervously clutching the arms of her chair. Bond gave her a reassuring smile.

'Now, if you please.' Sister Rose bent over a long printed form on expensive paper, 'I promise to be as quick as I can. Your name please Mister—er . . .''

'Bryce, John Bryce.'

She wrote busily. 'Permanent address?'

'Care of the Royal Zoological Society, Regent's Park, London, England.'

'Profession.'

'Ornithologist.'

'Oh dear,' she dimpled at him, 'could you please spell that?'

Bond did so.

'Thank you so much. Now, let me see, Purpose of Visit?'

'Birds,' said Bond. 'I am also a representative of the Audubon Society of New York. They have a lease of part of this island.'

'Oh, really.' Bond watched the pen writing down exactly what he had said. After the last words she put a neat query in brackets.

'And,' Sister Rose smiled politely in the direction of Honeychile, 'your wife? Is she also interested in birds?'

'Yes, indeed.'

'And her first name?'

'Honeychile.'

Sister Rose was delighted, 'What a pretty name.' She wrote busily. 'And now just your next of kin and then we're finished.'

Bond gave M's real name as next of kin for both of them. He described him as 'uncle' and gave his address as 'Managing Director, Universal Export, Regent's Park, London'.

Sister Rose finished writing and said, 'There, that's done. Thank you so much, Mr Bryce, and I do hope you both enjoy your stay.'

'Thank you very much. I'm sure we will.' Bond got up. Honeychile Rider did the same, her face still expressionless.

Sister Lily said, 'Now come along with me, you poor dears.' She walked to a door in the far wall. She stopped with her hand on the cut-glass doorknob. 'Oh deary me, now I've gone and forgotten the number of their rooms! It's the Cream Suite, isn't it, Sister?'

'Yes, that's right. Fourteen and fifteen.'

'Thank you, my dear. And now,' she opened the door, 'if you'll just follow me. I'm afraid it's a terribly long walk.' She shut the door behind them and led the way. 'The Doctor's often talked of putting in one of those moving stairway things, but you know how it is with a busy man,' she laughed gaily. 'So many other things to think of.'

'Yes, I expect so,' said Bond politely.

Bond took the girl's hand and they followed the motherly bustling figure down a hundred yards of lofty corridor in the same style as the reception room but lit at frequent intervals by discreetly expensive wall-brackets.

Bond answered with polite monosyllables the occasional twittering comments Sister Lily threw over her shoulder. His whole mind was focused on the extraordinary circumstances of their reception. He was

quite certain the two women had been genuine. Not a
look or a word had been dropped that was out of place.
It was obviously a front of some kind, but a solid one,
meticulously supported by the decor and the cast. The
lack of resonance in the room, and now in the corridor,
suggested that they had stepped from the Quonset hut
into the side of the mountain and that they were now
walking through its base. At a guess they would be
walking towards the west—towards the cliff-face with
which the island ended. There was no moisture on the
walls and the air was cool and pure with a strongish
breeze coming towards them. A lot of money and good
engineering had gone into the job. The pallor of the two
women suggested that they spent all their time inside the
mountain. From what Sister Lily had said it sounded as
if they were part of an inside staff that had nothing to
do with the strong-arm squad outside and perhaps
didn't even understand what sort of men they were.

It was grotesque, concluded Bond as they came nearer
to a door at the end of the corridor, dangerously grotesque,
but it was no good wondering about it. He could only
follow the lines of the gracious script. At least this was
better than the backstage of the island outside.

At the door, Sister Lily rang. They had been expected. The door opened at once. An enchanting
Chinese girl in a mauve and white flowered kimono
stood smiling and bowing as Chinese girls are supposed
to do. Again there was nothing but warmth and
welcome in the pale, flowerlike face. Sister Lily cried,
'Here they are at last, May! Mr and Mrs John Bryce.
And I know they must be exhausted so we must take
them straight to their rooms for some breakfast and a
sleep.' She turned to Bond. 'This is May. Such a dear
girl. She will be looking after you both. Anything you
want, just ring for May. She's a favourite with all our
patients.'

Patients, thought Bond. That's the second time she's
used the word. He smiled politely at the girl. 'How do
you do. Yes, we'd certainly both of us like to get to our
rooms.'

May embraced them both with a warm smile. She said in a low, attractive voice, 'I do hope you'll both be comfortable, Mr Bryce. I took the liberty of ordering breakfast as soon as I heard you had come in. Shall we . . . ?' Corridors branched off to left and right of double liftdoors set in the wall opposite. The girl led the way to the right. Bond and Honeychile followed with Sister Lily taking up the rear.

Numbered doors led off the corridor on either side. Now the decor was in the lightest pink with a dove grey carpet. The numbers on the doors were in the tens. The corridor came to an abrupt end with two doors side by side, 14 and 15. May opened the door of 14 and they followed her in.

It was a charming double bedroom in modern Miami style with dark green walls, dark polished mahogany floor with occasional thick white rugs, and well-designed bamboo furniture with a chintz of large red roses on a white background. There was a communicating door into a more masculine dressing-room and another that led into an extremely luxurious modern bathroom with a step-down bath and a bidet.

It was like being shown into the very latest Florida hotel suite—except for two details which Bond noticed. There were no windows and no inside handles to the doors.

May looked hopefully from one to the other.

Bond turned to Honeychile. He smiled at her. 'It looks very comfortable, don't you think, darling?'

The girl played with the edge of her skirt. She nodded, not looking at him.

There was a timid knock on the door and another girl, as pretty as May, tripped in with a loaded tray balanced on her upturned hand. She put it down on the centre table and pulled up two chairs. She whisked off the speckless linen cloth that covered the dishes and pattered out of the room. There was a delicious smell of bacon and coffee.

May and Sister Lily backed to the door. The older woman stopped on the threshold. 'And now we'll leave

you two dear people in peace. If you want anything, just
ring. The bells are by the bed. Oh, and by the way,
you'll find plenty of fresh clothes in the cupboards.
Chinese style, I'm afraid,' she twinkled apologetically,
'but I hope they're the right sizes. The wardrobe room
only got the measurements yesterday evening. The
Doctor has given strict orders that you're not to be
disturbed. He'd be delighted if you'd join him for
dinner this evening. He wants you to have the whole of
the rest of the day to yourselves—to get settled down,
you know.' She paused and looked from one to the
other in smiling inquiry. 'Shall I say you . . . ?'

'Yes, please,' said Bond. 'Tell the Doctor we shall be
delighted to join him for dinner.'

'Oh, I know he'll be so pleased.' With a last twitter
the two women softly withdrew and closed the door
behind them.

Bond turned towards Honeychile. She looked embarrassed. She still avoided his eyes. It occurred to Bond
that she could never have met such soft treatment or
seen such luxury in her life. To her, all this must be far
more strange and terrifying than what they had gone
through outside. She stood and fiddled at the hem of
her Man Friday skirt. There were streaks of dried sweat
and salt and dust on her face. Her bare legs were filthy
and Bond noticed that her toes were moving softly as
they gripped nervously into the wonderful thick pile
carpet.

Bond laughed. He laughed with real pleasure that her
fear had been drowned in the basic predicament of
clothes and how to behave, and he laughed at the picture they made—she in her rags and he in his dirty blue
shirt and black jeans and muddy canvas shoes.

He went to her and took her hands. They were cold.
He said, 'Honey, we're a couple of scarecrows. There's
only one problem. Shall we have breakfast first while
it's hot, or shall we get out of these rags and have a bath
and eat the breakfast when it's cold? Don't worry about
anything else. We're here in this wonderful little house

and that's all that matters. Now then, what shall we do?'

She smiled uncertainly. The blue eyes searched his face for reassurance. 'You're not worried about what's going to happen to us?' She nodded at the room. 'Don't you think this is all a trap?'

'If it's a trap we're in it. There's nothing we can do now but eat the cheese. The only question is whether we eat it hot or cold.' He pressed her hands. 'Really, Honey. Leave the worrying to me. Just think where we were an hour ago. Isn't this better? Now come on and decide the really important things. Bath or breakfast?'

She said reluctantly, 'Well, if you think . . . I mean—I'd rather get clean first.' She added quickly, 'But you've got to help me.' She jerked her head towards the bathroom door. 'I don't know how to work one of those places. What do you do?'

Bond said seriously, 'It's quite easy. I'll fix it all ready for you. While you're having your bath, I'll have my breakfast. I'll keep yours warm.' Bond went to one of the built-in clothes cupboards and ran the door back. There were half a dozen kimonos, some silk and some linen. He took out a linen one at random. 'You take off your clothes and get into this and I'll get the bath ready. Later on you can choose the things you want to wear for bed and dinner.'

She said gratefully, 'Oh yes, James. If you'll just show me . . .' She started to unbutton her shirt.

Bond wanted to take her in his arms and kiss her. Instead he said abruptly, 'That's fine, Honey,' and went into the bathroom and turned on the taps.

There was everything in the bathroom—Floris Lime bath essence for men and Guerlain bathcubes for women. He crushed a cube into the water and at once the room smelled like an orchid house. The soap was Guerlain's Sapoceti, *Fleurs des Alpes*. In a medicine cupboard behind the mirror over the washbasin were toothbrushes and toothpaste, Steradent toothpicks, Rose mouthwash, dental floss, Aspirin and Milk of

Magnesia. There was also an electric razor, Lentheric
after-shave lotion, and two nylon hairbrushes and
combs. Everything was brand new and untouched.

Bond looked at his filthy unshaven face in the mirror
and smiled grimly into the grey, sunburned castaway's
eyes. The coating on the pill was certainly of the very
finest sugar. It would be wise to expect that the medicine
inside would be of the bitterest.

He turned back to the bath and felt the water. It
would be too hot for someone who presumably had
never had a hot bath before. He let in some cold. As he
bent over, two arms were thrown round his neck. He
stood up. The golden body blazed in the white tiled
bathroom. She kissed him hard and clumsily on the lips.
He put his arms round her and crushed her to him, his
heart pounding. She said breathlessly at his ear, 'The
Chinese dress felt strange. Anyway, you told that
woman we were married.'

Bond's hand was on her left breast. Its peak was hard
with passion. Her stomach pressed against his. Why
not? Why not? Don't be a fool! This is a crazy time for
it. You're both in deadly danger. You must stay cold as
ice to have any chance of getting out of this mess. Later!
Later! Don't be weak.

Bond took his hand away from her breast and put it
round her neck. He rubbed his face against hers and
then brought his mouth round to hers and gave her one
long kiss.

He stood away and held her at arm's length. For a
moment they looked at each other, their eyes bright with
desire. She was breathing fast, her lips parted so that he
could see the glint of teeth. He said unsteadily, 'Honey,
get into that bath before I spank you.'

She smiled. Without saying anything she stepped
down into the bath and lay at full length. She looked up.
The fair hair on her body glittered up through the water
like golden sovereigns. She said provocatively, 'You've
got to wash me. I don't know what to do. You've got to
show me.'

Bond said desperately, 'Shut up, Honey. And stop

flirting. Just take the soap and the sponge and start scrubbing. Damn you! This isn't the time for making love. I'm going to have breakfast.' He reached for the door handle and opened the door. She said softly, 'James!' He looked back. She was sticking her tongue out at him. He grinned savagely back at her and slammed the door.

Bond went into the dressing-room and stood in the middle of the floor and waited for his heart to stop pounding. He rubbed his hands over his face and shook his head to get rid of the thought of her.

To clear his mind he went carefully over both rooms looking for exits, possible weapons, microphones— anything that would add to his knowledge. There were none of these things. There was an electric clock on the wall which said eight-thirty and a row of bells beside the double bed. They said, Room Service, Coiffeur, Mani- curist, Maid. There was no telephone. High up in a corner of both rooms was a small ventilator grille. Each was about two feet square. Useless. The doors ap- peaed to be of some light metal, painted to match the walls. Bond threw the whole weight of his body against one of them. It didn't give a millimetre. Bond rubbed his shoulder. The place was a prison—an exquisite prison. It was no good arguing. The trap had shut tight on them. Now the only thing for the mice to do was to make the most of the cheese.

Bond sat down at the breakfast table. There was a large tumbler of pineapple juice in a silver-plated bowl of crushed ice. He swallowed it down and lifted the cover off his individual hot-plate. Scrambled eggs on toast, four rashers of bacon, a grilled kidney and what looked like an English pork sausage. There were also two kinds of hot toast, rolls inside a napkin, mar- malade, honey and strawberry jam. The coffee was boiling hot in a large Thermos decanter. The cream smelled fresh.

From the bathroom came the sound of the girl crooning 'Marion'. Bond closed his ears to the sound and started on the eggs.

Ten minutes later, Bond heard the bathroom door open. He put down his toast and marmalade and covered his eyes with his hands. She laughed. She said, 'He's a coward. He's frightened of a simple girl.' Bond heard her rummaging in the cupboards. She went on talking, half to herself. 'I wonder why he's frightened. Of course if I wrestled with him I'd win easily. Perhaps he's frightened of that. Perhaps he's really not very strong. His arms and his chest look strong enough. I haven't seen the rest yet. Perhaps it's weak. Yes, that must be it. That's why he doesn't dare take his clothes off in front of me. H'm, now let's see, would he like me in this?' She raised her voice. 'Darling James, would you like me in white with pale blue birds flying all over me?'

'Yes, damn you,' said Bond through his hands. 'Now stop chattering to yourself and come and have breakfast. I'm getting sleepy.'

She gave a cry. 'Oh, if you mean it's time for us to go to bed, of course I'll hurry.'

There was a flurry of feet and Bond heard her sit down opposite. He took his hands down. She was smiling at him. She looked ravishing. Her hair was dressed and combed and brushed to kill, with one side falling down the side of the cheek and the other slicked back behind her ear. Her skin sparkled with freshness and the big blue eyes were alight with happiness. Now Bond loved the broken nose. It had become part of his thoughts of her and it suddenly occurred to him that he would be sad when she was just an immaculately beautiful girl like other beautiful girls. But he knew it would be no good trying to persuade her of that. She sat demurely, with her hands in her lap below the end of a cleavage which showed half her breasts and a deep vee of her stomach.

Bond said severely, 'Now listen, Honey. You look wonderful, but that isn't the way to wear a kimono. Pull it up right across your body and tie it tight and stop trying to look like a call girl. It just isn't good manners at breakfast.'

'Oh, you are a stuffy old beast.' She pulled her kimono an inch or two closer. 'Why don't you like playing? I want to play at being married.'

'Not at breakfast time,' said Bond firmly. 'Come on and eat up. It's delicious. And anyway, I'm filthy. I'm going to shave and have a bath.' He got up and walked round the table and kissed the top of her head. 'And as for playing, as you call it, I'd rather play with you than anyone in the world. But not now.' Without waiting for her answer he walked into the bathroom and shut the door.

Bond shaved and had a bath and a shower. He felt desperately sleepy. Sleep came to him in waves so that from time to time he had to stop what he was doing and bend his head down between his knees. When he came to brush his teeth he could hardly do it. Now he recognized the signs. He had been drugged. In the coffee or in the pineapple juice? It didn't matter. Nothing mattered. All he wanted to do was lie down on the tiled floor and shut his eyes. Bond weaved drunkenly to the door. He forgot that he was naked. That didn't matter either. Anyway the girl had finished her breakfast. She was in bed. He staggered over to her, holding on to the furniture. The kimono was lying in a pile on the floor. She was fast asleep, naked under a single sheet.

Bond gazed dreamily at the empty pillow beside her head. No! He found the switches and turned out the lights. Now he had to crawl across the floor and into his room. He got to his bed and pulled himself on to it. He reached out an arm of lead and jabbed at the switch on the bed-light. He missed it. The lamp crashed to the floor and the bulb burst. With a last effort Bond turned on his side and let the waves sweep over his head.

The luminous figures on the electric clock in the double room said nine-thirty.

At ten o'clock the door of the double room opened softly. A very tall thin figure was silhouetted against the lighted corridor. It was a man. He must have been six feet six tall. He stood on the threshold with his arms folded, listening. Satisfied, he moved slowly into the room and up to the bed. He knew the way exactly. He bent down and listened to the quiet breathing of the girl. After a moment he reached up to his chest and pressed a switch. A flashlight with a very broad diffused beam came on. The flashlight was attached to him by a belt that held it above the breast bone. He bent forward so that the soft light shone on the girl's face.

The intruder examined the girl's face for several minutes. One of his hands came up and took the sheet at her chin and softly drew the sheet down to the end of the bed. The hand that drew down the sheet was not a hand. It was a pair of articulated steel pincers at the end of a metal stalk that disappeared into a black silk sleeve. It was a mechanical hand.

The man gazed for a long time at the naked body, moving his chest to and fro so that every corner of the body came under the light. Then the claw came out again and delicately lifted a corner of the sheet from the bottom of the bed and drew it back over the girl. The man stood for another moment gazing down at the sleeping face, then he switched off the torch on his chest and moved quietly away across the room to the open door through which Bond was sleeping.

The man spent longer beside Bond's bed. He scrutinized every line, every shadow on the dark, rather cruel face that lay drowned, almost extinct, on the pillow. He watched the pulse in the neck and counted it and, when he had pulled down the sheet, he did the same with the area round the heart. He gauged the curve of the muscles on Bond's arms and thighs and looked thoughtfully at the hidden strength in the flat stomach. He even bent down close over the out-flung open right hand and examined its life and fate lines.

Finally, with infinite care, the steel claw drew the sheet back up to Bond's neck. For another minute the tall figure stood over the sleeping man, then it swished softly away and out into the corridor and the door closed with a click.

CHAPTER 14

Come into My Parlour

The electric clock in the cool dark room in the heart of the mountain showed four-thirty.

Outside the mountain, Crab Key had sweltered and stunk its way through another day. At the eastern end of the island, the mass of birds, Louisiana herons, pelicans, avocets, sandpipers, egrets, flamingoes and the few roseate spoonbills, went on with building their nests or fished in the shallow waters of the lake. Most of the birds had been disturbed so often that year that they had given up any idea of building. In the past few months they had been raided at regular intervals by the monster that came at night and burned down their roosting places and the beginnings of their nests. This year many would not breed. There would be vague movements to migrate and many would die of the nervous hysteria that seizes bird colonies when they no longer have peace and privacy.

At the other end of the island, on the guanera that gave the mountain its snow-covered look, the vast swarm of cormorants had passed their usual day of gorging themselves with fish and paying back the ounce of precious manure to their owner and protector. Nothing had interfered with *their* nesting season. Now they were noisily fiddling with the untidy piles of sticks that would be their nests—each pile at exactly sixty centimetres from the next, for the guanay is a quarrelsome bird and this sixty-centimetre ring represents their sparring space. Soon the females would be laying the three eggs from which their master's flock would be increased by an average of two young cormorants.

Below the peak, where the diggings began, the hundred or so negro men and women who were the labour force were coming to the end of the day's shift. Another fifty cubic yards of guano had been dug out of the mountainside and another twenty yards of terrace had been added to the working level. Below, the mountainside looked like terraced vineyards in Upper Italy, except that here there were no vines, only deep barren shelves cut in the mountainside. And here, instead of the stink of marsh gas on the rest of the island, there was a strong ammoniac smell, and the ugly hot wind that kept the diggings dry blew the freshly turned whitish-brown dust into the eyes and ears and noses of the diggers. But the workers were used to the smell and the dust, and it was easy, healthy work. They had no complaints.

The last iron truck of the day started off on the Decauderville Track that snaked down the mountainside to the crusher and separator. A whistle blew and the workers shouldered their clumsy picks and moved lazily down towards the high-wired group of Quonset huts that was their compound. Tomorrow, on the other side of the mountain, the monthly ship would be coming in to the deepwater quay they had helped to build ten years before, but which, since then, they had never seen. That would mean fresh stores and fresh goods and cheap jewellery at the canteen. It would be a holiday. There would be rum and dancing and a few fights. Life was good.

Life was good, too, for the senior outside staff—all

Chinese negroes like the men who had hunted Bond and Quarrel and the girl. They also stopped work in the garage and the machine shops and at the guard posts and filtered off to the 'officers' ' quarters. Apart from watch and loading duties, tomorrow would also be a holiday for most of them. They too would have their drinking and dancing, and there would be a new monthly batch of girls from 'inside'. Some 'marriages' from the last lot would continue for further months or weeks according to the taste of the 'husband', but for the others there would be some of the older girls who had had their babies in the creche and were coming back for a fresh spell of duty 'outside', and there would be a sprinkling of young ones who had come of age and would be 'coming out' for the first time. There would be fights over these and blood would be shed, but in the end the officers' quarters would settle down for another month of communal life, each officer with his woman to look after his needs.

Deep down in the cool heart of the mountain, far below this well-disciplined surface life, Bond awoke in his comfortable bed. Apart from a slight Nembutal headache he felt fit and rested. Lights were on in the girl's room and he could hear her moving about. He swung his feet to the ground and, avoiding the fragments of glass from the broken lamp, walked softly over to the clothes cupboard and put on the first kimono that came to his hand. He went to the door. The girl had a pile of kimonos out on the bed and was trying them on in front of the wall mirror. She had on a very smart one in sky-blue silk. It looked wonderful against the gold of her skin. Bond said, 'That's the one.'

She whirled round, her hand at her mouth. She took it down. 'Oh, it's you!' She smiled at him. 'I thought you'd never wake up. I've been to look at you several times. I'd made up my mind to wake you at five. It's half past four and I'm hungry. Can you get us something to eat?'

'Why not.' Bond walked across to her bed. As he passed her he put his arm round her waist and took her with him. He examined the bells. He pressed the one marked 'Room Service'. He said, 'What about the others? Let's have the full treatment.'

She giggled. 'But what's a manicurist?'

'Someone who does your nails. We must look our best for Doctor No.' At the back of Bond's mind was the urgent necessity to get his hands on some kind of weapon—a pair of scissors would be better than nothing. Anything would do.

He pressed two more bells. He let her go and looked round the room. Someone had come while they were asleep and taken away the breakfast things. There was a drink tray on a sideboard against the wall. Bond went over and examined it. It had everything. Propped among the bottles were two menus, huge double-folio pages covered with print. They might have been from the Savoy Grill, or the '21', or the Tour d'Argent. Bond ran his eye down one of them. It began with *Caviar double de Beluga* and ended with *Sorbet à la Champagne.* In between was every dish whose constituents would not be ruined by a deep freeze. Bond tossed it down. One certainly couldn't grumble about the quality of the cheese in the trap!

There was a knock on the door and the exquisite May came in. She was followed by two other twittering Chinese girls. Bond brushed aside their amiabilities, ordered tea and buttered toast for Honeychile and told them to look after her hair and nails. Then he went into the bathroom and had a couple of Aspirins and a cold shower. He put on his kimono again, reflected that he looked idiotic in it, and went back into the room. A beaming May asked if he would be good enough to select what he and Mrs Bryce could care to have for dinner. Without enthusiasm, Bond ordered caviar, grilled lamb cutlets and salad, and angels on horseback for himself. When Honeychile refused to make any suggestions, he chose melon, roast chicken à l' Anglaise and vanilla icecream with hot chocolate sauce for her.

May dimpled her enthusiasm and approval. 'The

Doctor asks if seven forty-five or eight would be convenient.'

Bond said curtly that it would.

'Thank you so much, Mr Bryce. I will call for you at seven forty-four.'

Bond walked over to where Honeychile was being ministered to at the dressing table. He watched the busy delicate fingers at work on her hair and her nails. She smiled at him excitedly in the mirror. He said gruffly, 'Don't let them make too much of a monkey out of you,' and went to the drink tray. He poured himself out a stiff Bourbon and soda and took it into his own room. So much for his idea of getting hold of a weapon. The scissors and files and probes were attached to the manicurist's waist by a chain. So were the scissors of the hairdresser. Bond sat down on his rumpled bed and lost himself in drink and gloomy reflections.

The women went. The girl looked in at him. When he didn't lift his head she went back into her room and left him alone. In due course Bond came into her room to get himself another drink. He said perfunctorily, 'Honey, you look wonderful.' He glanced at the clock on the wall and went back and drank his drink and put on another of the idiotic kimonos, a plain black one.

In due course there came the soft knock on the door and the two of them went silently out of the room and along the empty, gracious corridor. May stopped at the lift. Its doors were held open by another eager Chinese girl. They walked in and the doors shut. Bond noticed that the lift was made by Waygood Otis. Everything in the prison was de luxe. He gave an inward shudder of distaste. He noticed the reaction. He turned to the girl. 'I'm sorry, Honey. Got a bit of a headache.' He didn't want to tell her that all this luxury play-acting was getting him down, that he hadn't the smallest idea what it was all about, that he knew it was bad news, and that he hadn't an inkling of a plan of how to get them out of whatever situation they were in. That was the worst of it. There was nothing that depressed Bond's spirit so

much as the knowledge that he hadn't one line of either
attack or defence.

The girl moved closer to him. She said, 'I'm sorry,
James. I hope it will go away. You're not angry with me
about anything?'

Bond dredged up a smile. He said, 'No, darling. I'm
only angry with myself.' He lowered his voice: 'Now,
about this evening. Just leave the talking to me. Be
natural and don't be worried by Doctor No. He may be
a bit mad.'

She nodded solemnly. 'I'll do my best.'

The lift sighed to a stop. Bond had no idea how far
down they had gone—a hundred feet, two hundred?
The automatic doors hissed back and Bond and the girl
stepped out into a large room.

It was empty. It was a high-ceilinged room about sixty
feet long, lined on three sides with books to the ceiling.
At first glance, the fourth wall seemed to be made of
solid blue-black glass. The room appeared to be a com-
bined study and library. There was a big paper-strewn
desk in one corner and a central table with periodicals
and newspapers. Comfortable club chairs, upholstered
in red leather, were dotted about. The carpet was dark
green, and the lighting, from standard lamps, was sub-
dued. The only odd feature was that the drink tray and
sideboard were up against the middle of the long glass
wall, and chairs and occasional tables with ashtrays
were arranged in a semi-circle round it so that the room
was centred in front of the empty wall.

Bond's eye caught a swirl of movement in the dark
glass. He walked across the room. A silvery spray of
small fish with a bigger fish in pursuit fled across the
dark blue. They disappeared, so to speak, off the edge
of the screen. What was this? An aquarium? Bond
looked upwards. A yard below the ceiling, small waves
were lapping at the glass. Above the waves was a strip of
greyer blue-black, dotted with sparks of light. The
outlines of Orion were the clue. This was not an
aquarium. This was the sea itself and the night sky. The
whole of one side of the room was made of armoured

glass. They were under the sea, looking straight into its heart, twenty feet down.

Bond and the girl stood transfixed. As they watched, there was the glimpse of two great goggling orbs. A golden sheen of head and deep flank showed for an instant and was gone. A big grouper? A silver swarm of anchovies stopped and hovered and sped away. The twenty-foot tendrils of a Portuguese man-o'-war drifted slowly across the window, glinting violet as they caught the light. Up above there was the dark mass of its underbelly and the outline of its inflated bladder, steering with the breeze.

Bond walked along the wall, fascinated by the idea of living with this slow, endlessly changing moving picture. A big tulip shell was progressing slowly up the window from the floor level, a frisk of demoiselles and angel fish and a ruby-red moonlight snapper were nudging and rubbing themselves against a corner of the glass and a sea centipede quested along, nibbling at the minute algae that must grow every day on the outside of the window. A long dark shadow paused in the centre of the window and then moved slowly away. If only one could see more!

Obediently, two great shafts of light, from off the 'screen', lanced out into the water. For an instant they searched independently. Then they converged on the departing shadow and the dull grey torpedo of a twelve-foot shark showed up in all its detail. Bond could even see the piglike pink eyes roll inquisitively in the light and the slow pulse of the slanting gill-rakers. For an instant the shark turned straight into the converged beam and the white half-moon mouth showed below the flat reptile's head. It stood poised for a second and then, with an elegant, disdainful swirl, the great swept-back tail came round and with a lightning quiver the shark had gone.

The searchlights went out. Bond turned slowly. He expected to see Doctor No, but still the room was empty. It looked static and lifeless compared with the pulsing mysteries outside the window. Bond looked

back. What must this be like in the colours of day, when
one could see everything perhaps for twenty yards or
more? What must it be like in a storm when the waves
crashed noiselessly against the glass, delving almost to
the floor and then sweeping up and out of sight. What
must it be like in the evening when the last golden shafts
of the sun shone into the upper half of the room and the
waters below were full of dancing motes and tiny water
insects? What an amazing man this must be who had
thought of this fantastically beautiful conception, and
what an extraordinary engineering feat to have carried it
out! How had he done it? There could only be one way.
He must have built the glass wall deep inside the cliff
and then delicately removed layer after layer of the outside rock until the divers could prise off the last skin of
coral. But how thick was the glass? Who had rolled it
for him? How had he got it to the island? How many
divers had he used? How much, God in heaven, could it
have cost?

'One million dollars.'

It was a cavernous, echoing voice, with a trace of
American accent.

Bond turned slowly, almost reluctantly, away from
the window.

Doctor No had come through a door behind his desk.
He stood looking at them benignly, with a thin smile on
his lips.

'I expect you were wondering about the cost. My
guests usually think about the material side after about
fifteen minutes. Were you?'

'I was.'

Still smiling (Bond was to get used to that thin smile),
Doctor No came slowly out from behind the desk and
moved towards them. He seemed to glide rather than
take steps. His knees did not dent the matt, gunmetal
sheen of his kimono and no shoes showed below the
sweeping hem.

Bond's first impression was of thinness and erectness
and height. Doctor No was at least six inches taller than
Bond, but the straight immovable poise of his body

made him seem still taller. The head also was elongated and tapered from a round, completely bald skull down to a sharp chin so that the impression was of a reversed raindrop—or rather oildrop, for the skin was of a deep almost translucent yellow.

It was impossible to tell Doctor No's age: as far as Bond could see, there were no lines on the face. It was odd to see a forehead as smooth as the top of the polished skull. Even the cavernous indrawn cheeks below the prominent cheekbones looked as smooth as fine ivory. There was something Dali-esque about the eyebrows, which were fine and black and sharply up-swept as if they had been painted on as make-up for a conjurer. Below them, slanting jet black eyes stared out of the skull. They were without eyelashes. They looked like the mouths of two small revolvers, direct and un-blinking and totally devoid of expression. The thin fine nose ended very close above a wide compressed wound of a mouth which, despite its almost permanent sketch of a smile, showed only cruelty and authority. The chin was indrawn towards the neck. Later Bond was to notice that it rarely moved more than slightly away from centre, giving the impression that the head and the ver-tebra were in one piece.

The bizarre, gliding figure looked like a giant venomous worm wrapped in grey tin-foil, and Bond would not have been surprised to see the rest of it trailing slimily along the carpet behind.

Doctor No came within three steps of them and stopped. The wound in the tall face opened. 'Forgive me for not shaking hands with you,' the deep voice was flat and even. 'I am unable to.' Slowly the sleeves parted and opened. 'I have no hands.'

The two pairs of steel pincers came out on their gleaming stalks and were held up for inspection like the hands of a praying mantis. Then the two sleeves joined again.

Bond felt the girl at his side give a start.

The black apertures turned towards her. They slid down to her nose. The voice said flatly, 'It is a misfortune.' The eyes came back to Bond. 'You were admiring my aquarium.' It was a statement, not a question. 'Man enjoys the beasts and the birds. I decided to enjoy also the fish. I find them far more varied and interesting. I am sure you both share my enthusiasm.'

Bond said, 'I congratulate you. I shall never forget this room.'

'No.' Again a statement, perhaps with a sardonic inflection, of fact. 'But we have much to talk about. And so little time. Please sit down. You will have a drink? Cigarettes are beside your chairs.'

Doctor No moved to a high leather chair and folded himself down on to the seat. Bond took the chair opposite. The girl sat between them and slightly back.

Bond felt a movement behind him. He looked over his shoulder. A short man, a Chinese negro, with the build of a wrestler, stood at the drink tray. He was dressed in black trousers and a smart white jacket. Black almond eyes in a wide moon face met his and slid incuriously away.

Doctor No said, 'This is my bodyguard. He is expert in many things. There is no mystery about his sudden appearance. I always carry what is known as a walkie-talkie here,' he inclined his chin towards the bosom of his kimono. 'Thus I can summon him when he is needed. What will the girl have?'

Not 'Your Wife'. Bond turned to Honeychile. Her eyes were wide and staring. She said quietly, 'A Coca-Cola, please.'

Bond felt a moment of relief. At least she was not being got down by the performance. Bond said, 'And I would like a medium Vodka dry Martini—with a slice of lemon peel. Shaken and not stirred, please. I would prefer Russian or Polish vodka.'

Doctor No gave his thin smile an extra crease. 'I see you are also a man who knows what he wants. On this occasion your desires will be satisfied. Do you not find that it is generally so? When one wants a thing one gets it? That is my experience.'

'The small things.'

'If you fail at the large things it means you have not large ambitions. Concentration, focus—that is all. The aptitudes come, the tools forge themselves. "Give me a fulcrum and I will move the world"—but only if the desire to move the world is there.' The thin lips bent minutely downwards in deprecation. 'But this is chatter. We are making conversation. Instead, let us talk. Both of us, I am sure, prefer talk to conversation. Is the Martini to your liking? You have cigarettes—enough and the right sort to cosset your cancer? So be it. Sam-sam, put the shaker beside the man and another bottle of Coca-Cola beside the girl. It should now be eight-ten. We will have dinner at nine o'clock precisely.'

Doctor No sat slightly more upright in his chair. He inclined himself forward, staring at Bond. There was a moment's silence in the room. Then Doctor No said, 'And now Mister James Bond of the Secret Service, let us tell each other our secrets. First, to show you that I hide nothing, I will tell you mine. Then you will tell me yours.' Doctor No's eyes blazed darkly. 'But let us tell each other the truth.' He drew one steel claw out of the wide sleeve and held it upwards. He paused, 'I shall do so. But you must do the same. If you do not, these,' he pointed the claw at his eyes, 'will know that you are lying.'

Doctor No brought the steel claw delicately in front of each eye and tapped the centre of each eyeball.

Each eyeball in turn emitted a dull ting. 'These,' said Doctor No, 'see everything.'

CHAPTER 15

Pandora's Box

James Bond picked up his glass and sipped at it thoughtfully. It seemed pointless to go on bluffing. His story of representing the Audubon Society was anyway a thin one which could be punctured by anyone who knew about birds. It was obvious that his own cover was in shreds. He must concentrate on protecting the girl. To begin with he must reassure her.

Bond smiled at Doctor No. He said, 'I know about your contact in King's House, Miss Taro. She is your agent. I have recorded the fact and it will be divulged in certain circumstances'—Doctor No's expression showed no interest—'as will other facts. But, if we are to have a talk, let us have it without any more stage effects. You are an interesting man. But it is not necessary to make yourself more interesting than you are. You have suffered the misfortune of losing your hands. You wear mechanical hands. Many men wounded in the war wear them. You wear contact lenses instead of spectacles. You use a walkie-talkie instead of a bell to summon your servant. No doubt you have other tricks. But,

Doctor No, you are still a man who sleeps and eats and defecates like the rest of us. So no more conjuring tricks, please. I am not one of your guano diggers and I am not impressed by them.'

Doctor No inclined his head a fraction. 'Bravely spoken, Mister Bond. I accept the rebuke. I have no doubt developed annoying mannerisms from living too long in the company of apes. But do not mistake these mannerisms for bluff. I am a technician. I suit the tool to the material. I possess also a range of tools for working with refractory materials. However,' Doctor No raised his joined sleeves an inch and let them fall back in his lap, 'let us proceed with our talk. It is a rare pleasure to have an intelligent listener and I shall enjoy telling you the story of one of the most remarkable men in the world. You are the first person to hear it. I have not told it before. You are the only person I have ever met who will appreciate my story and also—' Doctor No paused for the significance of the last word to make itself felt—'keep it to himself.' He continued, 'The second of these considerations also applies to the girl.'

So that was it. There had been little doubt in Bond's mind ever since the Spandau had opened up on them, and since, even before then, in Jamaica, where the attempts on him had not been half-hearted. Bond had assumed from the first that this man was a killer, that it would be a duel to the death. He had had his usual blind faith that he would win the duel—all the way until the moment when the flame-thrower had pointed at him. Then he had begun to doubt. Now he knew. This man was too strong, too well equipped.

Bond said, 'There is no point in the girl hearing this. She has nothing to do with me. I found her yesterday on the beach. She is a Jamaican from Morgan's Harbour. She collects shells. Your men destroyed her canoe so I had to bring her with me. Send her away now and then back home. She won't talk. She will swear not to.'

The girl interrupted fiercely. 'I *will* talk! I shall tell everything. I'm not going to move. I'm going to stay with you.'

Bond looked at her. He said icily, 'I don't want you.'

Doctor No said softly, 'Do not waste your breath on these heroics. Nobody who comes to this island has ever left it. Do you understand? Nobody—not even the simplest fisherman. It is not my policy. Do not argue with me or attempt to bluff me. It is entirely useless.'

Bond examined the face. There was no anger in it, no obstinacy—nothing but a supreme indifference. He shrugged his shoulders. He looked at the girl and smiled. He said, 'All right, Honey. And I didn't mean it. I'd hate you to go away. We'll stay together and listen to what the maniac has to say.'

The girl nodded happily. It was as if her lover had threatened to send her out of the cinema and now had relented.

Doctor No said, in the same soft resonant voice, 'You are right, Mister Bond. That is just what I am, a maniac. All the greatest men are maniacs. They are possessed by a mania which drives them forward towards their goal. The great scientists, the artists, the philosophers, the religious leaders—all maniacs. What else but a blind singleness of purpose could have given focus to their genius, would have kept them in the groove of their purpose? Mania, my dear Mister Bond, is as priceless as genius. Dissipation of energy, fragmentation of vision, loss of momentum, the lack of follow-through—these are the vices of the herd.' Doctor No sat slightly back in his chair. 'I do not possess these vices. I am, as you correctly say, a maniac—a maniac, Mister Bond, with a mania for power. That'—the black holes glittered blankly at Bond through the contact lenses—'is the meaning of my life. That is why I am here. That is why you are here. That is why here exists.'

Bond picked up his glass and drained it. He filled it again from the shaker. He said, 'I'm not surprised. It's the old business of thinking you're the King of England, or the President of the United States, or God. The asylums are full of them. The only difference is that instead of being shut up, you've built your own asylum and shut yourself up in it. But why did you do it? Why does sitting shut up in this cell give you the illusion of power?'

Irritation flickered at the corner of the thin mouth. 'Mister Bond, power is sovereignty. Clausewitz's first principle was to have a secure base. From there one proceeds to freedom of action. Together, that is sovereignty. I have secured these things and much besides. No one else in the world possesses them to the same degree. They *cannot* have them. The world is too public. These things can only be secured in privacy. You talk of kings and presidents. How much power do they possess? As much as their people will allow them. Who in the world has the power of life or death over his people? Now that Stalin is dead, can you name any man except myself? And how do I possess that power, that sovereignty? Through privacy. Through the fact that nobody *knows*. Through the fact that I have to account to no one.'

Bond shrugged. 'That is only the illusion of power, Doctor No. Any man with a loaded revolver has the power of life and death over his neighbour. Other people beside you have murdered in secret and got away with it. In the end they generally get their deserts. A greater power than they possess is exerted upon them by the community. That will happen to you, Doctor No. I tell you, your search for power is an illusion because power itself is an illusion.'

Doctor No said equably, 'So is beauty, Mister Bond. So is art, so is money, so is death. And so, probably, is life. These concepts are relative. Your play upon words does not shake me. I know philosophy, I know ethics, and I know logic—better than you do, I daresay. But let us move away from this sterile debate. Let us return to where I began, with my mania for power, or, if you wish it, for the illusion of power. And please, Mister Bond,' again the extra crease in the fixed smile, 'please do not imagine that half an hour's conversation with you will alter the pattern of my life. Interest yourself rather in the history of my pursuit, let us put it, of an illusion.'

'Go ahead.' Bond glanced at the girl. She caught his

eyes. She put her hand up to her mouth as if to conceal a yawn. Bond grinned at her. He wondered when it would amuse Doctor No to crack her pose of indifference.

Doctor No said benignly, 'I shall endeavour not to bore you. Facts are so much more interesting than theories, don't you agree?' Doctor No was not expecting a reply. He fixed his eye on the elegant tulip shell that had now wandered half way up the outside of the dark window. Some small silver fish squirted across the black void. A bluish prickle of phosphorescence meandered vaguely. Up by the ceiling, the stars shone more brightly through the glass.

The artificiality of the scene inside the room—the three people sitting in the comfortable chairs, the drinks on the sideboard, the rich carpet, the shaded lights, suddenly seemed ludicrous to Bond. Even the drama of it, the danger, were fragile things compared with the progress of the tulip shell up the glass outside. Supposing the glass burst. Supposing the stresses had been badly calculated, the workmanship faulty. Supposing the sea decided to lean a little more heavily against the window.

Doctor No said, 'I was the only son of a German Methodist missionary and a Chinese girl of good family. I was born in Pekin, but on what is known as "the wrong side of the blanket". I was an encumbrance. An aunt of my mother was paid to bring me up.' Doctor No paused. 'No love, you see, Mister Bond. Lack of parental care.' He went on, 'The seed was sown. I went to work in Shanghai. I became involved with the Tongs, with their illicit proceedings. I enjoyed the conspiracies, the burglaries, the murders, the arson of insured properties. They represented revolt against the father figure who had betrayed me. I loved the death and destruction of people and things. I became adept in the technique of criminality—if you wish to call it that. Then there was trouble. I had to be got out of the way. The Tongs considered me too valuable to kill. I was smuggled to the United States. I settled in New York. I had been given a

letter of introduction, in code, to one of the two most
powerful Tongs in America—the Hip Sings. I never
knew what the letter said, but they took me on at once
as a confidential clerk. In due course, at the age of
thirty, I was made the equivalent of treasurer. The
treasury contained over a million dollars. I coveted this
money. Then began the great Tong Wars of the late
'twenties. The two great New York Tongs, my own, the
Hip Sings, and our rival, the On Lee Ongs, joined in
combat. Over the weeks, hundreds on both sides were
killed and their houses and properties burned to the
ground. It was a time of torture and murder and arson
in which I joined with delight. Then the riot squads
came. Almost the whole police force of New York was
mobilized. The two underground armies were prised
apart and the headquarters of the two Tongs were
raided and the ringleaders sent to jail. I was tipped off
about the raid on my own Tong, the Hip Sings. A few
hours before it was due, I got to the safe and rifled the
million dollars in gold and disappeared into Harlem and
went to ground. I was foolish. I should have left
America, gone to the farthest corner of the earth. Even
from the condemned cells in Sing Sing the heads of my
Tong reached out for me. They found me. The killers
came in the night. They tortured me. I would not say
where the gold was. They tortured me all through the
night. Then, when they could not break me, they cut off
my hands to show that the corpse was that of a thief,
and they shot me through the heart and went away. But
they did not know something about me. I am the one
man in a million who has his heart on the right side of
his body. Those are the odds against it, one in a million.
I lived. By sheer willpower I survived the operation and
the months in hospital. And all the time I planned and
planned how to get away with the money—how to keep
it, what to do with it.'

Doctor No paused. There was a slight flush at his
temples. His body fidgeted inside his kimono. His
memories had excited him. For a moment he closed his

eyes, composing himself. Bond thought, now! Shall I leap at him and kill him? Break off my glass and do it with the jagged stem?

The eyes opened. 'I am not boring you? You are sure? For an instant I felt your attention wandering.'

'No.' The moment had passed. Would there be others? Bond measured the inches of the leap: noted that the jugular vein was in full view above the neck of the kimono.

The thin purple lips parted and the story went on. 'It was, Mister Bond, a time for clear, firm decisions. When they let me out of the hospital I went to Silberstein, the greatest stamp dealer in New York. I bought an envelope, just one envelope, full of the rarest postage stamps in the world. It took weeks to get them together. But I didn't mind what I paid—in New York, London, Paris, Zurich. I wanted my gold to be mobile. I invested it all in these stamps. I had foreseen the World War. I knew there would be inflation. I knew the best would appreciate, or at least hold its value. And meanwhile I was changing my appearance. I had all my hair taken out by the roots, my thick nose made thin, my mouth widened, my lips sliced. I could not get smaller, so I made myself taller. I wore built up shoes. I had weeks of traction on my spine. I held myself differently. I put away my mechanical hands and wore hands of wax inside gloves. I changed my name to Julius No—the Julius after my father and the No for my rejection of him and of all authority. I threw away my spectacles and wore contact lenses—one of the first pairs ever built. Then I went to Milwaukee, where there are no Chinamen, and enrolled myself in the faculty of medicine. I hid myself in the academic world, the world of libraries and laboratories and classrooms and campuses. And there, Mister Bond, I lost myself in the study of the human body and the human mind. Why? Because I wished to know what this clay is capable of. I had to learn what my tools were before I put them to use on my next goal—total security from physical weaknesses, from material dangers and from the hazards of living. Then,

Mister Bond, from that secure base, armoured even against the casual slings and arrows of the world, I would proceed to the achievement of power—the power, Mister Bond, to do unto others what had been done unto me, the power of life and death, the power to decide, to judge, the power of absolute independence from outside authority. For that, Mister Bond, whether you like it or not, is the essence of temporal power.'

Bond reached for the shaker and poured himself a third drink. He looked at Honeychile. She seemed composed and indifferent—as if her mind was on other things. She smiled at him.

Doctor No said benignly, 'I expect you are both hungry. Pray be patient. I will be brief. So, if you recall, there I was, in Milwaukee. In due course, I completed my studies and I left America and went by easy stages round the world. I called myself "doctor" because doctors receive confidences and they can ask questions without arousing suspicion. I was looking for my headquarters. It had to be safe from the coming war, it had to be an island, it had to be entirely private, and it had to be capable of industrial development. In the end I purchased Crab Key. And here I have remained for fourteen years. They have been secure and fruitful years, without a cloud on the horizon. I was entertained by the idea of converting bird dung into gold, and I attacked the problem with passion. It seemed to me the ideal industry. There was a constant demand for the product. The birds require no care except to be left in peace. Each one is a simple factory for turning fish into dung. The digging of the guano is only a question of not spoiling the crop by digging too much. The sole problem is the cost of the labour. It was 1942. The simple Cuban and Jamaican labourer was earning ten shillings a week cutting cane. I tempted a hundred of them over to the island by paying them twelve shillings a week. With guano at fifty dollars a ton I was well placed. But on one condition—that the wages remained constant. I ensured that by isolating my community from world inflation. Harsh methods have had to be used from time to time,

but the result is that my men are content with their
wages because they are the highest wages they have ever
known. I brought in a dozen Chinese negroes with their
families to act as overseers. They receive a pound a week
per man. They are tough and reliable. On occasion I had
to be ruthless with them, but they soon learned.
Automatically my people increased in numbers. I added
some engineers and some builders. We set to work on
the mountain. Occasionally I brought in teams of
specialists on high wages. They were kept apart from the
others. They lived inside the mountain until their work
was done and then left by ship. They put in the lighting
and the ventilation and the lift. They built this room.
Stores and furnishings came in from all over the world.
These people built the sanatorium façade which will
cover my operations in case one day there is a shipwreck
or the Governor of Jamaica decides to pay me a call.'
The lips glazed into a smile. 'You must admit that I am
able, if I wish, to accord visitors a most fragrant reception—a wise precaution for the future! And gradually,
methodically, my fortress was built while the birds
defecated on top of it. It has been hard, Mister Bond.'
The black eyes did not look for sympathy or praise. 'But
by the end of last year the work was done. A secure,
well-camouflaged base had been achieved. I was ready
to proceed to the next step—an extension of my power
to the outside world.'

Doctor No paused. He lifted his arms an inch and
dropped them again resignedly in his lap. 'Mister Bond,
I said that there was not a cloud in the sky during all
these fourteen years. But one was there, all the time,
below the horizon. And do you know what it was? It
was a bird, a ridiculous bird called a roseate spoonbill! I
will not weary you with the details, Mister Bond. You
are already aware of some of the circumstances. The
two wardens, miles away in the middle of the lake, were
provisioned by launch from Cuba. They sent out their
reports by the launch. Occasionally, ornithologists from
America came by the launch and spent some days at the
camp. I did not mind. The area is out of bounds to my

men. The wardens were not allowed near my compounds. There was no contact. From the first I made it clear to the Audubon Society that I would not meet their representatives. And then what happens? One day, out of a clear sky, I get a letter by the monthly boat. The roseate spoonbills have become one of the bird wonders of the world. The Society gives me formal notification that they intend to build a hotel on their leasehold, near the river up which you came. Bird lovers from all over the world will come to observe the birds. Films will be taken. Crab Key, they told me in their flattering, persuasive letter, would become famous.

'Mister Bond,' the arms were raised and dropped back. Irony gathered at the edges of the set smile. 'Can you believe it? This privacy I had achieved! The plans I had for the future! To be swept aside because of a lot of old women and their birds! I examined the lease. I wrote offering a huge sum to buy it. They refused. So I studied these birds. I found out about their habits. And suddenly the solution was there. And it was easy. Man had always been the worst predator on these birds. Spoonbills are extremely shy. They frighten easily. I sent to Florida for a marsh buggy—the vehicle that is used for oil prospecting, that will cover any kind of terrain. I adapted it to frighten and to burn—not only birds, but humans as well, for the wardens would have to go too. And, one night in December, my marsh buggy howled off across the lake. It smashed the camp, both wardens were reported killed—though one, it turned out, escaped to die in Jamaica—it burned the nesting places, it spread terror among the birds. Complete success! Hysteria spread among the spoonbills. They died in thousands. But then I get a demand for a plane to land on my airstrip. There was to be an investigation. I decide to agree. It seemed wiser. An accident is arranged. A lorry goes out of control down the airstrip as the plane is coming in. The plane is destroyed. All signs of the lorry are removed. The bodies are reverently placed in coffins and I report the tragedy. As I expected, there is further investigation. A destroyer arrives. I receive the captain courteously. He and his officers are brought round by sea and then led inland. They are shown the remains of the camp. My men suggest that the wardens went mad with loneliness and fought each other. The survivor set fire to the camp and escaped in his fishing canoe. The airstrip is examined. My men report that the plane was coming in too fast. The tyres must have burst on impact. The bodies are handed over. It is very sad. The officers are satisfied. The ship leaves. Peace reigns again.'

Doctor No coughed delicately. He looked from Bond to the girl and back again, 'And that, my friends, is my story—or rather the first chapter of what I am confident will be a long and interesting tale. Privacy has been re-established. There are now no roseate spoonbills, so there will be no wardens. No doubt the Audubon Society will decide to accept my offer for the rest of their lease. No matter. If they start their puny operations again, other misfortunes will befall them. This has been a warning to me. There will be no more interference.'

'Interesting,' said Bond. 'An interesting case history. So that was why Strangways had to be removed. What did you do with him and his girl?'

'They are at the bottom of the Mona Reservoir. I sent three of my best men. I have a small but efficient machine in Jamaica. I need it. I have established a watch on the intelligence services in Jamaica and Cuba. It is necessary for my further operations. Your Mister Strangways became suspicious and started ferreting about. Fortunately, by this time, the routines of this man were known to me. His death and the girl's were a simple matter of timing. I had hoped to deal with you with similar expedition. You were fortunate. But I knew what type of a man you were from the files at King's House. I guessed that the fly would come to the spider. I was ready for you, and when the canoe showed up on the radar screen I knew you would not get away.'

Bond said, 'Your radar is not very efficient. There were two canoes. The one you saw was the girl's. I tell you she had nothing to do with me.'

'Then she is unfortunate. I happen to be needing a white woman for a small experiment. As we agreed earlier, Mister Bond, one generally gets what one wants.'

Bond looked thoughtfully at Doctor No. He wondered if it was worth while even trying to make a dent in this impregnable man. Was it worth wasting breath by threatening or bluffing? Bond had nothing but a miserable two of clubs up his sleeve. The thought of playing it almost bored him. Casually, indifferently he threw it down.

'Then you're out of luck, Doctor No. You are now a file in London. My thoughts on this case, the evidence of the poisoned fruit and the centipede and the crashed motor car, are on record. So are the names of Miss Chung and Miss Taro. Instructions were left with someone in Jamaica that my report should be opened and acted upon if I failed to return from Crab Key within three days.'

Bond paused. The face of Doctor No was impassive. Neither the eyes nor the mouth had flickered. The jugular vein throbbed evenly. Bond bent forward. He said softly, 'But because of the girl, and only because of her, Doctor No, I will strike a bargain. In exchange for our safe return to Jamaica, you may have a week's start. You may take your aeroplane and your packet of stamps and try to get away.'

Bond sat back. 'Any interest, Doctor No?'

CHAPTER 16

Horizons of Agony

A voice behind Bond said quietly, 'Dinner is served.'

Bond swung round. It was the bodyguard. Beside him was another man who might have been his twin. They stood there, two stocky barrels of muscle, their hands buried in the sleeves of their kimonos, and looked over Bond's head at Doctor No.

'Ah, nine o'clock already.' Doctor No rose slowly to his feet. 'Come along. We can continue our conversation in more intimate surroundings. It is kind of you both to have listened to me with such exemplary patience. I hope the modesty of my cuisine and my cellar will not prove a further imposition.'

Double doors stood open in the wall behind the two white-jacketed men. Bond and the girl followed Doctor No through into a small octagonal mahogany panelled room lit by a central chandelier in silver with storm glasses round the candles. Beneath it was a round mahogany table laid for three. Silver and glass twinkled warmly. The plain dark blue carpet was luxuriously deep. Doctor No took the centre high-backed chair and bowed the girl into the chair on his right. They sat down and unfolded napkins of white silk.

The hollow ceremony and the charming room maddened Bond. He longed to break it up with his own hands—to wind his silk napkin round Doctor No's throat and squeeze until the contact lenses popped out of the black, damnable eyes.

The two guards wore white cotton gloves. They served the food with a suave efficiency that was prompted by an occasional word in Chinese from Doctor No.

At first, Doctor No seemed preoccupied. He slowly ate through three bowls of different soup, feeding himself with a spoon with a short handle that fitted neatly between the pincers. Bond concentrated on hiding his fears from the girl. He sat relaxed and ate and drank with a forced good appetite. He talked cheerfully to the girl about Jamaica—about the birds and the animals and the flowers which were an easy topic for her. Occasionally his feet felt for hers under the table. She became almost gay. Bond thought they were putting on an excellent imitation of an engaged couple being given dinner by a detested uncle.

Bond had no idea if his thin bluff had worked. He didn't give much for their chances. Doctor No, and Doctor No's story, exuded impregnability. The incredible biography rang true. Not a word of it was impossible. Perhaps there were other people in the world with their private kingdoms—away from the beaten track, where there were no witnesses, where they could do what they liked. And what did Doctor No plan to do next, after he had squashed the flies that had come to annoy him? And if—when—he killed Bond and the girl, would London pick up the threads that Bond had picked up? Probably they would. There would be Pleydell-Smith. The evidence of the poisoned fruit. But where would Bond's replacement get with Doctor No? Not far. Doctor No would shrug his shoulders over the disappearance of Bond and Quarrel. Never heard of them. And there would be no link with the girl. In Morgan's Harbour they would think she had been drowned on one of her expeditions. It was hard to see what could interfere with Doctor No—with the second chapter of his life, whatever it was.

Underneath his chatter with the girl, Bond prepared for the worst. There were plenty of weapons beside his plate. When the cutlets came, perfectly cooked, Bond fiddled indecisively with the knives and chose the bread knife to eat them with. While he ate and talked, he edged the big steel meat knife towards him. An expansive gesture of his right hand knocked over his glass of champagne and in the split second of the crash his left hand flicked the knife into the deep sleeve of his kimono. In the midst of Bond's apologies and the confusion as he and the bodyguard mopped up the spilled champagne, Bond raised his left arm and felt the knife slip back to below his armpit and then fall inside the kimono against his ribs. When he had finished his cutlets he tightened the silk belt round his waist, shifting the knife across his stomach. The knife nestled comfortingly against his skin and gradually the steel grew warm.

Coffee came and the meal was ended. The two guards came and stood close behind Bond's chair and the girl's. They stood with their arms crossed on their chests, impassive, motionless, like executioners.

Doctor No put his cup softly down on its saucer. He laid his two steel claws down on the table in front of him. He sat a fraction more upright. He turned his body an inch in Bond's direction. Now there was no preoccupation in his face. The eyes were hard and direct. The thin mouth creased and opened. 'You have enjoyed your dinner, Mister Bond?'

Bond took a cigarette from the silver box in front of him and lit it. He played with the silver table-lighter. He smelled bad news coming. He must somehow pocket the lighter. Fire might perhaps be another weapon. He said easily, 'Yes. It was excellent.' He looked across at the girl. He leant forward in his chair and rested his fore-

arms on the table. He crossed them, enveloping the
lighter. He smiled at her. 'I hope I ordered what you
like.'

'Oh yes, it was lovely.' For her the party was still
going on.

Bond smoked busily, agitating his hands and forearms to create an atmosphere of movement. He turned
to Doctor No. He stubbed out his cigarette and sat back
in his chair. He folded his arms across his chest. The
lighter was in his left armpit. He smiled cheerfully. 'And
what happens now, Doctor No?'

'We can proceed to our after-dinner entertainment,
Mister Bond.' The thin smile creased and vanished. 'I
have examined your proposition from every angle. I do
not accept it.'

Bond shrugged his shoulders. 'You are unwise.'

'No, Mister Bond. I suspect that your proposition is a
gold brick. People in your trade do not behave as you
suggest. They make routine reports to their headquarters. They keep their chief aware of the progress of
their investigations. I know these things. Secret agents
do not behave as you suggest you have done. You have
been reading too many novels of suspense. Your little
speech reeked of grease-paint and cardboard. No,
Mister Bond, I do not accept your story. If it is true, I
am prepared to face the consequences. I have too much
at stake to be turned from my path. So the police come,
the soldiers come. Where are a man and a girl? What
man and what girl? I know nothing. Please go away.
You are disturbing my guanera. Where is your evidence? Your search warrant? The English law is strict,
gentlemen. Go home and leave me in peace with my
beloved cormorants. You see, Mister Bond? And let us
even say that the worst comes to the worst. That one of
my agents talks, which is highly improbable (Bond
remembered the fortitude of Miss Chung). What have I
to lose? Two more deaths on the charge sheet. But,
Mister Bond, a man can only be hanged once.' The tall
pear-shaped head shook gently from side to side. 'Have
you anything else to say? Any questions to ask? You

both have a busy night ahead of you. Your time is getting short. And I must get my sleep. The monthly ship is putting in tomorrow and I have the loading to supervise. I shall have to spend the whole day down on the quay. Well, Mister Bond?'

Bond looked across at the girl. She had gone deathly pale. She was gazing at him, waiting for the miracle he would work. He looked down at his hands. He examined his nails carefully. He said, playing for time, 'And then what? After your busy day with the bird dung, what comes next on your programme? What is the next chapter you think you're going to write?'

Bond didn't look up. The deep quiet authoritative voice came to him as if it was coming down from the night sky.

'Ah, yes. You must have been wondering, Mister Bond. You have the habit of inquiry. It persists even to the last, even into the shadows. I admire such qualities in a man with only a few hours to live. So I will tell you. I will turn over the next page. It will console you. There is more to this place than bird dung. Your instincts did not betray you.' Doctor No paused for emphasis. 'This island, Mister Bond, is about to be developed into the most valuable technical intelligence centre in the world.'

'Really?' Bond kept his eyes bent on his hands.

'Doubtless you know that Turks Island, about three hundred miles from here through the Windward Passage, is the most important centre for testing the guided missiles of the United States?'

'It is an important centre, yes.'

'Perhaps you have read of the rockets that have been going astray recently? The multi-stage SNARK, for instance, that ended its flight in the forests of Brazil instead of the depths of the South Atlantic?'

'Yes.'

'You recall that it refused to obey the telemetred instructions to change its course, even to destroy itself. It developed a will of its own?'

'I remember.'

'There have been other failures, decisive failures,

from the long list of prototypes—the ZUNI, MATADOR, PETREL, REGULUS, BOMARC—so many names, so many changes, I can't even remember them all. Well, Mister Bond,' Doctor No could not keep a note of pride out of his voice, 'it may interest you to know that the vast majority of those failures have been caused from Crab Key.'

'Is that so?'

'You do not believe me? No matter. Others do. Others who have seen the complete abandonment of one series, the MASTODON, because of its recurring navigational errors, its failure to obey the radio directions from Turks Island. Those others are the Russians. The Russians are my partners in this venture. They trained six of my men, Mister Bond. Two of those men are on watch at this moment, watching the radio frequencies, the beams on which these weapons travel. There is a million dollars' worth of equipment up above us in the rock galleries, Mister Bond, sending fingers up into the Heavy-side Layer, waiting for the signals, jamming them, countering beams with other beams. And from time to time a rocket soars up on its way a hundred, five hundred miles into the Atlantic. And we track it, as accurately as they are tracking it in the Operations Room on Turks Island. Then, suddenly, our pulses go out to the rocket, its brain is confused, it goes mad, it plunges into the sea, it destroys itself, it roars off at a tangent. Another test has failed. The operators are blamed, the designers, the manufacturers. There is panic in the Pentagon. Something else must be tried, different frequencies, different metals, a different radio brain. Of course,' Doctor No was fair, 'we too have our difficulties. We track many practice shoots without being able to get through to the brain of the new rocket. But then we communicate urgently with Moscow. Yes, they have even given us a cipher machine with our own frequencies and routines. And the Russians get thinking. They make suggestions. We try them out. And then, one day, Mister Bond, it is like catching the attention of a man in a crowd. Up in the stratosphere the rocket acknowledges our signal. We are recognized and we can speak to it and change its mind.' Doctor No paused. 'Do you not find that interesting, Mister Bond, this little sideline to my business in guano? It is, I assure you, most profitable. It might be still more so. Perhaps Communist China will pay more. Who knows? I already have my feelers out.'

Bond lifted his eyes. He looked thoughtfully at Doctor No. So he *had* been right. There *had* been more, much more, in all this than met the eye. This was a big game, a game that explained everything, a game that was certainly, in the international espionage market, well worth the candle. Well, well! Now the pieces in the puzzle fell firmly into place. For this it was certainly worth scaring away a few birds and wiping out a few people. Privacy? Of course Doctor No would have to kill him and the girl. Power? This was it. Doctor No had really got himself into business.

Bond looked into the two black holes with a new respect. He said, 'You'll have to kill a lot more people to keep this thing in your hands, Doctor No. It's worth a lot of money. You've got a good property here—a better one than I thought. People are going to want to cut themselves a piece of this cake. I wonder who will get to you first and kill you. Those men up there', he gestured towards the ceiling, 'who were trained in Moscow? They're the technicians. I wonder what Moscow is telling them to do? You wouldn't know that, would you?'

Doctor No said, 'You persist in underestimating me, Mister Bond. You are an obstinate man, and stupider than I had expected. I am aware of these possibilities. I have taken one of these men and made him into a private monitor. He has duplicates of the ciphers and of the cipher machine. He lives in another part of the mountain. The others think that he died. He watches on all the routine times. He gives me a second copy of all the traffic that passes. So far, the signals from Moscow have been innocent of any sign of conspiracy. I am thinking of these things constantly, Mister Bond. I take precautions and I shall take further precautions. As I said, you underestimate me.'

'I don't underestimate you, Doctor No. You're a very careful man, but you've got too many files open on you. In my line of business, the same thing applies to me. I know the feeling. But you've got some really bad ones. The Chinese one, for instance. I wouldn't like to have that one. The F.B.I. should be the least painful—robbery and false identity. But do you know the Russians as well as I do? You're a "best friend" at the moment. But the Russians don't have partners. They'll want to take you over—buy you out with a bullet. Then there's the file you've started with my Service. You really want me to make that one fatter? I shouldn't do it if I were you, Doctor No. They're a tenacious lot of people in my Service. If anything happens to me and the girl, you'll find Crab Key's a very small and naked little island.'

'You cannot play for high stakes without taking risks, Mister Bond. I accept the dangers and, so far as I can, I have equipped myself against them. You see, Mister Bond,' the deep voice held a hint of greed, 'I am on the edge of still greater things. The Chapter Two to which I referred holds the promise of prizes which no one but a fool would throw away because he was afraid. I have told you that I can bend the beams on which these rockets fly, Mister Bond. I can make them change course and ignore their radio control. What would you say, Mister Bond, if I could go further? If I could bring them down into the sea near this island and salvage the secrets of their construction. At present American destroyers, far out in the South Atlantic, salvage these missiles when they come to the end of their fuel and parachute down into the sea. Sometimes the parachutes fail to open. Sometimes the self-destruction devices fail to operate. No one on Turks Island would be surprised if every now and then the prototype of a new series broke off its flight and came down near Crab Key. To begin with, at least, it would be put down to mechanical failure. Later, perhaps, they would discover that other radio signals besides theirs were guiding their rockets. A jamming war would start. They would try and locate the origin of the false signals. Directly I found they were looking for me, I would have one last fling. Their rockets would go mad. They would land on Havana, on Kingston. They would turn round and home on Miami. Even without warheads, Mister Bond, five tons of metal arriving at a thousand miles an hour can cause plenty of damage in a crowded town. And then what? There would be panic, a public outcry. The experiments would have to cease. The Turks Island base would have to close down. And how much would Russia pay for that to happen, Mister Bond? And how much for each of the prototypes I captured for them? Shall we say ten million dollars for the whole operation? Twenty million? It would be a priceless victory in the armaments race. I could name my figure. Don't you agree, Mister Bond? And don't you agree that these considerations make your arguments and threats seem rather puny?'

Bond said nothing. There was nothing to say. Suddenly he was back in the quiet room high up above Regent's Park. He could hear the rain slashing softly against the window and M's voice, impatient, sarcastic, saying, 'Oh, some damned business about birds . . . holiday in the sun'll do you good . . . routine inquiry.' And he, Bond, had taken a canoe and a fisherman and a picnic lunch and had gone off—how many days, how many weeks ago?—'to have a look'. Well, he had had his look into Pandora's Box. He had found out the answers, been told the secrets—and now? Now he was going to be politely shown the way to his grave, taking the secrets with him and the waif he had picked up and dragged along with him on his lunatic adventure. The bitterness inside Bond came up into his mouth so that for a moment he thought he was going to retch. He reached for his champagne and emptied the glass. He said harshly, 'All right, Doctor No. Now let's get on with the cabaret. What's the programme—knife, bullet, poison, rope? But make it quick, I've seen enough of you.'

Doctor No's lips compressed into a thin purple line. The eyes were hard as onyx under the billiard ball forehead and skull. The polite mask had gone. The Grand Inquisitor sat in the high-backed chair. The hour had struck for the *peine forte et dure.*

Doctor No spoke a word and the two guards took a step forward and held the two victims above the elbows, forcing their arms back against the sides of their chairs. There was no resistance. Bond concentrated on holding the lighter in his armpit. The white-gloved hands on his biceps felt like steel bands. He smiled across at the girl. 'I'm sorry about this, Honey. I'm afraid we're not going to be able to play together after all.'

The girl's eyes in the pale face were blue-black with fear. Her lips trembled. She said, 'Will it hurt?'

'Silence!' Doctor No's voice was the crack of a whip. 'Enough of this foolery. Of course it will hurt. I am interested in pain. I am also interested in finding out how much the human body can endure. From time to time I make experiments on those of my people who have to be punished. And on trespassers like yourselves. You have both put me to a great deal of trouble. In exchange I intend to put you to a great deal of pain. I shall record the length of your endurance. The facts will be noted. One day my findings will be given to the world. Your deaths will have served the purposes of science. I never waste human material. The German experiments on live humans during the war were a great benefit to science. It is a year since I put a girl to death in the fashion I have chosen for you, woman. She was a negress. She lasted three hours. She died of terror. I have wanted a white girl for comparison. I was not surprised when your arrival was reported. I get what I want.' Doctor No sat back in his chair. His eyes were now fixed on the girl, watching her reactions. She stared back at him, half hypnotized, like a bush mouse in front of a rattlesnake.

Bond set his teeth.

'You are a Jamaican, so you will know what I am talking about. This island is called Crab Key. It is called by that name because it is infested with crabs, land crabs—what they call in Jamaica "black crabs". You know them. They weigh about a pound each and they are as big as saucers. At this time of year they come up in thousands from their holes near the shore and climb up towards the mountain. There, in the coral uplands, they go to ground again in holes in the rock and spawn their broods. They march up in armies of hundreds at a time. They march through everything and over everything. In Jamaica they go through houses that are in their path. They are like the lemmings of Norway. It is a compulsive migration.' Doctor No paused. He said softly, 'But there is a difference. The crabs devour what they find in their path. And at present, woman, they are "running". They are coming up the mountainside in their tens of thousands, great red and orange and black waves of them, scuttling and hurrying and scraping against the rock above us at this moment. And tonight, in the middle of their path, they are going to find the naked body of a woman pegged out—a banquet spread for them—and they will feel the warm body with their feeding pincers, and one will make the first incision with his fighting claws and then . . . and then . . .'

There was a moan from the girl. Her head fell forward slackly on to her chest. She had fainted. Bond's body heaved in his chair. A string of obscenities hissed out between his clenched teeth. The huge hands of the guard were like fire round his arms. He couldn't even move the chair-legs on the floor. After a moment he desisted. He waited for his voice to steady, then he said, with all the venom he could put into the words, 'You bastard. You'll fry in hell for this.'

Doctor No smiled thinly. 'Mister Bond, I do not admit the existence of hell. Console yourself. Perhaps they will start at the throat or the heart. The movement of the pulse will attract them. Then it will not be long.' He spoke a sentence in Chinese. The guard behind the girl's chair leant forward and plucked her bodily out of the chair as if she had been a child and slung the inert body over his shoulder. Between the dangling arms the hair fell down in a golden shower. The guard went to the door and opened it and went out, closing it noiselessly behind him.

For a moment there was silence in the room. Bond thought only of the knife against his skin and of the lighter under his armpit. How much damage could he do with the two pieces of metal? Could he somehow get within range of Doctor No?

Doctor No said quietly, 'You said that power was an illusion, Mister Bond. Do you change your mind? My power to select this particular death for the girl is surely not an illusion. However, let us proceed to the method of your departure. That also has its novel aspects. You see, Mister Bond, I am interested in the anatomy of courage—in the power of the human body to endure. But how to measure human endurance? How to plot a graph of the will to survive, the tolerance of pain, the conquest of fear? I have given much thought to the problem, and I believe I have solved it. It is, of course, only a rough and ready method, and I shall learn by experience as more and more subjects are put to the test. I have prepared you for the experiment as best I could. I gave you a sedative so that your body should be rested and I have fed you well so that you may be at full strength. Future—what shall I call them—patients, will have the same advantages. All will start equal in that respect. After that it will be a question of the individual's courage and powers of endurance.' Doctor No paused, watching Bond's face. 'You see, Mister Bond, I have just finished constructing an obstacle race, an assault course against death. I will say no more about it because the element of surprise is one of the constituents of fear. It is the unknown dangers that are the worst, that bear most heavily on the reserves of courage. And I flatter myself that the gauntlet you will run contains a rich assortment of the unexpected. It will be particularly interesting, Mister Bond, that a man of your physical qualities is to be my first competitor. It will be most interesting to observe how far you get down the course I have devised. You should put up a worthy target figure for future runners. I have high expectations of you. You should go far, but when, as is inevitable, you have finally failed at an obstacle, your body will be recovered and I shall most meticulously examine the physical state of your remains. The data will be recorded. You will be the first dot on a graph. Something of an honour, is it not, Mister Bond?'

Bond said nothing. What the hell did all this mean? What could this test consist of? Would it be possible to survive it? Could he conceivably escape from it and get to the girl before it was too late, even if it was only to kill her and save her from her torture? Silently Bond gathered his reserves of courage, steeling his mind against the fear of the unknown that already had him by the throat, focusing his whole will on survival. Somehow, above all else, he must cling to his weapons.

Doctor No rose and stepped away from his chair. He walked slowly to the door and turned. The menacing black holes looked back at Bond from just below the lintel of the door. The head was inclined a fraction. The purple lips creased back. 'Run a good race for me, Mister Bond. My thoughts, as they say, will be with you.'

Doctor No turned away and the door closed softly behind the long thin gunmetal back.

CHAPTER 17

The Long Scream

There was a man on the lift. The doors were open, waiting. James Bond, his arms still locked to his sides, was marched in. Now the dining-room would be empty. How soon would the guards go back, start clearing away the dinner, notice the missing things? The doors hissed shut. The liftman stood in front of the buttons so that Bond could not see which he had pressed. They were going up. Bond tried to estimate the distance. The lift sighed to a stop. The time seemed rather less than when he had come down with the girl. The doors opened on to an uncarpeted corridor with rough grey paint on the stone walls. It ran about twenty yards straight ahead.

'Hold it, Joe,' said Bond's guard to the liftman. 'Be right with you.'

Bond was marched down the corridor past doors numbered with letters of the alphabet. There was a faint hum of machinery in the air and behind one door Bond thought he could catch the crackle of radio static. It sounded as if they might be in the engine-room of the

mountain. They came to the end door. It was marked
with a black Q. It was ajar and the guard pushed Bond
into the door so that it swung open. Through the door
was a grey painted stone cell about fifteen feet square.
There was nothing in it except a wooden chair on which
lay, laundered and, neatly folded, Bond's black canvas
jeans and his blue shirt.

The guard let go of Bond's arms. Bond turned and
looked into the broad yellow face below the crinkly
hair. There was a hint of curiosity and pleasure in the
liquid brown eyes. The man stood holding the door
handle. He said, 'Well, this is it, bud. You're at the
starting gate. You can either sit here and rot or find
your way out on to the course. Happy landings.'

Bond thought it was just worth trying. He glanced
past the guard to where the liftman was standing beside
his open doors, watching them. He said softly, 'How
would you like to earn ten thousand dollars, guaran-
teed, and a ticket to anywhere in the world?' He
watched the man's face. The mouth spread in a wide
grin to show brownish teeth worn to uneven points by
years of chewing sugar cane.

'Thanks, Mister. I'd rather stay alive.' The man made
to close the door. Bond whispered urgently, 'We could
get out of here together.'

The thick lips sneered. The man said, 'Shove it!' The
door shut with a solid click.

Bond shrugged his shoulders. He gave the door a cur-
sory glance. It was made of metal and there was no
handle on the inside. Bond didn't waste his shoulder on
it. He went to the chair and sat down on the neat pile of
his clothes and looked round the cell. The walls were entirely naked except for a ventilation grille of thick wire
in one corner just below the ceiling. It was wider than
his shoulders. It was obviously the way out into the
assault course. The only other break in the walls was a
thick glass porthole, no bigger than Bond's head, just
above the door. Light from the corridor filtered through
it into the cell. There was nothing else. It was no good
wasting any more time. It would now be about ten-

thirty. Outside, somewhere on the slope of the mountain, the girl would already be lying, waiting for the rattle of claws on the grey coral. Bond clenched his teeth at the thought of the pale body spreadeagled out there under the stars. Abruptly he stood up. What the hell was he doing sitting still. Whatever lay on the other side of the wire grille, it was time to go.

Bond took out his knife and the lighter and threw off the kimono. He dressed in the trousers and shirt and stowed the lighter in his hip pocket. He tried the edge of the knife with his thumb. It was very sharp. It would be better still if he could get a point on it. He knelt on the floor and began whittling the rounded end on the stone. After a precious quarter of an hour he was satisfied. It was no stiletto, but it would serve to stab as well as cut. Bond put the knife between his teeth and set the chair below the grille and climbed on to it. The grille! Assuming he could tear it off its hinges, the frame of quarter-inch wire might straighten into a spear. That would make a third weapon. Bond reached up with crooked fingers.

The next thing he knew was a searing pain up his arm and the crack of his head hitting the stone floor. He lay, stunned, with only the memory of a blue flash and the hiss and crackle of electricity to tell him what had hit him.

Bond got to his knees and stayed there. He bent his head down and shook it slowly from side to side like a wounded animal. He noticed a smell of burning flesh. He lifted his right hand up to his eyes. There was the red smear of an open burn across the inside of his fingers. Seeing it brought the pain. Bond spat out a four-letter word. Slowly he got to his feet. He squinted up at the wire grille as if it might strike at him again, like a snake. Grimly he set the chair upright against the wall. He picked up his knife and cut a strip off the discarded kimono and tied it firmly across his fingers. Then he climbed up again on to the chair and looked at the grille. He was meant to get through it. The shock had been to soften him up—a taste of pain to come. Surely he had fused the blasted thing. Surely they would have switched off the current. He looked at it only for an instant, then the fingers of his left hand crooked and went straight up to the impersonal wire mesh. His fingers went through the wire rim and gripped.

Nothing! Nothing at all—just wire. Bond grunted. He felt his nerves slacken. He tugged at the wire. It gave an inch. He tugged again and it came away in his hand and dangled down from two strands of copper flex and got down from the chair. Yes, there was a join in the frame. He set to work unravelling the mesh. Then using the chair as a hammer, he straightened the heavy wire.

After ten minutes, Bond had a crooked spear about four feet long. One end, where it had originally been cut by the pliers, was jagged. It would not pierce a man's clothes, but it would be good enough for the face and neck. By using all his strength and the crack at the bottom of the metal door, Bond turned the blunt end into a clumsy crook. He measured the wire against his leg. It was too long. He bent it double and slipped the spear down a trouser leg. Now it hung from his waistband to just above the knee. He went back to the chair and climbed up again and reached, nervously, for the edge of the ventilator shaft. There was no shock. Bond heaved up and through the opening and lay on his stomach looking along the shaft.

The shaft was about four inches wider than Bond's shoulders. It was circular and of polished metal. Bond reached for his lighter, blessing the inspiration that had made him take it, and flicked it on. Yes, zinc sheeting that looked new. The shaft stretched straight ahead, featureless except for the ridges where the sections of pipe joined. Bond put the lighter back in his pocket and snaked forward.

It was easy going. Cool air from the ventilating system blew strongly in Bond's face. The air held no smell of the sea—it was the canned stuff that comes from an air-conditioning plant. Doctor No must have adapted one of the shafts to his purpose. What hazards had he built into it to test out his victims? They would be ingenious and painful—designed to reduce the resistance of the victim. At the winning post, so to speak, there would be the *coup de grâce*—if the victim ever got that far. It would be something conclusive, something from which there would be no escape, for there would be no prizes in this race except oblivion—an oblivion, thought Bond, he might be glad to win. Unless of course Doctor No had been just a bit too clever. Unless he had underestimated the will to survive. That, thought Bond, was his only hope—to try to survive the intervening hazards, to get through at least to the last ditch.

There was a faint luminosity ahead. Bond approached it carefully, his senses questing in front of him like antennae. It grew brighter. It was the glint of light against the end of the lateral shaft. He went on until his head touched the metal. He twisted over on his back. Straight above him, at the top of fifty yards or so of vertical shaft, was a steady glimmer. It was like looking up a long gun barrel. Bond inched round the square bend and stood upright. So he was supposed to climb straight up this shining tube of metal without a foothold! Was it possible? Bond expanded his shoulders. Yes, they gripped the sides. His feet could also get a temporary purchase, though they would slip except where the ridges at the joints gave him an ounce of upward leverage. Bond shrugged his shoulders and kicked off his shoes. It was no good arguing. He would just have to try.

Six inches at a time, Bond's body began to worm up the shaft—expand shoulders to grip the sides, lift feet, lock knees, force the feet outwards against the metal and, as the feet slipped downwards with his weight, contract shoulders and raise them a few inches higher. Do it again, and again and again and again. Stop at each tiny bulge where the sections joined and use the millimetre of extra support to get some breath and measure the next lap. Otherwise don't look up, think only of the inches of metal that have to be conquered one by one. Don't worry about the glimmer of light that never grows brighter or nearer. Don't worry about losing your grip and falling to smash your ankles at the bottom of the shaft. Don't worry about cramp. Don't worry about your screaming muscles or the swelling bruises on your shoulders and the sides of your feet. Just take the silver inches as they come, one by one, and conquer them.

But then the feet began to sweat and slip. Twice Bond lost a yard before his shoulders, scalding with the friction, could put on the brake. Finally he had to stop altogether to let his sweat dry in the downward draught of air. He waited for a full ten minutes, staring at his faint reflection in the polished metal, the face split in half by the knife between the teeth. Still he refused to look up to see how much more there was. It might be too much to bear. Carefully Bond wiped each foot against a trouser-leg and began again.

Now half Bond's mind was dreaming while the other half fought the battle. He wasn't even conscious of the strengthening breeze or the slowly brightening light. He saw himself as a wounded caterpillar crawling up a waste pipe towards the plug-hole of a bath. What would he see when he got through the plug-hole? A naked girl drying herself? A man shaving? Sunlight streaming through an open window into an empty bathroom?

Bond's head bumped against something. The plug was in the plug-hole! The shock of disappointment made him slip a yard before his shoulders got a fresh grip. Then he realized. He was at the top! Now he noticed the bright light and the strong wind. Feverishly, but with a more desperate care, he heaved up again until his head touched. The wind was coming into his left ear. Cautiously he turned his head. It was another lateral shaft. Above him light was shining through a thick porthole. All he had to do was inch himself round and grip the edge of the new shaft and somehow gather enough strength to heave himself in. Then he would be able to lie down.

With an extra delicacy, born of panic that something might now go wrong, that he might make a mistake and plummet back down the shaft to land in a crackle of bone, Bond, his breath steaming against the metal, carried out the manoeuvre and, with his last ounce of strength, jackknifed into the opening and crumpled full length on his face.

Later—how much later?—Bond's eyes opened and his body stirred. The cold had woken him from the fringe of total unconsciousness into which his body had plunged. Painfully he rolled over on his back, his feet and shoulders screaming at him, and lay gathering his wits and summoning more strength. He had no idea what time it was or whereabouts he was inside the mountain. He lifted his head and looked back at the porthole above the yawning tube out of which he had come. The light was yellowish and the glass looked thick. He remembered the porthole in Room Q. There had been nothing breakable about that one, nor, he guessed, would there be here.

Suddenly, behind the glass, he saw movement. As he watched, a pair of eyes materialized from behind the electric light bulb. They stopped and looked at him, the bulb making a yellow glass nose between them. They gazed incuriously at him and then they were gone. Bond's lips snarled back from his teeth. So his progress was going to be observed, reported back to Doctor No!

Bond said out loud, viciously, '—— them all,' and turned sullenly back on his stomach. He raised his head and looked forward. The tunnel shimmered away into blackness. Come on! No good hanging about. He picked up his knife and put it back between his teeth and winced his way forward.

Soon there was no more light. Bond stopped from time to time and used the lighter, but there was nothing but blackness ahead. The air began to get warmer in the shaft, and, perhaps fifty yards further, definitely hot. There was the smell of heat in the air, metallic heat. Bond began to sweat. Soon his body was soaked and he had to pause every few minutes to wipe his eyes. There came a right hand turn in the shaft. Round it the metal of the big tube was hot against his skin. The smell of heat was very strong. There came another right-angled turn. As soon as Bond's head got round he quickly pulled out his lighter and lit it and then snaked back and lay panting. Bitterly he examined the new hazard, probing it, cursing it. His light had flickered on discoloured, oyster-hued zinc. The next hazard was to be heat!

Bond groaned aloud. How could his bruised flesh stand up to that? How could he protect his skin from the metal? But there wasn't anything he could do about it. He could either go back, or stay where he was, or go on. There was no other decision to make, no other shift or excuse. There was one, and only one, grain of consolation. This would not be heat that would kill, only maim. This would not be the final killing ground—only one more test of how much he could take.

Bond thought of the girl and of what she was going through. Oh well. Get on with it. Now, let's see. . . .

Bond took his knife and cut off the whole front of his shirt and sliced it into strips. The only hope was to put some wrapping round the parts of his body that would have to bear the brunt—his hands and his feet. His knees and elbows would have to get along with their single covering of cotton fabric. Wearily he set to work, cursing softly.

Now he was ready. One, two, three . . .

Bond turned the corner and forged forward into the heat stench.

Keep your naked stomach off the ground! Contract your shoulders! Hands, knees, toes; hands, knees, toes. Faster, faster! Keep going fast so that each touch on the ground is quickly taken over by the next.

The knees were getting it worst, taking the bulk of Bond's weight. Now the padded hands were beginning to smoulder. There was a spark, and another one, and then a worm of red as the sparks began to run. The smoke from the stuff smarted in Bond's sweating eyes. God, he couldn't do any more! There was no air. His lungs were bursting. Now his two hands shed sparks as he thrust them forward. The stuff must be nearly gone. Then the flesh would burn. Bond lurched and his bruised shoulder hit the metal. He screamed. He went on screaming, regularly, with each contact of hand or knee or toes. Now he was finished. Now it was the end. Now he would fall flat and slowly fry to death. No! He must drive on, screaming, until his flesh was burned to the bone. The skin must have already gone from his knees. In a moment the balls of his hands would meet the metal. Only the sweat running down his arms could be keeping the pads of stuff damp. Scream, scream, scream! It helps the pain. It tells you you're alive. Go on! Go on! It can't be much longer. This isn't where you're supposed to die. You are still alive. Don't give up! You can't!

Bond's right hand hit something that gave before it. There was a stream of ice-cold air. His other hand hit, then his head. There was a tinny noise. Bond felt the lower edge of an asbestos baffle scrape down his back. He was through. He heard the baffle bang shut. His hands came up against solid wall. They quested to left and right. It was a right-angled bend. His body followed blindly round the corner. The cool air felt like daggers in his lungs. Gingerly he laid his fingers down on the metal. It was cold! With a groan Bond fell on his face and lay still.

Sometime later the pain revived him. Bond turned sluggishly over on his back. Vaguely he noticed the lighted porthole above him. Vaguely he took in the eyes gazing down on him. Then he let the black waves take him away again.

Slowly, in the darkness, the blisters formed across the skin and the bruised feet and shoulders stiffened. The sweat dried on the body and then on the rags of clothing, and the cool air soaked down into the overheated lungs and began its insidious work. But the heart beat on, strongly and regularly inside the tortured envelope, and the healing sorceries of oxygen and rest pumped life back into the arteries and veins and recharged the nerves.

Years later, Bond awoke. He stirred. As his eyes opened and met the other pair, inches away behind the glass, pain took him and shook him like a rat. He waited for the shock to die. He tried again, and then again, until he had measured the strength of his adversary. Then Bond, to hide himself away from the witness, turned over on his stomach and took the full blast of it. Again he waited, exploring his body for its reactions, testing the strength of the resolve that was left in the batteries. How much more could he take now? Bond's lips drew back from his teeth and he snarled into the darkness. It was an animal sound. He had come to the end of his human reactions to pain and adversity. Doctor No had got him cornered. But there were animal reserves of desperation left and, in a strong animal, those reserves are deep.

Slowly, agonizingly, Bond snaked a few yards away from the eyes and then reached for his lighter and lit it. Ahead there was only the black full moon, the yawning circular mouth that led into the stomach of death. Bond put back the lighter. He took a deep breath and got to his hands and knees. The pain was no greater, only different. Slowly, stiffly, he winced forward.

The cotton fabric at Bond's knees and elbows had burned away. Numbly his mind registered the moisture as his blisters burst against the cool metal. As he moved, he flexed his fingers and toes, testing the pain. Slowly he got the measure of what he could do, what hurt most. This pain is supportable, he argued to himself. If I had been in an aeroplane crash, they would only diagnose superficial contusions and burns. I would be out of hospital in a few days. There's nothing wrong with me. I'm a survivor from the crash. It hurts, but it's nothing. Think of the bits and pieces of the other passengers. Be thankful. Put it out of your mind. But, nagging behind these reflections, was the knowledge that he had not yet had the crash—that he was still on his way towards it, his resistance, his effectiveness reduced. When would it come? What shape would it take? How much more was he to be softened up before he reached the killing ground?

Ahead in the darkness the tiny red pin-points might

have been an hallucination, specks before the eyes as a result of exhaustion. Bond stopped and screwed up his eyes. He shook his head. No, they were still there. Slowly he snaked closer. Now they were moving. Bond stopped again. He listened. Above the quiet thumping of his heart there was a soft, delicate rustling. The pin-points had increased in number. Now there were twenty or thirty, shifting to and fro, some quickly, some slowly, all over the circle of blackness ahead. Bond reached for his lighter. He held his breath as he lit the little yellow flame. The red pin-points went out. Instead, a yard ahead of him, very narrow mesh wire, almost as fine as muslin, blocked the shaft.

Bond inched forward, the lighter held before him. It was some sort of a cage with small things living in it. He could hear them scuttling back, away from the light. A foot away from the mesh he dowsed the light and waited for his eyes to get used to the dark. As he waited, listening, he could hear the tiny scuttling back towards him, and gradually the forest of red pin-points gathered again, peering at him through the mesh.

What was it? Bond listened to the pounding of his heart. Snakes? Scorpions? Centipedes?

Carefully he brought his eyes close up to the little glowing forest. He inched the lighter up beside his face and suddenly pressed the lever. He caught a glimpse of tiny claws hooked through the mesh and of dozens of thick furry feet and of furry sacklike stomachs topped by big insect heads that seemed to be covered with eyes. The things plopped hurriedly off the wire on to the tin and scurried back and huddled in a grey-brown furry mass at the end of the cage.

Bond squinted through the mesh, moving the light back and forward. Then he dowsed the light, to save fuel, and let the breath come through his teeth in a quiet sigh.

They were spiders, giant tarantulas, three or four inches long. There were twenty of them in the cage. And somehow he had to get past them.

Bond lay and rested and thought while the red eyes

gathered again in front of his face.

How deadly were these things? How much of the tales about them was myth? They could certainly kill animals, but how mortal to men were these giant spiders with the long soft friendly fur of a borzoi? Bond shuddered. He remembered the centipede. The touch of the tarantulas would be much softer. They would be like tiny teddy bears' paws against one's skin—until they bit and emptied their poison sacs into you.

But again, would this be Doctor No's killing ground? A bite or two perhaps—to send one into a delirium of pain. The horror of having to burst through the mesh in the darkness—Doctor No would not have reckoned with Bond's lighter—and squash through the forest of eyes, crushing some soft bodies, but feeling the jaws of the others lance home. And then more bites from the ones that had caught in the clothing. And then the creeping agony of the poison. That would have been the way Doctor No's mind would have worked—to send one screaming on one's way. To what? To the final fence?

But Bond had the lighter and the knife and the wire spear. All he needed was the nerve, and infinite, infinite precision.

Bond softly opened the jaws of the lighter and pulled the wick out an inch with his thumb and fingernail to give a bigger flame. He lit it and, as the spiders scuttled back, he pierced the thin wire mesh with his knife. He made a hole near the frame and cut down sideways and round. Then he seized the flap of wire and wrenched it out of the frame. It tore like stiff calico and came away in one piece. He put the knife back between his teeth and snaked through the opening. The spiders cowered before the flame of the lighter and crowded back on top of each other. Bond slid the wire spear out of his trousers and jabbed the blunt, doubled wire into the middle of them. He jabbed again and again, fiercely pulping the bodies. When some of the spiders tried to escape towards him he waved the light at them and smashed the fugitives one by one. Now the living spiders were attacking the dead and wounded and all Bond had to do was bash and bash into the writhing, sickening mess of blood and fur.

Slowly all movement slackened and then ceased. Were they all dead? Were some shamming? The flame of the lighter was beginning to die. He would have to chance it. Bond reached forward and shovelled the dead mess to one side. Then he took his knife from between his teeth and reached out and slashed open the second curtain of wire, bending the flap down over the heap of pulped bodies. The light flickered and became a red glow. Bond gathered himself and shot his body over the bloody pile of corpses and through the jagged frame.

He had no idea what bits of metal he touched or whether he had put his knee or his foot among the spiders. All he knew was that he had got through. He heaved himself yards on along the shaft and stopped to gather his breath and his nerve.

Above him a dim light came on. Bond squinted sideways and upwards, knowing what he would see. The slanting yellow eyes behind the thick glass looked keenly down at him. Slowly, behind the bulb, the head moved from side to side. The eyelids dropped in mock pity. A closed fist, the thumb pointing downwards in farewell and dismissal, inserted itself between the bulb and the glass. Then it was withdrawn. The light went out. Bond turned his face back to the floor of the shaft and rested his forehead on the cool metal. The gesture said that he was coming into the last lap, that the observers had finished with him until they came for his remains. It took an extra ounce of heart out of Bond that there had been no gesture of praise, however small, that he had managed to survive so far. These Chigroes hated him. They only wanted him to die, and as miserably as possible.

Bond's teeth ground softly together. He thought of the girl and the thought gave him strength. He wasn't dead yet. Damn it, he wouldn't die! Not until the heart was torn from his body.

Bond tensed his muscles. It was time to go. With extra care he put his weapons back in their places and painfully began to drag himself on into the blackness.

The shaft was beginning to slope gently downwards. It made the going easier. Soon the slope grew steeper so that Bond could almost slide along under the momentum of his weight. It was a blessed relief not to have to make the effort with his muscles. There was a glimmer of grey light ahead, nothing more than a lessening of the darkness, but it was a change. The quality of the air seemed to be different. There was a new, fresh smell to it. What was it? The sea?

Suddenly Bond realized that he was slipping down the shaft. He opened his shoulders and spread his feet to slow himself. It hurt and the braking effect was small. Now the shaft was widening. He could no longer get a grip! He was going faster and faster. A bend was just ahead. And it was a bend downwards!

Bond's body crashed into the bend and round it. Christ, he was diving head downwards! Desperately Bond spread his feet and hands. The metal flayed his skin. He was out of control, diving, diving down a gun barrel. Far blow there was a circle of grey light. The open air? The sea? The light was tearing up at him. He fought for breath. Stay alive, you fool! Stay alive!

Head first, Bond's body shot out of the shaft and fell through the air, slowly, slowly, down towards the gunmetal sea that waited for him a hundred feet below.

CHAPTER 18

Killing Ground

Bond's body shattered the mirror of the dawn sea like a bomb.

As he had hurtled down the silver shaft towards the widening disc of light, instinct had told him to get his knife from between his teeth, to get his hands forward to break his fall, and to keep his head down and his body rigid. And, at the last fraction of a second when he glimpsed the up-rushing sea, he had managed to take a gulp of breath. So Bond hit the water in the semblance of a dive, his outstretched clenched fists cleaving a hole for his skull and shoulders, and though, by the time he had shot twenty feet below the surface, he had lost consciousness, the forty-mile-an-hour impact with the water failed to smash him.

Slowly the body rose to the surface and lay, head down, softly rocking in the ripples of the dive. The water-choked lungs somehow contrived to send a last message to the brain. The legs and arms thrashed clumsily. The head turned up, water pouring from its open mouth. It sank. Again the legs jerked, instinctively trying to get the body upright in the water. This time, coughing horribly, the head jerked above the surface and stayed there. The arms and legs began to move feebly, paddling like a dog, and, through the red and black curtain, the bloodshot eyes saw the lifeline and told the sluggish brain to make for it.

The killing ground was a narrow deep water inlet at the base of the towering cliff. The lifeline towards which Bond struggled, hampered by the clumsy spear in his trouser-leg, was a strong wire fence, stretched from the rock walls of the inlet and caging it off from the open sea. The two-feet squares of thick wire were suspended from a cable six feet above the surface and disappeared, algae encrusted, into the depths.

Bond got to the wire and hung, crucified. For fifteen minutes he stayed like that, his body occasionally racked with vomiting, until he felt strong enough to turn his head and see where he was. Blearily his eyes took in the towering cliffs above him and the narrow vee of softly breathing water. The place was in deep grey shadow, cut off from the dawn by the mountain, but out at sea there was the pearly iridescence of first light that meant that for the rest of the world the day was dawning. Here it was dark and gloomy and brooding.

Sluggishly Bond's mind puzzled over the wire fence. What was its purpose, closing off this dark cleft of sea? Was it to keep things out, or keep them in? Bond gazed vaguely down into the black depths around him. The wire strands vanished into nothingness below his clinging feet. There were small fish round his legs below the waist. What were they doing? They seemed to be feeding, darting in towards him and then backing away, catching at black strands. Strands of what? Of cotton from his rags? Bond shook his head to clear it. He looked again. No, they were feeding off his blood.

Bond shivered. Yes, blood was seeping off his body, off the torn shoulders, the knees, the feet, into the water. Now for the first time he felt the pain of the sea water on his sores and burns. The pain revived him, quickened his mind. If these small fish liked it, what

about barracuda and shark? Was that what the wire
fence was for, to keep man-eating fish from escaping to
sea? They why hadn't they been after him already? To
hell with it! The first thing was to crawl up the wire and
get over to the other side. To put the fence between him
and whatever lived in this black aquarium.

Weakly, foothold by foothold, Bond climbed up the
wire and over the top and down again to where he could
rest well above the water. He hooked the thick cable
under his arms and hung, a bit of washing on a line, and
gazed vaguely down at the fish that still fed from the
blood that dripped off his feet.

Now there was nothing much left of Bond, not many
reserves. The last dive down the tube, the crash of impact and the half-death from drowning had squeezed
him like a sponge. He was on the verge of surrender, on
the verge of giving one small sigh and then slipping back
into the soft arms of the water. How beautiful it would
be to give in at last and rest—to feel the sea softly take
him to its bed and turn out the light.

It was the explosive flight of the fish from their
feeding ground that shook Bond out of his death-
dreaming. Something had moved far below the surface.
There was a distant shimmer. Something was coming
slowly up on the landward side of the fence.

Bond's body tautened. His hanging jaw slowly shut
and the slackness cleared from his eyes. With the electric
shock of danger, life flooded back into him, driving out
the lethargy, pumping back the will to survive.

Bond uncramped the fingers that, a long time ago, his
brain had ordered not to lose his knife. He flexed his
fingers and took a fresh grip of the silver-plated handle.
He reached down and touched the crook of the wire
spear that still hung inside his trouser-leg. He shook his
head sharply and focused his eyes. Now what?

Below him the water quivered. Something was stirring
in the depths, something huge. A great length of
luminescent greyness showed, poised far down in the
darkness. Something snaked up from it, a whiplash as
thick as Bond's arm. The tip of the thong was swollen to

a narrow oval, with regular budlike markings. It swirled through the water where the fish had been and was withdrawn. Now there was nothing but the huge grey shadow. What was it doing? Was it . . . ? Was it tasting the blood?

As if in answer, two eyes as big as footballs slowly swam up and into Bond's vision. They stopped, twenty feet below his own, and stared up through the quiet water at his face.

Bond's skin crawled on his back. Softly, wearily, his mouth uttered one bitter four-lettered word. So this was the last surprise of Doctor No, the end of the race!

Bond stared down, half hypnotized, into the wavering pools of eyes far below. So this was the giant squid, the mythical kraken that could pull ships beneath the waves, the fifty-foot-long monster that battled with whales, that weighed a ton or more. What else did he know about them? That they had two long seizing tentacles and ten holding ones. That they had a huge blunt beak beneath eyes that were the only fishes' eyes that worked on the camera principle, like a man's. That their brains were efficient, that they could shoot backwards through the water at thirty knots, by jet-propulsion. That explosive harpoons burst in their jellied mantle without damaging them. That . . . but the bulging black and white targets of the eyes were rising up towards him. The surface of the water shivered. Now Bond could see the forest of tentacles that flowered out of the face of the thing. They were weaving in front of the eyes like a bunch of thick snakes. Bond could see the dots of the suckers on their undersides. Behind the head, the great flap of the mantle softly opened and closed, and behind that the jellied sheen of the body disappeared into the depths. God, the thing was as big as a railway engine!

Softly, discreetly, Bond snaked his feet and then his arms through the squares in the wire, lacing himself into them, anchoring himself so that the tentacles would have either to tear him to bits or wrench down the wire barrier with him. He squinted to right and left. Either way it was twenty yards along the wire to the land. And movement, even if he was capable of it, would be fatal. He must stay dead quiet and pray that the thing would lose interest. If it didn't . . . Softly Bond's fingers clenched on the puny knife.

The eyes watched him, coldly, patiently. Delicately, like the questing trunk of an elephant, one of the long seizing tentacles broke the surface and palped its way up the wire towards his leg. It reached his foot. Bond felt the hard kiss of the suckers. He didn't move. He dared not reach down and lose the grip of his arms through the wire. Softly the suckers tugged, testing the amount of yield. It was not enough. Like a huge slimy caterpillar, the tentacle walked slowly on up the leg. It got to the bloody, blistered kneecap and stopped there, interested. Bond's teeth gritted with the pain. He could imagine the message going back down the thick tentacle to the brain: Yes, it's good to eat! And the brain signalling back: then get it! Bring it to me!

The suckers walked on up the thigh. The tip of the tentacle was pointed, then it splayed out so that it almost covered the width of Bond's thigh and then tapered off to a wrist. That was Bond's target. He would just have to take the pain and the horror and wait for the wrist to come within range.

A breeze, the first soft breeze of early morning, whispered across the metal surface of the inlet. It raised small waves that slapped gently against the sheer walls of the cliff. A wedge of cormorants took off from the guanera, five hundred feet above the inlet, and, cackling softly, made out to sea. As they swept over, the noise that had disturbed them reached Bond—the triple blast of a ship's siren that means it is ready to take on cargo. It came from Bond's left. The jetty must be round the corner from the northern arm of the inlet. The tanker from Antwerp had come in. Antwerp! Part of the world outside—the world that was a million miles away, out of Bond's reach—surely out of his reach for ever. Just round that corner, men would be in the galley, having breakfast. The radio would be playing. There would be

the sizzle of bacon and eggs, the smell of coffee . . .
breakfast cooking . . .

The suckers were at his hip. Bond could see into the
horny cups. A stagnant sea smell reached him as the
hand slowly undulated upwards. How tough was the
mottled grey-brown jelly behind the hand? Should he
stab? No, it must be a quick hard slash, straight across,
like cutting a rope. Never mind about cutting into his
own skin.

Now! Bond took a quick glance into the two football
eyes, so patient, so incurious. As he did so the other
seizing arm broke the surface and shot straight up at his
face. Bond jerked back and the hand curled into a fist
round the wire in front of his eyes. In a second it would
shift to an arm or shoulder and he would be finished.
Now!

The first hand was on his ribs. Almost without taking
aim, Bond's knife-hand slashed down and across. He
felt the blade bite into the puddingy flesh and then the
knife was almost torn from his grips as the wounded
tentacle whipped back into the water. For a moment the
sea boiled around him. Now the other hand let go the
wire and slapped across his stomach. The pointed hand
stuck like a leech, all the power of the suckers furiously
applied. Bond screamed as the suckers bit into his flesh.
He slashed madly, again and again. God, his stomach
was being torn out! The wire shook with the struggle.
Below him the water boiled and foamed. He would have
to give in. One more stab, this time into the back of the
hand. It worked! The hand jerked free and snaked
down and away leaving twenty red circles, edged with
blood, across his skin.

Bond had no time to worry about them. Now the
head of the squid had broken the surface and the sea
was being thrashed into foam by the great heaving
mantle round it. The eyes were glaring up at him, redly,
venomously, and the forest of feeding arms was at his
feet and legs, tearing the cotton fabric away and flailing
back. Bond was being pulled down, inch by inch. The
wire was biting into his armpits. He could even feel his

spine being stretched. If he held on he would be torn in half. Now the eyes and the great triangular beak were right out of the water and the beak was reaching up for his feet. There was one hope, only one!

Bond thrust his knife between his teeth and his hand dived for the crook of the wire spear. He tore it out, got it between his two hands and wrenched the doubled wire almost straight. He would have to let go with one arm to stoop and get within range. If he missed, he would be torn to shreds on the fence.

Now, before he died of the pain! Now, now!

Bond let his whole body slip down the ladder of wire and lunged through and down with all his force.

He caught a glimpse of the tip of his spear lancing into the centre of a black eyeball and then the whole sea erupted up at him in a fountain of blackness and he fell and hung upside down by the knees, his head an inch from the surface of the water.

What had happened? Had he gone blind? He could see nothing. His eyes were stinging and there was a horrible fish taste in his mouth. But he could feel the wire cutting into the tendons behind his knees. So he must be alive! Dazedly Bond let go the spear from his trailing hand and reached up and felt for the nearest strand of wire. He got a hold and reached up his other hand and slowly, agonizingly, pulled himself up so that he was sitting in the fence. Streaks of light came into his eyes. He wiped a hand across his face. Now he could see. He gazed at his hand. It was black and sticky. He looked down at his body. It was covered with black slime, and blackness stained the sea for twenty yards around. Then Bond realized. The wounded squid had emptied its ink sac at him.

But where was the squid? Would it come back? Bond searched the sea. Nothing, nothing but the spreading stain of black. Not a movement. Not a ripple. Then don't wait! Get away from here! Get away quick! Wildly Bond looked to right and left. Left was towards the ship, but also towards Doctor No. But right was towards nothing. To build the wire fence the men must have come from the left, from the direction of the jetty. There would be some sort of a path. Bond reached for the top cable and frantically began to edge along the swaying fence towards the rocky headland twenty yards away.

The stinking, bleeding, black scarecrow moved its arms and legs quite automatically. The thinking, feeling apparatus of Bond was no longer part of his body. It moved alongside his body, or floated above it, keeping enough contact to pull the strings that made the puppet work. Bond was like a cut worm, the two halves of which continue to jerk forward although life has gone and been replaced by the mock life of nervous impulses. Only, with Bond, the two halves were not yet dead. Life was only in abeyance in them. All he needed was an ounce of hope, an ounce of reassurance that it was still worth while trying to stay alive.

Bond got to the rock face. Slowly he let himself down to the bottom rung of wire. He gazed vaguely at the softly heaving sheen of water. It was black, impenetrable, as deep as the rest. Should he chance it? He must! He could do nothing until he had washed off the caking slime and blood, the horrible stale fish-smell. Moodily, fatalistically, he took off the rags of his shirt and trousers and hung them on the wire. He looked down at his brown and white body, striped and pockmarked with red. On an instinct he felt his pulse. It was slow but regular. The steady thump of life revived his spirits. What the hell was he worrying about? He was alive. The wounds and bruises on his body were nothing—absolutely nothing. They looked ugly, but nothing was broken. Inside the torn envelope, the machine was quietly, solidly ticking over. Superficial cuts and abrasions, bloody memories, deathly exhaustion—these were hurts that an accident ward would sneer at. Get on, you bastard! Get moving! Clean yourself and wake up. Count your blessings. Think of the girl. Think of the man you've somehow got to find and kill. Hang on to life like you've hung on to the knife between your teeth. Stop being sorry for yourself. To hell with what happened just now. Get down into the water and wash!

Ten minutes later, Bond, his wet rags clinging to his scrubbed, stinging body and his hair slicked back out of his eyes, climbed over the top of the headland.

Yes, it was as he had guessed. A narrow rocky track, made by the feet of the workers, led down the other side and round the bulge of the cliff.

From close by came various sounds and echoes. A crane was working. He could hear the changing beat of its engine. There were iron ship-noises and the sound of water splashing into the sea from a bilge pump.

Bond looked up at the sky. It was pale blue. Clouds tinged with golden pink were trailing away towards the horizon. Far above him the cormorants were wheeling round the guanera. Soon they would be going off to feed. Perhaps even now they were watching the scout groups far out at sea locating the fish. It would be about six o'clock, the dawn of a beautiful day.

Bond, leaving drops of blood behind him, picked his way carefully down the track and along the bottom of the shadowed cliff. Round the bend, the track filtered through a maze of giant, tumbled boulders. The noises grew louder. Bond crept softly forward, watching his foot for loose stones. A voice called out, startlingly close, 'Okay to go?' There was a distant answer: 'Okay.' The crane engine accelerated. A few more yards. One more boulder. And another. Now!

Bond flattened himself against the rock and warily inched his head round the corner.

CHAPTER 19

A Shower of Death

Bond took one long comprehensive look and pulled back.

He leant against the cool face of rock and waited for his breathing to get back to normal. He lifted his knife close up to his eyes and carefully examined the blade. Satisfied, he slipped it behind him and down the waistband of his trousers up against his spine. There it would be handy but protected from hitting against anything. He wondered about the lighter. He took it out of his hip pocket. As a hunk of metal it might be useful, but it wouldn't light any more and it might scrape against the rock. He put it down on the ground away from his feet.

Then Bond sat down and meticulously went over the photograph that was in his brain.

Round the corner, not more than ten yards away, was the crane. There was no back to the cabin. Inside it a man sat at the controls. It was the Chinese negro boss, the driver of the marsh buggy. In front of him the jetty ran twenty yards out into the sea and ended in a T. An aged tanker of around ten thousand tons deadweight was secured alongside the top of the T. It stood well out of the water, its decks perhaps twelve feet above the quay. The tanker was called *Blanche,* and the *Ant* of Antwerp showed at her stern. There was no sign of life on board except one figure lolling at the wheel in the enclosed bridge. The rest of the crew would be below, battened away from the guano dust. From just to the right of the crane, an overhead conveyor-belt in a corrugated-iron housing ran out from the cliff-face. It was carried on high stanchions above the jetty and stopped just short of the hold of the tanker. Its mouth ended in a huge canvas sock, perhaps six feet in diameter. The purpose of the crane was to lift the wire-framed mouth of the sock so that it hung directly over the hold of the tanker and to move it to right or left to give even distribution. From out of the mouth of the sock, in a solid downward jet, the scrambled-egg-coloured guano dust was pouring into the hold of the tanker at a rate of tons a minute.

Below, on the jetty, to the left and to leeward of the drifting smoke of the guano dust, stood the tall, watchful figure of Doctor No.

That was all. The morning breeze feathered the deep-water anchorage, still half in shadow beneath the towering cliffs, the conveyor-belt thudded quietly on its rollers, the crane's engine chuffed rhythmically. There was no other sound, no other movement, no other life apart from the watch at the ship's wheel, the trusty working at the crane, and Doctor No, seeing that all went well. On the other side of the mountain men would be working, feeding the guano to the conveyor-belt that rumbled away through the bowels of the rock, but on this side no one was allowed and no one was necessary. Apart from aiming the canvas mouth of the conveyor, there was nothing else for anyone to do.

Bond sat and thought, measuring distances, guessing at angles, remembering exactly where the crane driver's hands and feet were on the levers and pedals. Slowly, a thin, hard smile broke across the haggard, sun-burned face. Yes! It was on! It could be done. But softly, gently, slowly! The prize was almost intolerably sweet.

Bond examined the soles of his feet and his hands. They would serve. They would have to serve. He reached back and felt the handle of the knife. Shifted it an inch. He stood up and took several slow deep breaths, ran his hands through his salt- and sweat-matted hair, rubbed them harshly up and down his face and then down the tattered sides of his black jeans. He gave a final flex to his fingers. He was ready.

Bond stepped up to the rock and inched an eye round. Nothing had changed. His guess at the distances had been right. The crane driver was watchful, absorbed. The neck above the open khaki shirt was naked, offered, waiting. Twenty yards away, Doctor No, also with his back to Bond, stood sentry over the thick rich cataract of whity-yellow dust. On the bridge, the watch was lighting a cigarette.

Bond looked along the ten yards of path that led past the back of the crane. He picked out the places he would put each foot. Then he came out from behind the rock and ran.

Bond ran to the right of the crane, to a point he had chosen where the lateral side of the cabin would hide him from the driver and the jetty. He got there and stopped, crouching, listening. The engine hurried on, the conveyor-belt rumbled steadily out of the mountain above and behind him. There was no change.

The two iron footholds at the back of the cabin, inches away from Bond's face, looked solid. Anyway the noise of the engine would drown small sounds. But he would have to be quick to yank the man's body out of the seat and get his own hands and feet on the controls. The single stroke of the knife would have to be mortal. Bond felt along his own collarbone, felt the soft triangle of skin beneath which the jugular pumped, remembered the angle of approach behind the man's back, reminded himself to force the blade and hold it in.

For a final second he listened, then he reached behind his back for the knife and went up the iron steps and into the cabin with the stealth and speed of a panther.

At the last moment there was no need to hurry. Bond stood behind the man's back, smelling him. He had time to raise his knife hand almost to the roof of the cabin, time to summon every ounce of strength, before he swept the blade down and into the square inch of smooth, brownish-yellow skin.

The man's hands and legs splayed away from the controls. His face strained back towards Bond. It seemed to Bond that there was a flash of recognition in the bulging eyes before the whites rolled upwards. Then a strangled noise came from the open mouth and the big body rolled sideways off its iron seat and crashed to the floor.

Bond's eyes didn't even follow it as far as the ground. He was already in the seat and reaching for the pedals and levers. Everything was out of control. The engine was running in neutral, the wire hawser was tearing off the drum, the tip of the crane was bending slowly forwards like a giraffe's neck, the canvas mouth of the conveyor-belt had wilted and was now pouring its column of dust between the jetty and the ship. Doctor No was staring upwards. His mouth was open. Perhaps he was shouting something.

Coolly, Bond reined the machine in, slowly easing the levers and pedals back to the angles at which the driver had been holding them. The engine accelerated, the gears bit and began to work again. The hawser slowed on the spinning drum and reversed, bringing the canvas mouth up and over the ship. The tip of the crane lifted and stopped. The scene was as before. Now!

Bond reached forward for the iron wheel which the driver had been handling when Bond had caught his first glimpse of him. Which way to turn it? Bond tried to the left. The tip of the crane veered slightly to the right. So be it. Bond spun the wheel to the right. Yes, by God, it was answering, moving across the sky, carrying the mouth of the conveyor with it.

Bond's eyes flashed to the jetty. Doctor No had moved. He had moved a few paces to a stanchion that Bond had missed. He had a telephone in his hand. He

was getting through to the other side of the mountain.
Bond could see his hand frantically jiggling the receiver
arm, trying to attract attention.

Bond whirled the director wheel. Christ, wouldn't it
turn any faster? In seconds Doctor No would get
through and it would be too late. Slowly the tip of the
crane arced across the sky. Now the mouth of the conveyor was spewing the dust column down over the side
of the ship. Now the yellow mound was marching
silently across the jetty. Five years, four, three, two!
Don't look round, you bastard! Arrh, got you! Stop the
wheel! Now, *you* take it, Doctor No!

At the first brush of the stinking dust column, Doctor
No had turned. Bond saw the long arms fling wide as if
to embrace the thudding mass. One knee rose to run.
The mouth opened and a thin scream came up to Bond
above the noise of the engine. Then there was a brief
glimpse of a kind of dancing snowman. And then only a
mound of yellow bird dung that grew higher and higher.

'God'! Bond's voice gave back an iron echo from the
walls of the cabin. He thought of the screaming lungs
stuffing with the filthy dust, the body bending and then
falling under the weight, the last impotent kick of the
heels, the last flash of thought—rage, horror,
defeat?—and then the silence of the stinking tomb.

Now the yellow mountain was twenty feet high. The
stuff was spilling off the sides of the jetty into the sea.
Bond glanced at the ship. As he did so, there came three
blasts on its siren. The noise crashed round the cliff.
There came a fourth blast which didn't stop. Bond
could see the watch holding on to the lanyard as he
craned out of the bridge window, looking down. Bond
took his hands off the controls and let them rip. It was
time to go.

He slipped off the iron seat and bent over the dead
body. He took the revolver out of the holster and
looked at it. He smiled grimly—Smith & Wesson .38,
the regular model. He slipped it down inside his waistband. It was fine to feel the heavy cold metal against his

skin. He went to the door of the cabin and dropped down to the ground.

An iron ladder ran up the cliff behind the crane to where the conveyor-housing jutted out. There was a small door in the corrugated iron wall of the housing. Bond scrambled up the ladder. The door opened easily, letting out a puff of guano dust, and he clambered through.

Inside, the clanking of the conveyor-belt over its rollers was deafening, but there were dim inspection lights in the stone ceiling of the tunnel and a narrow cat-walk that stretched away into the mountain alongside the hurrying river of dust. Bond moved quickly along it, breathing shallowly against the fishy ammoniac smell. At all costs he must get to the end before the significance of the ship's siren and of the unanswered telephone overcame the fear of the guards.

Bond half ran and half stumbled through the echoing, stinking tunnel. How far would it be? Two hundred yards? And then what? Nothing for it but to break out of the tunnel mouth and start shooting—cause a panic and hope for the best. He would get hold of one of the men and wring out of him where the girl was. Then what? When he got to the place on the mountainside, what would he find? What would be left of her?

Bond ran on faster, his head down, watching the narrow breadth of planking, wondering what would happen if he missed his footing and slipped into the rushing river of guano dust. Would he be able to get off the belt again or would he be whirled away and down until he was finally spewed out on to the burial mound of Doctor No?

When Bond's head hit into the soft stomach and he felt the hands at his throat, it was too late to think of his revolver. His only reaction was to throw himself down and forward at the legs. The legs gave against his shoulder and there was a shrill scream as the body crashed down on his back.

Bond had started the heave that would hurl his at-

tacker sideways and on to the conveyor-belt when the
quality of the scream and something light and soft
about the impact of the body froze his muscles.

It couldn't be!

As if in answer, sharp teeth bit deeply into the calf of
his right leg and an elbow jabbed viciously, knowl-
edgeably, backwards into his groin.

Bond yelled with the pain. He tried to squirm
sideways to protect himself, but even as he shouted
'Honey!' the elbow thudded into him again.

The breath whistled through Bond's teeth with the
agony. There was only one way to stop her without
throwing her on to the conveyor-belt. He took a firm
grip of one ankle and heaved himself to his knees. He
stood upright, holding her slung over his shoulder by
one leg. The other foot banged against his head, but
half-heartedly, as if she too realized that something was
wrong.

'Stop it, Honey! It's me!'

Through the din of the conveyor-belt, Bond's shout
got through to her. He heard her cry 'James!' from
somewhere near the floor. He felt her hands clutch at
his legs. 'James, James!'

Bond slowly let her down. He turned and knelt and
reached for her. He put his arms round her and held her
tightly to him. 'Oh Honey, Honey. Are you all right?'
Desperately, unbelieving, he strained her to him.

'Yes, James! Oh, yes!' He felt her hands at his back
and his hair. 'Oh, James, my darling!' she fell against
him, sobbing.

'It's all right, Honey.' Bond smoothed her hair. 'And
Doctor No's dead. But now we've got to run for it.
We've got to get out of here. Come on! How can we get
out of the tunnel? How did you get here? We've got to
hurry!'

As if in comment, the conveyor-belt stopped with a
jerk.

Bond pulled the girl to her feet. She was wearing a
dirty suit of workmen's blue dungarees. The sleeves and
legs were rolled up. The suit was far too big for her. She

looked like a girl in a man's pyjamas. She was powdered white with the guano dust except where the tears had marked her cheeks. She said breathlessly, 'Just up there! There's a side tunnel that leads to the machine shops and the garage. Will they come after us?'

There was no time to talk. Bond said urgently, 'Follow me!' and started running. Behind him her feet padded softly in the hollow silence. They came to the fork where the side tunnel led off into the rock. Which way would the man come? Down the side tunnel or along the catwalk in the main tunnel? The sound of voices booming far up the side tunnel answered him. Bond drew the girl a few feet up the main tunnel. He brought her close to him and whispered, 'I'm sorry, Honey. I'm afraid I'm going to have to kill them.'

'Of course.' The answering whisper was matter of fact. She pressed his hand and stood back to give him room. She put her hands up to her ears.

Bond eased the gun out of his waistband. Softly he broke the cylinder sideways and verified with his thumb that all six chambers were loaded. Bond knew he wasn't going to like this, killing again in cold blood, but these men would be the Chinese negro gangsters, the strong-arm guards who did the dirty work. They would certainly be murderers many times over. Perhaps they were the ones who had killed Strangways and the girl. But there was no point in trying to ease his conscience. It was kill or be killed. He must just do it efficiently.

The voices were coming closer. There were three men. They were talking loudly, nervously. Perhaps it was many years since they had even thought of going through the tunnel. Bond wondered if they would look round as they came out into the main tunnel. Or would he have to shoot them in the back?

Now they were very close. He could hear their shoes scuffing the ground.

'That makes ten bucks you owe me, Sam.'

'Not after tonight it won't be. Roll them bones, boy. Roll them bones.'

'No dice for me tonight, feller. I'm goin' to cut

maself a slice of de white girl.'

'Haw, haw, haw.'

The first man came out, then the second, then the third. They were carrying their revolvers loosely in their right hands.

Bond said sharply, 'No, you won't.'

The three men whirled round. White teeth glinted in open mouths. Bond shot the rear man in the head and the second man in the stomach. The front man's gun was up. A bullet whistled past Bond and away up the main tunnel. Bond's gun crashed. The man clutched at his neck and spun slowly round and fell across the conveyor-belt. The echoes thundered slowly up and down the tunnel. A puff of fine dust rose in the air and settled. Two of the bodies lay still. The man with the stomach shot writhed and jerked.

Bond tucked his hot gun into the waistband of his trousers. He said roughly to the girl, 'Come on.' He reached for her hand and pulled her after him into the mouth of the side tunnel. He said, 'Sorry about that, Honey,' and started running, pulling her after him by the hand. She said, 'Don't be stupid.' Then there was no sound but the thud of their naked feet on the stone floor.

The air was clean in the side tunnel and it was easier going but, after the tension of the shooting, pain began to crowd in again and take possession of Bond's body. He ran automatically. He hardly thought of the girl. His whole mind was focused on taking the pain and on the problems that waited at the end of the tunnel.

He couldn't tell if the shots had been heard and he had no idea what opposition was left. His only plan was to shoot anyone who got in his way and somehow get to the garage and the marsh buggy. That was their only hope of getting away from the mountain and down to the coast.

The dim yellow bulbs in the ceiling flicked by overhead. Still the tunnel stretched on. Behind him, Honey stumbled. Bond stopped, cursing himself for not having thought of her. She reached for him and for a moment she leaned against him panting. 'I'm sorry, James. It's just that . . .'

Bond held her to him. He said anxiously, 'Are you hurt, Honey?'

'No, I'm all right. It's just that I'm so terribly tired. And my feet got rather cut on the mountain. I fell a lot in the dark. If we could walk a bit. We're nearly there. And there's a door into the garage before we get to the machine shop. Couldn't we go in there?'

Bond hugged her to him. He said, 'That's just what I'm looking for, Honey. That's our only hope of getting away. If you can stick it till we get there, we've got a real chance.'

Bond put his arm round her waist and took her weight. He didn't trust himself to look at her feet. He knew they must be bad. It was no good being sorry for each other. There wasn't time for it if they were to stay alive.

They started moving again, Bond's face grim with the extra effort, the girl's feet leaving bloody footsteps on the ground, and almost immediately she whispered urgently and there was a wooden door in the wall of the tunnel and it was ajar and no sound came from the other side.

Bond took out his gun and gently eased the door open. The long garage was empty. Under the neon lights the black and gold painted dragon on wheels looked like a float waiting for the Lord Mayor's Show. It was pointing towards the sliding doors and the hatch of the armoured cabin stood open. Bond prayed that the tank was full and that the mechanic had carried out his orders to get the damage fixed.

Suddenly, from somewhere outside, there was the sound of voices. They came nearer, several of them, jabbering urgently.

Bond took the girl by the hand and ran forward. There was only one place to hide—in the marsh buggy. The girl scrambled in. Bond followed, softly pulling the door shut behind him. They crouched, waiting. Bond thought: only three rounds left in the gun. Too late he remembered the rack of weapons on the wall of the garage. Now the voices were outside. There came the clang of the door being slid back on its runners and a confusion of talk.

'How d'ya know they were shootin'?'

'Couldn't been nuthen else. I should know.'

'Better take rifles. Here, Joe! Take that one, Lemmy! An' some pineapples. Box under da table.'

There was the metallic noise of bolts being slid home and safety catches slicked.

'Some feller must a gone nuts. Couldn't ha been da Limey. You ever seen da big pus-feller in da creek? Cheessus! An' da rest of da tricks da Doc fixed up in da tube? An' dat white gal. She cain't have been in much shape dis mornin'. Any of you men bin to have a look?'

'Nossir.'

'No.'

'No.'

'Haw, haw. I'se sho surprised at you fellers. Dat's a fine piece of ass out dere on de crab walk.'

More rattling and shuffling of feet, then, 'Okay let's go! Two abreast till we gets to da main tunnel. Shoot at da legs. Whoever's makin' trouble, da Doc'll sure want him to play wit.'

'Tee-hee.'

Feet echoed hollowly on the concrete. Bond held his breath as they filed by. Would they notice the shut door of the buggy? But they went on down the garage and into the tunnel and the noise of them slowly faded away.

Bond touched the girl's arm and put his finger to his lips. Softly he eased open the door and listened again. Nothing. He dropped to the ground and walked round the buggy and went to the half-open entrance. Cautiously he edged his head round. There was no one in sight. There was a smell of frying food in the air that brought the saliva to Bond's mouth. Dishes and pans clattered in the nearest building, about twenty yards away, and from one of the further Quonsets came the sound of a guitar and a man's voice singing a calypso.

Dogs started to bark half-heartedly and then were silent. The Dobermann pinschers.

Bond turned and ran back to the end of the garage. No sound came from the tunnel. Softly Bond closed the tunnel door and locked and bolted it. He went to the arms-rack on the wall and chose another Smith & Wesson and a Remington carbine. He verified that they were loaded and went to the door of the marsh buggy and handed them in to the girl. Now the entrance door. Bond put his shoulder to it and softly eased it wide open. The corrugated iron rumbled hollowly. Bond ran back and scrambled through the open hatch and into the driver's seat. 'Shut it, Honey,' he whispered urgently and bent and turned the ignition key.

The needle on the gauge swung to Full. Pray God the damned thing would start up quickly. Some diesels were slow. Bond stamped his foot down on the starter.

The grinding rattle was deafening. It must be audible all over the compound! Bond stopped and tried again. The engine fluttered and died. And again, and this time the blessed thing fired and the strong iron pulse hammered as Bond revved it up. Now, gently into gear. Which one? Try this. Yes, it bit. Brake off, you bloody fool! Christ, it had nearly stalled. But now they were out and on the track and Bond rammed his foot down to the floor.

'Anyone after us?' Bond had to shout above the noise of the diesel.

'No. Wait! Yes, there's a man come out of the huts! And another! They're waving and shouting at us. Now some more are coming out. One of them's run off to the right. Another's gone back into the hut. He's coming out with a rifle. He's lying down. He's firing!'

'Close the slot! Lie down on the floor!' Bond glanced at the speedometer. Twenty. And they were on a slope. There was nothing more to get out of the machine. Bond concentrated on keeping the huge bucking wheels on the track. The cabin bounced and swayed on the springs. It was a job to keep his hands and feet on the controls. An iron fist clanged against the cabin. And another. What was the range? Four hundred? Good shooting! But that would be the lot. He shouted, 'Take a look, Honey! Open the slot an inch.'

'The man's got up. He's stopped firing. They're all looking after us—a whole crowd of them. Wait, there's something else. The dogs are coming! There's no one with them. They're just tearing down the track after us. Will they catch us?'

'Doesn't matter if they do. Come and sit by me, Honey. Hold tight. Mind your head against the roof.' Bond eased up on the throttle. She was beside him. He grinned sideways at her. 'Hell, Honey. We've made it. When we get down to the lake I'll stop and shoot up the dogs. If I know those brutes I've only got to kill one and the whole pack'll stop to eat him.'

Bond felt her hand at his neck. She kept it there as they swayed and thundered down the track. At the lake, Bond went on fifty yards into the water and turned the machine round and put it in neutral. Through the oblong slot he could see the pack streaming round the last bend. He reached down for the rifle and pushed it through the aperture. Now the dogs were in the water and swimming. Bond kept his finger on the trigger and sprayed bullets into the middle of them. One floundered, kicking. Then another and another. He could hear their snarling screams above the clatter of the engine. There was blood in the water. A fight had started. He saw one dog leap on one of the wounded ones and sink its teeth into the back of its neck. Now they all seemed to have gone berserk. They were milling around in the frothing bloody water. Bond emptied his magazine among them and dropped the gun on the floor. He said, 'That's that, Honey,' and put the machine into gear and swung it round and began rolling at an easy speed across the shallow lake towards the distant gap in the mangroves that was the mouth of the river.

For five minutes they moved along in silence. Then Bond put a hand on the girl's knee and said, 'We should be all right now, Honey. When they find the boss is dead there'll be panic. I guess some of the brighter ones will try and get away to Cuba in the plane or the launch. They'll worry about their skins, not about us. All the same, we'll not take the canoe out until it's dark. I guess it's about ten by now. We should be at the coast in an hour. Then we'll rest up and try and get in shape for the trip. Weather looks all right and there'll be a bit more moon tonight. Think you can make it?'

Her hand squeezed his neck. 'Of course I can, James. But what about you? Your poor body! It's nothing but burns and bruises. And what are those red marks across your stomach?'

'Tell you later. I'll be okay. But you tell me what happened to you last night. How in hell did you manage to get away from the crabs? What went wrong with that bastard's plan? All night long I could only think of you out there being slowly eaten to death. God, what a thing to have dreamed up! What happened?'

The girl was actually laughing. Bond looked sideways. The golden hair was tousled and the blue eyes were heavy with lack of sleep, but otherwise she might just be coming home from a midnight barbecue.

'That man thought he knew everything. Silly old fool.' She might have been talking about a stupid schoolteacher. 'He's much more impressed by the black crabs than I am. To begin with, I don't mind any animal touching me, and anyway those crabs wouldn't think of even nipping someone if they stay quite still and haven't got an open sore or anything. The whole point is that they don't really like meat. They live mostly on plants and things. If he was right and he did kill a black girl that way, either she had an open wound or she must have died of fright. He must have wanted to see if I'd stand it. Filthy old man. I only fainted down there at dinner because I knew he'd have something much worse for you.'

'Well, I'm damned. I wish to heaven I'd known that. I thought of you being picked to pieces.'

The girl snorted. 'Of course it wasn't very nice having my clothes taken off and being tied down to pegs in the ground. But those black men didn't dare touch me. They just made jokes and then went away. It wasn't very comfortable out there on the rock, but I was thinking of you and of how I could get at Doctor No and kill him. Then I heard the crabs beginning to run—that's what we call it in Jamaica—and soon they came scurrying and rattling along—hundreds of them. I just lay still and thought of you. They walked round me and over me. I might have been a rock for all they cared. They tickled a bit. One annoyed me by trying to pull out a bit of my hair. But they don't smell or anything, and I just waited for the early morning when they crawl into holes and go to sleep. I got quite fond of them. They were company. Then they got fewer and fewer and finally stopped coming and I could move. I pulled at all the pegs in turn and then concentrated on my right hand one. In the end I got it out of the crack in the rock and the rest was easy. I got back to the buildings and began scouting about. I got into the machine shop near the garage and found this filthy old suit. Then the conveyor thing started up not far away and I thought about it and I guessed it must be taking the guano through the mountain. I knew you must be dead by then,' the quiet voice was matter of fact, 'so I thought I'd get to the conveyor somehow and get through the mountain and kill Doctor No. I took a screwdriver to do it with.' She giggled. 'When we ran into each other, I'd have stuck it into you only it was in my pocket and I couldn't get to it. I found the door in the back of the machine shop and walked through and into the main tunnel. That's all.' She caressed the back of his neck. 'I ran along watching my step and the next thing I knew was your head hitting me in the stomach.' She giggled again. 'Darling, I hope I didn't hurt you too much when we were fighting. My nanny told me always to hit men there.'

Bond laughed. 'She did, did she?' He reached out and caught her by the hair and pulled her face to him. Her mouth felt its way round his cheek and locked itself against his.

The machine gave a sideways lurch. The kiss ended. They had hit the first mangrove roots at the entrance to the river.

CHAPTER 20

Slave-Time

'You're quite sure of all this?'

The Acting Governor's eyes were hunted, resentful. How could these things have been going on under his nose, in one of Jamaica's dependencies? What would the Colonial Office have to say about it? He already saw the long, pale blue envelope marked 'Personal. For Addressee Only', and the foolscap page with those very wide margins: 'The Secretary of State for the Colonies has instructed me to express to you his surprise . . .'

'Yes, sir. Quite sure.' Bond had no sympathy for the man. He hadn't liked the reception he had had on his last visit to King's House, nor the mean comments on Strangways and the girl. He liked the memory of them even less now that he knew his friend and the girl were at the bottom of the Mona Reservoir.

'Er—well we mustn't let any of this get out to the Press. You understand that? I'll send my report in to the Secretary of State by the next bag. I'm sure I can rely on your . . .'

'Excuse me, sir.' The Brigadier in command of the Caribbean Defence Force was a modern young soldier of thirty-five. His military record was good enough for him to be unimpressed by relics from the Edwardian era of Colonial Governors, whom he collectively referred to as 'feather-hatted fuddy-duddies'. 'I think we can assume that Commander Bond is unlikely to communicate with anyone except his Department. And if I may say so, sir, I submit that we should take steps to clear up Crab Key without waiting for approval from London. I can provide a platoon ready to embark by this evening. H.M.S. *Narvik* came in yesterday. If the programme of receptions and cocktail parties for her could possibly be deferred for forty-eight hours or so . . .' The Brigadier let his sarcasm hang in the air.

'I agree with the Brigadier, sir.' The voice of the Police Superintendent was edgy. Quick action might save him from a reprimand, but it would have to be quick. 'And in any case I shall have to proceed immediately against the various Jamaicans who appear to be implicated. I'll have to get the divers working at Mona. If this case is to be cleaned up we can't afford to wait for London. As Mister—er—Commander Bond says, most of these negro gangsters will probably be in Cuba by now. Have to get in touch with my opposite number in Havana and catch up with them before they take to the hills or go underground. I think we ought to move at once, sir.'

There was silence in the cool shadowy room where the meeting was being held. On the ceiling above the massive mahogany conference table there was an unexpected dapple of sunlight. Bond guessed that it shone up through the slats of the jalousies from a fountain or a lily pond in the garden outside the tall windows. Far away there was the sound of tennis balls being knocked about. Distantly a young girl's voice called, 'Smooth. Your serve, Gladys.' The Governor's children? Secretaries? From one end of the room King George VI, from the other end the Queen, looked down the table with grace and good humour.

'What do you think, Colonial Secretary?' The Governor's voice was hustled.

Bond listened to the first few words. He gathered that Pleydell-Smith agreed with the other two. He stopped listening. His mind drifted into a world of tennis courts and lily ponds and kings and queens, of London, of people being photographed with pigeons on their heads in Trafalgar Square, of the forsythia that would soon be blazing on the bypass roundabouts, of May, the treasured housekeeper in his flat off the King's Road, getting up to brew herself a cup of tea (here it was eleven o'clock. It would be six o'clock in London), of the first tube trains beginning to run, shaking the ground beneath his cool, dark bedroom. Of the douce weather of England: the soft airs, the 'heat' waves, the cold spells—'The only country where you can take a walk every day of the year'—Chesterfield's Letters? And then Bond thought of Crab Key, of the hot ugly wind beginning to blow, of the stink of the marsh gas from the mangrove swamps, the jagged grey, dead coral in whose holes the black crabs were now squatting, the black and red eyes moving swiftly on their stalks as a shadow—a cloud, a bird—broke their small horizons. Down in the bird colony the brown and white and pink birds would be stalking in the shallows, or fighting or nesting, while up on the guanera the cormorants would be streaming back from their breakfast to deposit their milligramme of rent to the landlord who would no longer be collecting. And where would the landlord be? The men from the S.S. *Blanche* would have dug him out. The body would have been examined for signs of life and then put somewhere. Would they have washed the yellow dust off him and dressed him in his kimono while the Captain radioed Antwerp for instructions? And where had Doctor No's soul gone to? Had it been a bad soul or just a mad one? Bond thought of the burned twist down in the swamp that had been Quarrel. He remembered the soft ways of the big body, the innocence in the grey, horizon-seeking eyes, the simple lusts and desires, the reverence for superstitions and instincts, the childish faults, the loyalty and even love that Quarrel had given him—the warmth, there was only one word for it, of the man. Surely he hadn't gone to the same place as Doctor No. Whatever happened to dead people, there was surely one place for the warm and another for the cold. And which, when the time came, would he, Bond, go to?

The Colonial Secretary was mentioning Bond's name. Bond pulled himself together.

'. . . survived is quite extraordinary. I do think, sir, that we should show our gratitude to Commander Bond and to his Service by accepting his recommendations. It does seem, sir, that he has done at least three-quarters of the job. Surely the least we can do is look after the other quarter.'

The Governor grunted. He squinted down the table at Bond. The chap didn't seem to be paying much attention. But one couldn't be sure with these Secret Service fellows. Dangerous chaps to have around, sniffing and snooping. And their damned Chief carried a lot of guns in Whitehall. Didn't do to get on the wrong side of him. Of course there was something to be said for sending the *Narvik*. News would leak, of course. All the Press of the world would be coming down on his head. But then suddenly the Governor saw the headlines: 'GOVERNOR TAKES SWIFT ACTION . . . ISLAND'S STRONG MAN INTERVENES . . . THE NAVY'S THERE!' Perhaps after all it would be better to do it that way. Even go down and see the troops off himself. Yes, that was it, by jove. Cargill, of the *Gleaner,* was coming to lunch. He'd drop a hint or two to the chap and make sure the story got proper coverage. Yes, that was it. That was the way to play the hand.

The Governor raised his hands and let them fall flat on the table in a gesture of submission. He embraced the conference with a wry smile of surrender.

'So I am overruled, gentlemen. Well, then,' the voice was avuncular, telling the children that just this once . . . 'I accept your verdict. Colonial Secretary, will you please call upon the commanding officer of H.M.S. *Narvik* and explain the position. In strict confidence, of course. Brigadier, I leave the military arrangements in your hands. Superintendent, you will know what to do.' The Governor rose. He inclined his head regally in the direction of Bond. 'And it only remains to express my appreciation to Commander—er—Bond, for his part in this affair. I shall not fail to mention your assistance, Commander, to the Secretary of State.'

Outside the sun blazed down on the gravel sweep. The interior of the Hillman Minx was a Turkish bath. Bond's bruised hands cringed as they took the wheel.

Pleydell-Smith leant through the window. He said, 'Ever heard the Jamaican expression "rarse"?'

'No.'

' "Rarse, man" is a vulgar expression meaning—er—"stuff it up". If I may say so, it would have been appropriate for you to have used the expression just now. However,' Pleydell-Smith gave a wave of his hand which apologized for his Chief and dismissed him, 'is there anything else I can do for you? You really think you ought to go back to Beau Desert? They were quite definite at the hospital that they want to have you for a week.'

'Thanks,' said Bond shortly, 'but I've got to get back. See the girl's all right. Would you tell the hospital I'll be back tomorrow? You got off that signal to my Chief?'

'Urgent rates.'

'Well, then,' Bond pressed the self-starter, 'I guess that's the lot. You'll see the Jamaica Institute people about the girl, won't you? She really knows the hell of a lot about the natural history side of the island. Not from books either. If they've got the right sort of job . . . Like to see her settled. I'll take her up to New York myself and see her through the operation. She'd be ready to start in a couple of weeks after that. Incidentally,' Bond looked embarrassed, 'she's really the hell of a fine girl. When she comes back . . . if you and your wife . . . You know. Just so there's someone to keep an eye on her.'

Pleydell-Smith smiled. He thought he had the picture. He said, 'Don't worry about that. I'll see to it. Betty's rather a hand at that sort of thing. She'll like taking the girl under her wing. Nothing else? See you later in the week, anyway. That hospital's the hell of a place in this heat. You might care to spend a night or two with us before you go ho—I mean to New York. Glad to have you—er—both.'

'Thanks. And thanks for everything else.' Bond put the car into gear and went off down the avenue of flaming tropical shrubbery. He went fast, scattering the gravel on the bends. He wanted to get the hell away from King's House, and the tennis, and the kings and queens. He even wanted to get the hell away from the kindly Pleydell-Smith. Bond liked the man, but all he wanted now was to get back across the Junction Road to Beau Desert and away from the smooth world. He swung out past the sentry at the gates and on to the main road. He put his foot down.

The night voyage under the stars had been without incident. No one had come after them. The girl had done most of the sailing. Bond had not argued with her. He had lain in the bottom of the boat, totally collapsed, like a dead man. He had woken once or twice and listened to the slap of the sea against the hull and watched her quiet profile under the stars. Then the cradle of the soft swell had sent him back to sleep and to the nightmares that reached out after him from Crab Key. He didn't mind them. He didn't think he would ever mind a nightmare now. After what had happened the night before, it would have to be strong stuff that would ever frighten him again.

The crunch of a nigger-head against the hull had woken him. They were coming through the reef into Morgan's Harbour. The first quarter moon was up, and inside the reef the sea was a silver mirror. The girl had brought the canoe through under sail. They slid across the bay to the little fringe of sand and the bows under Bond's head sighed softly into it. She had had to help him out of the boat and across the velvet lawn and into the house. He had clung to her and cursed her softly as she had cut his clothes off him and taken him into the shower. She had said nothing when she had seen his battered body under the lights. She had turned the water full on and taken soap and washed him down as if he had been a horse. Then she led him out from under the water and dabbed him softly dry with towels that were soon streaked with blood. He had seen her reach for the bottle of Milton. He had groaned and taken hold of the washbasin and waited for it. Before she had begun to put it on him, she had come round and kissed him on the lips. She had said softly, 'Hold tight, my darling. And cry. It's going to hurt,' and as she splashed the murderous stuff over his body the tears of pain had run out of his eyes and down his cheeks without shame.

Then there had been a wonderful breakfast as the dawn flared up across the bay, and then the ghastly drive over to Kingston to the white table of the surgery in the emergency ward. Pleydell-Smith had been summoned. No questions had been asked. Merthiolate had been put on the wounds and tannic ointment on the burns. The efficient negro doctor had written busily in the duty report. What? Probably just 'Multiple burns and contusions'. Then, with promises to come into the private ward on the next day, Bond had gone off with Pleydell-Smith to King's House and to the first of the meetings that had ended with the full-dress conference. Bond had enciphered a short signal to M via the Colonial Office which he had coolly concluded with: 'REGRET MUST AGAIN REQUEST SICK LEAVE STOP SURGEONS REPORT FOLLOWS STOP KINDLY INFORM ARMOURER SMITH AND WESSON INEFFECTIVE AGAINST FLAME-THROWER ENDIT.'

Now, as Bond swung the little car down the endless S-bends towards the North Shore, he regretted the gibe. M wouldn't like it. It was cheap. It wasted cipher groups. Oh, well! Bond swerved to avoid a thundering red bus with 'Brownskin Gal' on the destination plate. He had just wanted M to know that it hadn't quite been a holiday in the sun. He would apologize when he sent in his written report.

Bond's bedroom was cool and dark. There was a plate of sandwiches and a Thermos full of coffee beside the turned-down bed. On the pillow was a sheet of paper with big childish writing. It said, 'You are staying with me tonight. I can't leave my animals. They were fussing. And I can't leave you. And you owe me slave-time. I will come at seven. Your H.'

In the dusk she came across the lawn to where Bond was sitting finishing his third glass of Bourbon-on-the-rocks. She was wearing a black and white striped cotton skirt and a tight sugar-pink blouse. The golden hair smelled of cheap shampoo. She looked incredibly fresh and beautiful. She reached out her hand and Bond took it and followed her up the drive and along a narrow well-trodden path through the sugar cane. It wound along for quite a way through the tall whispering sweet-scented jungle. Then there was a patch of tidy lawn up against thick broken stone walls and steps that led down to a heavy door whose edges glinted with light.

She looked up at him from the door. 'Don't be frightened. The cane's high and they're most of them out.'

Bond didn't know what he had expected. He had vaguely thought of a flat earthen floor and rather damp walls. There would be a few sticks of furniture, a broken bedstead covered with rags, and a strong zoo smell. He had been prepared to be careful about hurting her feelings.

Instead it was rather like being inside a very large tidy cigar-box. The floor and ceiling were of highly polished cedar that gave out a cigar-box smell and the walls were panelled with wide split bamboo. The light came from a dozen candles in a fine silver chandelier that hung from the centre of the ceiling. High up in the walls there were three square windows through which Bond could see the dark blue sky and the stars. There were several pieces of good nineteenth-century furniture. Under the chandelier a table was laid for two with expensive-looking old-fashioned silver and glass.

Bond said, 'Honey, what a lovely room. From what you said I thought you lived in a sort of zoo.'

She laughed delightedly. 'I got out the old silver and things. It's all I've got. I had to spend the day polishing it. I've never had it out before. It does look rather nice, doesn't it? You see, generally there are a lot of little cages up against the wall. I like having them with me. It's company. But now that you're here . . .' She paused. 'My bedroom's in there,' she gestured at the other door. 'It's very small, but there's room for both of us. Now come on. I'm afraid it's cold dinner—just lobsters and fruit.'

Bond walked over to her. He took her in his arms and kissed her hard on the lips. He held her and looked down into the shining blue eyes. 'Honey, you're a wonderful girl. You're one of the most wonderful girls I've ever known. I hope the world's not going to change you too much. D'you really want to have that operation? I love your face—just as it is. It's part of you. Part of all this.'

She frowned and freed herself. 'You're not to be serious tonight. Don't talk about these things. I don't want to talk about them. This is my night with you. Please talk about love. I don't want to hear about anything else. Promise? Now come on. You sit there.'

Bond sat down. He smiled up at her. He said, 'I promise.'

She said, 'Here's the mayonnaise. It's not out of a bottle. I made it myself. And take some bread and butter.' She sat down opposite him and began to eat, watching him. When she saw that he seemed satisfied she said, 'Now you can start telling me about love. Everything about it. Everything you know.'

Bond looked across into the flushed, golden face. The eyes were bright and soft in the candlelight, but with the same imperious glint they had held when he had first seen her on the beach and she had thought he had come to steal her shells. The full red lips were open with ex-

citement and impatience. With him she had no
inhibitions. They were two loving animals. It was
natural. She had no shame. She could ask him anything
and would expect him to answer. It was as if they were
already in bed together, lovers. Through the tight cotton
bodice the points of her breasts showed, hard and
roused.

Bond said, 'Are you a virgin?'

'Not quite. I told you. That man.'

'Well . . .' Bond found he couldn't eat any more. His
mouth was dry at the thought of her. He said, 'Honey, I
can either eat or talk love to you. I can't do both.'

'You're going over to Kingston tomorrow. You'll get
plenty to eat there. Talk love.'

Bond's eyes were fierce blue slits. He got up and went
down on one knee beside her. He picked up her hand
and looked into it. At the base of the thumb the Mount
of Venus swelled luxuriously. Bond bent his head down
into the warm soft hand and bit softly into the swelling.
He felt her other hand in his hair. He bit harder. The
hand he was holding curled round his mouth. She was
panting. He bit still harder. She gave a little scream and
wrenched his head away by the hair.

'What are you doing?' Her eyes were wide and dark.
She had gone pale. She dropped her eyes and looked at
his mouth. Slowly she pulled his head towards her.

Bond put out a hand to her left breast and held it
hard. He lifted her captive, wounded hand and put it
round his neck. Their mouths met and clung, exploring.

Above them the candles began to dance. A big hawk-
moth had come in through one of the windows. It
whirred round the chandelier. The girl's closed eyes
opened, looked at the moth. Her mouth drew away. She
smoothed the handful of his hair back and got up, and
without saying anything took down the candles one by
one and blew them out. The moth whirred away
through one of the windows.

The girl stood away from the table. She undid her
blouse and threw it on the floor. Then her skirt. Under
the glint of moonlight she was a pale figure with a cen-

tral shadow. She came to Bond and took him by the hand and lifted him up. She undid his shirt and slowly, carefully took it off. Her body, close to him, smelled of new-mown hay and sweet pepper. She led him away from the table and through a door. The filtering moonlight shone down on a single bed. On the bed was a sleeping-bag, its mouth laid open.

The girl let go his hand and climbed into the sleeping-bag. She looked up at him. She said, practically, 'I bought this today. It's a double one. It cost a lot of money. Take those off and come in. You promised. You owe me slave-time.'

'But . . .'

'Do as you're told.'

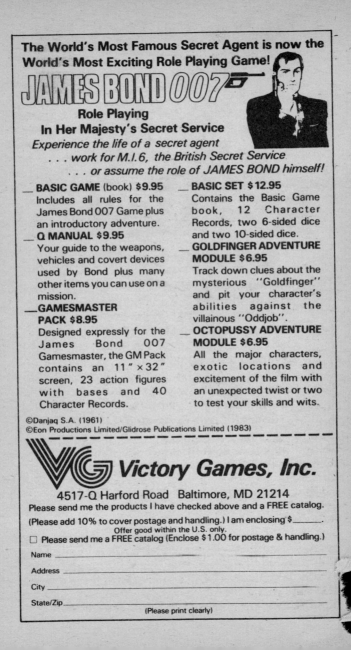